Acclaim for Geraldo J.Uscategui and

The Rumdog Chronicles

"Couldn' t put this book down once I started. I became absorbed in the character and wanted to know more. Loved the ending." - Judy B, Amazon Customer

"This book was sad, funny and gripping all at the same time. I couldn' t put it down. Finished reading this book in one sitting. The ending was awesome!" -Phyllis D

"This book is a must read. Once I started reading the book it was hard to put it down. I went from laughing out loud to say Oh my God..." -Jackie S, Amazon Customer

"This is an in-depth, gripping sneek peak into Rumdog' s soul. I could not put this book down. I was on an emotional roller coaster. I laughed uncontrollably followed by my heart being ripped out...its descriptive journey stuns you into having nothing but compassion for this self-destructive loon." -Jen, Amazon Customer

"Wow! What a page turner and emotional rollercoaster. I felt a wide range of feels throughout Rumdog's entire story, and at various points, had to check myself in public from bursting out in tears or laughing out loud... I hope this work is a first of many in the indubitably captivating storyline known as Rumdog. -Ande C

"The best part of reading to me is being able to vividly picture the words and immerse yourself in to the story as if it were happening. I enjoyed reading this book immensely. When you find a book that you don't want to put down, you have got a good one. Get it today!" -Tanya S, Amazon Customer

"This is an amazing, well written book. The author is a masterful storyteller who makes you feel every emotion. Looking forward to more of his work. I am telling everyone, this is a must read." -Anita Bullock, RJC

"Great read! Highly recommended! I thoroughly enjoyed this book. Excellent read. The tale was full of twists and hilarious moments. -Amazon Customer

The**RUMDOG**

CHRONICLES

Geraldo Jose Uscategui

For My Beautiful Babes

Gabriela and Joshua

You are and will always be

The rhythm

of the beat of my heart

CONTENTS

Prologue

Noun

A separate introductory section of a literary or musical work.

Synonyms: introduction, foreword, preface

Preamble, prelude

There are dreams and then there are memories. The kind that come to me almost every single night. It seems that I have a favorite. My brother Gilbert and I are sitting on the floor in a living room that is not our own. We could never afford such nice furnishings. We are not allowed to sit on the furniture, even if it's covered in thick plastic all year round. She's yelling at us again, in Spanish. Someone had dared to put his mouth on the gallon of milk, and not bothered to use a cup. I know it was Gilbert, but we have a bond called loyalty that neither one of us will ever forget. We will pay the price together, on our knees. I am always the one to break first. One tear is all it usually takes to break the dam as the tiny but relentless grains of raw rice strewn out in the corner of the kitchen begin to dig deeper and deeper into my skin. My own weight and a little thing called gravity is all that is needed to teach the lesson yet again. We are not allowed to face each other. Instead, we face the same direction with our noses pressed firmly against the wall. Somehow, Gilbert knows that I am close to my breaking point. He whispers, "Don't let her see you cry," but it is too late. Her heavy hand is on my shoulder, pressing down.

I always wake up right about then. Sometimes with a jolt, and other times my eyes simply flutter open as I instinctively wake up and look to see how much rice is still embedded in the skin of my knees. I reach for Nina, but she is no longer in my bed. I am alone, but I'm fine now. I've had more than my share of fun since then. Not once have I ever dreamt about the laughter.

RD

First Impressions

I cannot remember the first time that I came to know the Rumdog. I met him at some point during my childhood and ever since then, he's just always been around. He was a different kind of kid that seemed a little older than he actually was. Physically, he was nothing to fear, and aesthetically there was nothing more to him than his smile.

He was awkward and skinny, with facial features that somehow didn't match the rest of his face. However, he wore that smile just about every day. On most days, he wore it like a suffocating mask, even when the last thing he wanted to do was flash those pearly whites at everyone, but he wore it nonetheless.

Everything I was, he was the opposite. Where I was outgoing, he was withdrawn and private. Nobody knew him, and moreover nobody wanted to know him. I was the kid that excelled in school and even had the chance to skip grades in my middle school years, but Rumdog couldn't care less about grades or conforming to whatever the teachers wanted him to do. He was known to walk out of class without permission or consent in the middle of the period, and I was the kid that would sit in class until the bell rang, even if it meant having an accident in my own seat. He was a tough kid, of that there was no doubt, who had been born of heartbreak and unimaginable hurt. And to put it bluntly, I was soft. Whenever something happened, if there was a fight at school or someone on the street we lived on was brawling, I always managed to barely miss it. Not Rumdog, he always managed to get right into the fight, always arriving right on time to stick his neck out for his buddies.

Nevertheless, he and I were inseparable. Where I went he went. Where I succeeded or failed, he was always the first one to pat me on the back or kick me in the ass. We are acquaintances still, and while I hardly ever see him these days, it's a comfort to know that he will always come to my side at a moment's notice, even if I don't want him to.

When I started writing many moons ago, I questioned whether anyone would ever care or take the time to read me. Would someone ever pick up a book or story that I had penned, absorb all my words and somehow digest and comprehend whatever it was I was trying to convey? Many nights, I have started writing and somewhere along the way decided it was rubbish before the night was over. I knew that if I ever hoped to be a successful writer, it would have to be something interesting and titillating. Not only a story full of excitement, but also a story full of peaks and valleys of emotion and vulnerability. I have no such tales.

I look at my life now and I have to admit, I really can't complain. I'm happily divorced, I have great kids, a decent job, and I've never had any problems making friends or meeting women. I'm not rich and I live from paycheck to paycheck like the next guy. Sure, sometimes I get a little carried away with my expenditure, and I will live from paycheck to a few days before I get my next paycheck. It's the very common story of just about every divorcee, so I won't bore you with all the details of how I get by. Once or twice a week I treat myself to a nice dinner out, whether it be alone or with friends, and I'll even have myself quite a few drinks.

One evening, during one of the weeks that I had been wise about my budget, I was sitting at a bar having a few innocent after work drinks before I headed home. I was just about to order myself a bite to eat since I was already out. As I was perusing the menu, for some reason or another, Rumdog popped into my head as it dawned on me that I had not seen him or heard from him in quite some time. It's scary how my mind works sometimes, because minutes after I thought of him, who suddenly walked in but Rumdog himself looking like he could really use a drink. It was almost as if I had conjured him somehow. The look on his face didn't suggest that he was there to have a few drinks like I was, but instead he looked like a man that was planning on having his mail delivered to his bar stool. He was hard to read sometimes.

We saw each other right away. It was no surprise since the place wasn't crowded at all, but when I think about it, we never really made plans. We always run into each other in random places. He's a sports fanatic and a barfly just like me, so it's almost harder to not run into each other. He pulled out the stool right next to me and without ever uttering a word, he had a rum and coke delivered to him almost instantaneously. He thanked the bartender and picked up his drink to extend his cheers with me as I raised my whisky to him in return.

He looked at my glass with distaste and asked me, "You're still drinking that swill, huh?"

I nodded and told him that he would never quite comprehend that whisky was simply mother's milk, but I couldn't possibly expect a savage like him to understand that. He quickly suggested that I go fuck myself, and without missing a beat, he remarked that it'd been a while since he'd seen me last.

He asked me, "So, how are you doing?" He was always good like that.

He could pepper you with admiration and ridicule in the same sentence, but sometimes, due to his deadpan delivery, you were never quite sure which one was the insult and which was the compliment. I always admired that about him. He spoke his mind, and was so free with his words that people hardly ever took offense. Not that he cared one bit if you did.

That day, however, he seemed like something was on his mind and usually he was a lot better at camouflaging his inner sentiment, disguising it with humor as he playfully lobbed insults back and forth with the other drunks in the bar. He still wore that trademark smile, but even back when we were kids, I had suspected that perhaps there had always been something hiding behind it. Whatever it was, it had gnawed on him internally for so many years that all he could do was try to drown it, until he was drunk most of the time.

That was the exact thought that was going through my mind at that point. He was a drunk. He was fully functional and still responsible for the most part, but he had lost control of his alcoholism long ago. He was still a good guy, with a sharp sense of humor that could keep you in stitches for hours at a time, but he could be very dangerous and unpredictable when he slipped into one of his binges. That night it seemed he might be in the early beginnings of one of his infamous marathons, during which he would drink one or two bottles of booze every night of the week. It would end eventually after a week or two with him crashing into a corpse like coma, waking up with almost no recollection and on more than one occasion, having no clue where he had left his car or how he had gotten back to his home. The blackouts were far and few in between, but as is their nature, blackouts usually prefer to arrive unannounced. He would go weeks of drinking, yet he would have total recall of everything he had done and said. Then one night would start out as any other, but he would wake up the next day not having a clue what had transpired after a certain point in the evening.

He once "misplaced" his car after a New Year's Eve party and didn't find it until after the first week of the New Year. He had tried retracing his steps, but had no luck at any of the bars and clubs he had visited that night. Finally, when he was ready to declare the car stolen, a friend called and told him that the truck was parked near his house. Everyone had a good laugh at the length of time it had taken him to find his car but his nights didn't always end with a funny anecdote. One night, for no reason whatsoever from what I heard, and after a great amount of alcohol, he took it upon himself to remove the mirrors of every single parked car using only his fists. He walked around an entire city block, punching every mirror, and laughing like a madman while his hands bled from all the shards of glass in his skin. He was bleeding profusely and ranting about a dog. While he was certainly angry, he never stopped laughing the entire time.

He was a complex individual, but if you smartly kept yourself at a safe distance, all you could really see was what he wanted you to see. That got me wondering, especially on this particular night at the bar, what exactly had happened to Rumdog that had made him this way. I didn't know of anything traumatic that had happened to him ever since we had been friends. Whatever it was, it had to be something that had taken place in his early, formative years. Perhaps it was all the shots I had that night, or maybe I had finally realized that the story I had been searching for had been sitting right in front of me all along. I asked him, quite abruptly, what was on his mind? His expression suggested that he had no clue what I was talking about, but I prodded a little deeper as I went on to suggest that he looked like a man that felt a need to shed a great weight from his shoulders. His face changed at that moment and I felt a sudden pang of regret. Inexplicably, I feared that he was going to hit me. I was always a quick thinker, so while he momentarily appraised me and my intentions, I took advantage of his uncertainty and asked him if there was anything that he wanted to unload. I told him that I never really knew what he was thinking and that I just wanted to know what made him tick after all these years of friendship.

He saw right through me. A smile started on the corner of his mouth and just like it had always done, it stopped halfway across his face. I thought it was a good sign that I wasn't going to be assaulted that night and I felt relieved, but I wasn't really

8

sure that I could press my luck any further. He ordered two shots of whisky, and I took the fact that he had been willing to indulge in my swill as a sign that he wasn't cross with me for trying to invade his privacy. He knew that I had been a frustrated writer and though we had shared ideas of possible stories and screenplays to write someday, we were always inebriated whenever we conspired, so it was usually a foggy memory by the next morning. As I stated earlier, he saw right through me, because the following words that came out of his mouth made me blush with shame.

He asked, "You want to write my story, don't you?"

I felt like a jerk. I had tried to pry into his life and somehow fancied myself to own a bit of subtlety but my motive had been embarrassingly naked. When the shots arrived, again we raised them and extended our cheer, but when we finished knocking them down the hatch his expression changed yet again. He was suddenly stern and solemn. I thought to myself that perhaps this was the first time that I had seen the real face of the Rumdog. We had been acquainted for a long time, but for the second time in minutes, I felt yet another pang of regret. Maybe he was going to say something that I would wish I had never heard, and something that I had been better off never knowing. What if he were to confess to some horrific crime and then had to kill me immediately after we left the bar, rousing me into a dark alleyway with the false promises of telling me the rest of his story. I had definitely had too much to drink. Again and quite inexplicably, I felt like I was about to have some sort of panic attack.

The moments that he took to express his next thought felt like an eternity, and before he spoke, I almost said; "Hey man forget it!" But before I had a chance to interject, he looked at me and told me that he too, had thought of someday putting his experiences on paper. He didn't know how to, or where to start, but it was something that had been on his mind for quite some time. All my timidity instantly vanished as I absorbed what he had said and tried unsuccessfully to not sound too eager.

"Let's do it," I said.

He gave me a not so long, but hard stare and nodded his head slowly.

Then he said, "Yes, lets! We can't do it here obviously."

"That is fine with me," I replied.

He laid down some ground rules, insisting that I never reveal anything he said to me until his entire story was complete. I readily agreed. Then he said something that was both curious and odd but I agreed nonetheless. He told me that some strange and incredible things had happened to him, and that my job was simply to write and not ask questions, unless it was absolutely necessary. Again, I agreed, but he had one last request.

"Most importantly, whatever I say to you, I need you to believe that it is the absolute truth!"

At that point, a beautiful woman came over and gently placed her hand on Rumdog's shoulder. It was an incredibly light touch, but certainly telling, indicating that she was without a doubt his lover. She looked somewhat familiar, but she certainly wasn't someone I had met before. I could never forget a face like that. Her voice was heavenly.

"Baby, I'm going to wait outside. You don't have to rush," she said to him.

He nodded at her, and then looked back at me. "Sorry to cut this short pal, but I have to go."

I was certainly incorrect about the length of time he would be staying at the bar that night, but who could blame him? The woman was stunning. He peeled off a few twenty-dollar bills and laid them on the bar.

He turned to me and said, "It's always good to see you brother. Remember what I said, nothing but the truth. You think you can handle that?"

I nodded in agreement and all I could say was, "When do we start?"

He said to me, "Whenever you want to, you just make sure you come over with a bottle of rum." And we shook on it.

The things that the Rumdog would later confess to me were both jarring and sometimes unbelievable. I often wondered how it is that some people make it in the real world while some fall by the wayside and never quite grasp the ability or desire to be a productive member of society. Some kids just don't have a chance and from the day they are born, are short changed and discounted. They go through horrific things in their formative years or sometimes even younger. They are expected to get over it and be a normal person, act just as unfazed as those of us that had lived a charmed life. In some ways, I guess that I can agree with those that say that we all have problems and it's an eat-or-be-eaten kind of life.

Lions aren't expected to say please and thank you when they devour another living being, but aren't we as humans supposed to be better? There are people in this world that grew up in a jungle like atmosphere, kill or be killed. They have a vastly different and sharply acute perspective on how things should be. I don't know what kind of person I would be if I had grown up and walked in the same shoes as Rumdog, but you can decide for yourself how you could have triumphed over years of poverty and sadness without losing so much of yourself in the process. The thing is, there are people in this world that have endured worse things and have triumphed. There are people that have not had so much as a ripple in their pond, yet still could not maintain a functional life. Each person has their own story and each person deals with it in their own manner. Still, I ask myself, what kind of person would I be?

One thing about Rumdog, and it's something that almost anyone that knows him will tell you, is that he appreciates the people that he has in his life. He's definitely a scarred individual with too much loss behind him, especially for someone his age, but he has a unique way of looking at things. After he had told me about all the people that he had lost in his time, I asked him what was it exactly that kept him ticking. What was it about himself that made it so easy for him to cope and to keep on, regardless of whatever pained experience he had endured. He seemed to give it just a little bit of thought, but he answered me quite quickly considering the question, suggesting to me that he had probably given this some thought before this moment.

I was quite incorrect about his ability to cope. He actually has a very tough time carrying on with day-to-day operations, yet he does so without complaint. What he went on to express to me was a long explanation of how life has its own way of maintaining checks and balances. I never really thought about it that way but now that I have heard his point of view, it's definitely a sound and lucid argument for why and how people come and go into your life. Sometimes, it seems, you will have people come into your life just at the precise moment that you needed, but the truth is that it was you that left that door open to let someone new in. Using a simpler arithmetic, why would you open the window on a hot summer's night, if not to let in

11

the breeze?

It's also a fact that some relationships, whether they are romantic or otherwise, also tend to have a shelf life. People take it personal when someone moves on with their life, and it just might be that their time and role in your life has met its expiration date. You simply cannot keep everyone in your life that you cared about at one point or another. The Rumdog has a pragmatic sense of the value an individual may have in his life and a keen sense of when that time has come and gone. So while his way of letting people go seems dismissive and impersonal, it has actually given him a peace of mind, feeling no ill will when someone else decides that perhaps his own role in their lives has come to an end. He wishes them well and may even raise his glass, wishing nothing but luck and good spirits for the future. His rationale is that not everyone you meet is destined to be in your life for all eternity. As they say, a reason and a season. When you do reach an impasse, the parting need not be bitter or scorned.

People cry harder over break-ups than they do at funerals. You would think that it would be harder to lose someone who you will not see for the rest of your natural life, but instead they mourn and long for someone that they will probably see much sooner than later. It took years, however, for this to sink in. He was guilty of holding on too long on more than one occasion, choosing to hyper-romanticize the most toxic of pairings in the name of love and trying to make it work. It took years of loss to make him understand that sometimes the loss, painful and searing to the heart as it may be, is sometimes necessary in order to make room for what lies ahead.

When he walked into the bar that night and after he agreed to let me put his life on paper, it was then that I realized that perhaps both of us had left the window open. It wasn't easy to get Rumdog nailed down for an actual face-to-face sit down. When we finally met up again, I was completely revved up and ready to go. We sat down in his living room, each with a bottle of our chosen poison.

He leaned back in his chair and said, "You do remember the rules, right?"

I nodded quickly, confirming that I was well aware of the rules he had relayed to me at the bar. Then he said, "I guess I should start at my beginning."

The Rumdog Speaks

I'm going to tell you my story. I may bounce around a bit and confuse you but my only excuse is that my memory does not work chronologically. I can only remember things as they pop into my head. For some reason, this is what jumped into my brain as my introduction to you. It's not exactly a feel good tale that paints me in any sort of positive light, but it's certainly a peek into the things that happen when I go too far with my drinking and lose control.

The night started innocently like any other, and then it wasn't. Just like that. I slowly tried to open my eyes, and when I came to, it seemed that I had somehow fallen asleep in a dense forest. This is kind of a hard thing to do in Brooklyn. Then I heard the yelling. As I started to step back from the tree that was in my face, its coarse branches scratching my face, I saw my friend Cee and he had a look of astonishment on his face. Next to him was a guy in a clip-on tie that looked vaguely familiar. He was the one doing all the yelling. I realized that my penis was out and I quickly tried to put it away. At that point, I realized that maybe this night had gotten away from me for I had no clue how I had gotten there. This had happened before.

Of course, this wasn't really my fault. I had called Cee sometime right after work hours. I had told him a few friends and I were going to a party to do some boozing at a karaoke bar. After Cee's customary seventeen questions regarding, crowd, attire, and menu, he finally agreed to meet me there. By the time he arrived, I was already annoyed as I was being unsuccessful in getting myself drunk. As I recall, the bartender was getting on my nerves with his short pour of rum and very long pour of soda. The drinks were so weak that I had started to order a shot of Jagermeister with every drink. Still, I gave the bartender a generous tip with every round I bought. When Cee finally arrived, I ordered vodka and cranberry for him and a rum and coke for myself. The bartender did his little short pour trick again. Enough was enough. When he tried to put the bottle back down, I put two fingers under the bottle of rum and didn't let him put it back down as the rum continued to pour into the glass.

After a few moments of staring at each other, he finally said, "I guess you'll let me know when to stop." I gave it another second and then let him put the bottle down.

I said, "Hey buddy, I'm paying for my drinks and giving you a nice tip every single time, at least have the decency to get me drunk."

He didn't short pour me again after that. In fact, he put me on my ass and he made a nice amount of money that night. Cee said he had never seen anyone do that to a bartender before and I just shrugged my shoulders. I just really didn't want to continue paying ten bucks a glass for rum flavored soda. Funny thing, I hate soda. It's actually too acidic and gassy for me, way too strong for my blood. So much so that if I don't dilute the soda with about half a glass of rum I just cannot drink it. I don't know how kids drink it, or adults for that matter. Soda by itself is awful and undrinkable.

Well, the night went on. We drank and I sang a few tunes slightly off key. The night was certainly typical. I met a few girls, got a few phone numbers, and got lucky enough to kiss one of them before it was time to go. I was smart enough not to drive that night, so instead of a cab we decided that it was still early enough to take the New York City subway home. As we were walking towards the train station, Cee spotted a restaurant.

He froze in his tracks and said, "Dick, we gotta get some wings."

I don't know why he always called me "Dick". I won't say that he's being ingenuous or even inaccurate because it certainly applies, but somewhere along the way in the twenty years that I've known him, he decided he was going to address me as "Dick". And I answer to it.

On that particular night, in my drunken stupor, I whole-heartedly disagreed on our need for chicken wings. And let me tell you something, the one thing I love more than booze is wings. However, after all that I had drank that night, I was finished. I told Cee there was no way I was stopping for wings in the middle of the night. Besides, I had to take care of some things early in the am.

He said, "Dick, let's get wings, I'll treat."

Hold on a second. As a person with a wing fetish saying no was hard enough. Now he said he was buying and there was no way my ample brown ass was going to turn down free wings. I'm just not emotionally equipped to do such a thing. So we went of course, and got the wings. I also got two colossal rum and cokes in fish bowl sized glasses to wash them down. We ended up in an argument with a few black girls about who was currently the best female rapper in the Hip-Hop game and thankfully, we somehow avoided coming to blows. Eventually the manager came over and told us that they were closing so it was time for us to go. That's when things started to get a little foggy for me. I slammed the rest of my drink, we paid our tab, and that's when I noticed that the whole restaurant was dark. They had just been waiting on us to leave so that they could lock up. We were at the exit when Cee stopped abruptly. He handed me his bag and asked the manager if he could use the bathroom before we left. That's when things got extremely foggy. I don't know how long Cee was in the bathroom but he must have taken quite a bit of time in there.

I fell asleep while I was waiting for him. I remember waking up and thinking to myself that I should probably pee before I left. I leaned up against one of the trees and started to go. I woke up to screaming and yelling, and as far as I knew, I didn't see what the big deal was all about. That's when I realized that I wasn't in the forest at all. I was actually standing in the lobby of a restaurant, and I was pissing on their Christmas tree. The manager of the restaurant was going ape shit and screaming about calling the cops. I thought it would be best if we left immediately

I pulled Cee by the coat and yelled, "Run!"

We started running down the street in absolute hysterics, with my pants undone, mind you. The manager from the restaurant was still yelling but we could hardly hear him by then. We were laughing way too hard. We ran about two blocks to the train and that's when we really started to laugh so hard that I almost had myself an asthma attack. I literally had to drop down to one knee at the train station because I was getting light headed from laughing that much.

It was a long train ride home, and both Cee and I fell asleep. When I awoke, miraculously we were at my subway stop. I shook Cee and told him to make a run for the door. We barely made it, but Cee forgot his bag on the train. The doors almost closed on us but I managed to get my foot in the door as I tried to get back on. The train conductor was a few train cars down the station and he started to yell for us to let go of the door. He had no intentions of opening the doors to let us back in.

After a brief standoff, I screamed in a woman's voice, "My baby, my baby is on the train!"

I could see the conductor's face and it was pure panic. He popped his head back into his booth and the doors opened almost instantly. Cee ran into the train and retrieved his bag, then jumped off the train again. We were still laughing as were leaving the train station, especially when the conductor's car went past us, and he was giving us the filthiest of looks.

We went up the stairs and sat down again at the train stop going in the opposite direction because we had missed Cee's stop a few stations before. I told Cee that I'd wait with him until his train came, and it was a good long wait. Finally, the train arrived and when it came to a full stop, guess who was glaring right at us? It was the same conductor that was operating the train that we were on earlier. He must have gone to the last stop, which was Coney Island, and turned the train back around. I covered my mouth because I started to laugh instantly and because I could see the level of "pissed" this guy was at. He wanted to jump out of the train and kick our asses but what could he really do. There weren't many people on the station but we weren't alone by any means so he was forced to open the doors. I gave Cee a quick five and told him to hit me up when he got home. I waved at the conductor and wished him a good night but he was in no mood for pleasantries.

I stuck my hands in my pockets and started to walk home, and I began to laugh to myself. Pissing on a Christmas tree was a new low for me. Still, I laughed. Can you imagine what would have happened had the tree been plugged in? I think being electrocuted to death while peeing on a Christmas tree would certainly be front-page news. That would have been a shame because I really enjoy the holidays and I believe people would get the wrong idea if my last act on this earth was peeing all over a Christmas tree. It would be a misrepresentation of my Christmas spirit. However, none of that would have happened if not for alcohol. There is a component to it, which makes for a lot of fun. And it makes me wonder if any of the funny little things that have happened to me would have ever taken place if not for the presence of alcohol. It also makes me wonder if I would be able to cope with the things that happened during my childhood if I wasn't constantly drowning myself in rum every chance that I got.

Why do I drink?

Now we are getting somewhere. I've been through years of therapy and enough time on a couch to make you scratch your head. I think that my story is a colorful one, yet it's somehow both simple and complex to see how I turned out to be me. My story is somewhat sad at times. Simultaneously, my story can be viewed as hilarious, but I'll let you decide for yourself. I guess the best I can do to somehow unravel my tangled frame of mind is to start with my early memories.

My family has never had any money to speak of. We were poor amongst the poor. I really didn't know any better because as far as I was concerned, everyone we knew was probably in the same boat as us. To me we weren't poor. We were normal and maybe just a little bit poorer than anyone else.

I was second generation welfare, barely surviving from day to day and my family was getting by on public assistance. I think the earliest memory I possess may be the New York City blackout of 1977. We lived on the fourth floor of a building in Brooklyn. It was a big tenement on the corner of East 2nd street and Cortelyou Road. We were playing in the front courtyard of the building at about 8:30 pm or so. Back then, there was nothing else to do but play outside of your own building within earshot of your parents. The block was lined with streetlights so everyone was out in the summer heat because it was way too hot to stay inside. All of a sudden, it was pitch black outside. Some people started yelling about a blackout as all the neighborhood mothers began to gather their children. My mother went to me immediately. I had just started to cry before I felt her grabbing my hand and proceeded to take me upstairs. I was a little scared of this thing they called a blackout but I had no clue what it meant. All of a sudden, there were sounds of broken glass coming from all over the neighborhood as people began to loot all the stores on the avenue. My mother hurried her pace to get us all in safely. I closed my eyes as tight as I could, shaking from the sound of one shattering window after another. I can remember that staircase very well. It would become a remembered route for me but it was never a good thing. I was still too young to understand it, but that particular staircase haunted me. The staircase was nothing more than a path leading to and away from the bad. There was some looting and fighting outside and

I could hear the police car sirens blaring down the street as the police attempted to get everything under control. I could hear all of the looting through the broken windows along the stairs. My mother was carrying me, with my legs wrapped around her waist. I buried my head into her nape and prayed that I would get away from the sounds and screaming before it had a chance to reach me. It was all going on right down the street but for the most part we were kept away from the chaos outside that day. That awful staircase always stayed with me, but I have never really figured out why.

I have certain memories that sometimes flash into my mind when I don't expect them to. My recall is both a gift and a curse. I cannot control it. I have the ability to remember the smallest details and seemingly unimportant happenings throughout my life. Another unpleasant memory I have of that building is the fire. There was a neighbor that was some kind of Santero. For those of you who don't know what that is, it's someone who practices Santeria. He may consider himself a male witch or a medium.

The guy next door had statues and candles burning in his apartment, which happened to be right next to ours, so it's easy to guess what happened next. Having candles burning in a closet is usually a good idea, No? Of course, the items in his closet caught fire and it didn't take long to spread. His apartment was ablaze and he came screaming out of the apartment, pounding on everyone's door. We opened the door and the hallway was completely filled with black smoke. Right away, we all started coughing and inhaling the toxic smoke. There was no way that we were going out that way. The fire escape was our only alternative. We opened the window and started to go down the only possible way out. While we were on our way down, we were knocking on everyone's windows trying to warn them as best we could.

Human panic is really something to watch. There were two women sitting at their table wearing robes with their hair in curlers, and one of them was reading. I knocked loudly on the window and yelled "Fire!"

They both stood up and looked at each other momentarily before they started screaming as well, and running in circles around the table. We kept going down the fire escape and repeated the action of knocking on windows over and over again.

18

When we hit the second floor fire escape, there was nowhere else to go. The ladder was too heavy for us to lift. Windows were breaking, as we were showered with broken glass, and people were scampering out of their apartments and onto the fire escape. It was complete chaos. I glanced upward and the flames from the apartment that was ablaze were now visible as the fire exploded through the front window. Everyone started to huddle together, all of us trapped on the second floor landing of the fire escape. We had run out of room. My brother, Indio, was stuck halfway between the second and third floor holding Sandy, our family dog.

All of a sudden, the ladder shot straight up and off the hook. It came down all the way to the ground floor, landing with a heavy thud, and everyone started to climb down. I had my legs and arms wrapped around my mom, facing her as she came down the ladder. Everyone started to thank this guy named Louie, who was at the foot of the ladder helping people down and grabbing children that were being passed to him. He was a local guy who was also rumored to be a junkie. But as everyone came down the ladder, he had instantly become a celebrity. People were hugging him and thanking him profusely.

He just kept saying, "Okay, no problem."

Before long, the fire department came and everyone was across the street safely. My brother couldn't climb down with the dog, so the firefighters went up there with the ladder truck with the bucket at the end of it. They had to coax poor frightened Sandy into the bucket. Thankfully, she wasn't an aggressive dog. I think she was just happy and thankful as the rest of us to get off that rickety fire escape. They got her and Indio safely into the bucket and everyone started cheering and clapping. It was a scene straight out of Hollywood. Nobody had died.

The tide turned on Louie somewhere around then. People started saying it was he that started the fire. That he was a junkie and was probably paid by the landlord to burn the place down. Why else would he be standing next to the fire escape? It couldn't be a coincidence. The poor guy had changed from hero to villain in moments. I can still remember his face. He denied it of course, but his expression was unforgettable. He was shocked and hurt by the accusation. He walked away before the fire department or anyone else could thank him or ask him anything. No one suspected that the fire had started in the apartment closet next to ours. No one knew the circumstances or just how much of a hero this guy really was, because he had saved us all. Human nature is and always will be the great betrayer. A whole building full of families was still alive today and it was only because this guy had done something. However, nobody believed that a junkie like him could possibly be capable of such a heroic act. He disappeared after that night.

The next time I saw him would be almost 20 years later. When I first saw him, I didn't say anything. I knew exactly who he was but I didn't know what to say. It was merely coincidence that we had run into each other outside a bar when I stepped out to smoke a cigarette.

I asked, "You're Louie, right?"

And a look of instant panic came on his face. Where I'm from, people generally don't like someone they don't recognize knowing their name. He froze for a minute and I could tell that he was nervous. I urged him to relax and told him that I used to live on Cortelyou Road when I was a kid. He looked instantly relieved.

"Yeah, I used to live out there," he said.

I told him my name, who my mom was, and he said he didn't really remember her. Then I said, "You saved us. You saved all of us from that fire."

He remembered me instantly as he made the connection. He went on to say that he also remembered my sister and my brothers. He asked how everybody was doing and I told him that it was sad to say but we weren't too well at all. I gave him a brief history of our plight and he nodded solemnly. We chatted for a few minutes as we both smoked, and we spoke briefly about the fire. He explained that it was a really rough time for him and that many people were saying crazy things about him. I told him that I understood. I didn't back then, but I understood now. No matter what people say, he was a hero. He saved many lives that day. When he goes for his face to face with the big guy upstairs, he could honestly say that he had a lot of saved souls under his belt. And maybe we wouldn't be standing here having this conversation if he hadn't been there and did what he did.

He pondered this for a minute and then he said, "I hope so."

We shook hands and thanked each other again, and then Louie went on his way.

I never saw him again. So maybe life changed for him. Maybe hearing what I said to him made some sense and he saved himself right back. Whatever happened to him, I had said my piece and I was glad to have said it. I still drive through that neighborhood and I often see that apartment building. When I do, it all comes back to me. It feels like I'm driving and I can see the road ahead of me but in my mind I can see everything back then clear as day. I can still hear glass cracking under everyone's shoes as we went back up the stairs. I can still smell the acrid smoke in my nostrils as we climbed down the fire escape. There was a lot of damage to our apartment and or course the apartment next door was destroyed. Finally, when they let us back in, my mom carried me up the stairs on her back because I hadn't enough time to put on a pair of shoes. There was broken glass everywhere and it was pitch black in the building. Somehow, the power had gone off and I was a scared little boy, once again being led through the dark staircase. Everything we owned smelled of smoke for a long time no matter how many times we washed it. I can't really recall how long before things went back to normal, but chaos in the night was becoming a theme in our lives. Thus, began my aversion to the dark. It was not that I feared it, but more that I did not trust it. Soon after, something happened that made me wish that I had stayed in the dark with my eyes clamped shut forever.

Madeline

The place was cursed. Of that, I have little doubt. While we were living there, I had also managed to get my face bitten by a dog I was attempting to befriend. The dog bit the right side of my face, leaving a scar under my lip that still remains. Whenever I am getting dressed, combing my hair, or brushing my teeth, I am always reminded of the bite. Believe it or not, it only got worse. Maybe about a year after the fire, I saw something that is chiseled into memory and still remains. I was five years old at the time, so if I were to estimate, I would guess I had about two gigs of memory at that point. Gilbert and I were playing in the living room, when I heard my sister Vilma knocking on the bathroom door and yelling my sister Madeline's name.

Madeline, who was my mother's oldest child, was born with Down syndrome and needless to say, had a lot of issues. She would often hurt herself, so she spent a lot of time going in and out of mental institutions. She was home with us for a little while at that point in time, and I surmise Vilma had noticed that Madeline had been in the bathroom for way too long. She went to check on Madeline to make sure everything was ok. She knocked several times loudly and started to call out Madeline's name to no avail. Gilbert and I were always curious little creatures so we followed her to the bathroom to see what all the fuss was about. Once she had gotten in to the bathroom, all I could hear was blood curdling screams coming from her. I can also vividly remember being hit with a blast of cold air.

She ran out of the bathroom and after forbidding us to go in, Vilma ran to the phone. While she was on the phone, Gilbert and I snuck into the bathroom to see for ourselves what exactly was going on, but there was nothing to see. The bathroom was completely empty and spotless. The only thing that seemed odd was that the window was wide open. It was winter, which made the bathroom feel like an icebox. Before I got a grasp of what was going on, I saw Gilbert jump up onto the tub and stick his head out of the window. He was there for only a second and when he jumped back down off the tub, he was wearing a look of both horror and sadness. He looked at me and immediately, his eyes watered. He warned me not to look and ran out of the bathroom, starting to scream along with my sister, who was still screaming into the phone.

Being the ever-willful child, I promptly jumped up on the tub and since I was still tiny, I had to struggle to climb up to the window sill. I was very cold, and I could see the cold whispers of breath escaping my mouth as I pulled myself up with all my might, so that I could see out of the window. My head was almost all the way out of the window, and then I saw it.

Four flights down, in the alleyway where everyone deposited their garbage, Madeline was sprawled out in the snow in a pool of blood. I froze for a moment and just stared at everything seemingly happening in slow motion. People were yelling for someone to call an ambulance. The neighbors were all coming to their windows to see what was going on, and just like me, they instantly regretted that decision. As quickly as they looked, they shut the window, some of them taking the time to make the sign of the cross across their chest before they shut the curtains trying to forget what they had just witnessed.

Madeline's arm was backwards, her hand at an impossible angle behind her, and the pool of blood in the snow slowly grew bigger. When things happen around me, I have the ability to become hyper-aware. I recognize it now when it occurs but I was still quite young so this was one of my first experiences with it. Even though it seems physically impossible, I could hear the blood spilling out onto the fresh fallen snow. I could hear all of the onlookers hushed and mournful voices. She was lying face down. Her lower half had landed and crushed a few garbage cans with the impact of her body falling four stories down. Four stories up, I could hear her ragged and labored breathing. I had seen enough. Some people on the street had spotted her and ran over to offer their help but not much could be done. There was a crowd that was gathering around her and little by little, the group backed away from her as the circle of blood grew wider in circumference as it poured out of her body. I lowered myself off the window sill and jumped back down into the tub. I walked out of the bathroom still trying to make sense of what I had just seen. I stayed in the hallway, staring at the bathroom, imagining the door as yet another evil portal that would somehow take me. I feared I would end up like Madeline if I had dared step through it again.

I remember my sister then pulling my shoulder and telling me not to go into the bathroom. She was shaking and crying and I was so mentally jarred that I couldn't answer her. Knowing what I know now, I was obviously in shock, but what does a little boy know about shock or mental trauma. The Fire Department arrived and a bunch of cops came to the apartment asking questions, but all I could do was stare at the bathroom door.

Miraculously, my sister survived but she had extensive injuries. Madeline was in the hospital for a long time and afterwards she went to a mental institution on Roosevelt Island for some time after that. It was more than a year before I saw her again. She was able to communicate a bit before she had attempted to take flight that cold winter day, but by the time I had seen her again, the incident had changed her, damaged her further. She had a different look in her eyes, almost like she wasn't there anymore.

Once in a while, she'd look at you and notice that you were in the room, but other than that, there was no more acknowledgement in her eyes. I don't know how much longer we lived in that apartment building after that incident, but I was scared to go into that bathroom by myself afterward. I hated to bathe and I would beg my mother to stand by the door because I was terrified to use that bathroom by myself.

After some time passed, we moved into a halfway decent apartment in the Borough Park section of Brooklyn. It was right around 1980 or so, and that was the last time I ever saw Madeline. I still don't know until this day what happened to her. I don't speak much of her, because the truth is that I don't know much. I think it's too painful for my mother to talk about. The slightest mention sends my mom to the bedroom she has at Vilma's house, where she'll disappear for a day or two, or until she forgives the mere mention of her lost child.

The little things that I do know, does nothing positive for my disposition and frame of mind. It bothers me immensely to know that her life was just not a happy life but a miserable, forlorn existence, which was no fault of her own. She was born sick, and the seven years that I knew her, were full of hospitals and institution visits on Sunday's.

Whether she had mistakenly fell from the window that day, or decided that she had given up on life, we'll never know. The cruelty of it all is that she survived and was even further disabled, physically as well as mentally afterward. There are several rumors and stories as to how exactly she disappeared but none was ever confirmed as the truth. My oldest brother Indio once told Gilbert and I that Madeline had been sitting on the steps in front of the building one day, when a car pulled up to the curb. Allegedly, the guy in the car told her to get into the car and take a ride, and she obliged. She was never seen again. He warned us that we better behave and do exactly what he said or the same thing could happen to us.

Another story was that my mother had checked her into yet another mental institution, and when it came to visiting day, they had simply lost her. Whether she had escaped or if it was human error, the story still ended with Madeline never to be seen again. Vilma has tried several times to find her, or find out what exactly happened to her, but as of yet, it has been one fruitless search after another. It's sad to say that all I know about my sister Madeline, you now know.

The last time we saw my sister was in 1980. It was more than thirty-five years ago, and not a day goes by that I don't think about her. I think of just how tough her life was from the very beginning, and it breaks my heart to know that she had so much to deal with from her very first breath. I will also never know when or if she took her last breath. It also hurts to never know if she ever felt happiness, or if she missed us. Did she know enough to love us? Did she even understand the concept of love and family? She had not asked to be born, nor had she ever hurt anyone in her time here, yet she did nothing but suffer her entire time here. It really doesn't seem fair, does it? I've wrestled with that my entire life, and it was one of my first of many bouts with doubt regarding "God's plan." I fail to see the point of Madeline's poor tortured soul.

The Book of Gil

My brother Gilbert was probably the funniest and angriest person I have ever come across. He was a wonderful brother and he would never let harm come to me, no matter how hard I tried to get myself killed. He never tried to understand me or to figure out my rational, instead he simply disagreed with just about everything I have ever thought or said. If I said it, it was wrong. However, no matter what, at the end of the day I was his little brother.

He was a good-looking kid, and he was tough as nails. Nobody, but nobody messed with Gilbert in the neighborhood. The few that were unwise enough to try him quickly regretted it. When he balled his huge hand into a fist, his punches felt like you were being hit in the head with a roll of quarters, and I was on the receiving end of those punches my fair share of the time. But he did his best by me. We actually had different fathers. It mattered not. We slept in the same bed until we were teens, and went through the same struggles, same sadness, and same disappointments as any other set of brothers would. As much as we fought and as much as we disagreed, we loved each other dearly. We would do anything for each other.

Whenever one of us would get a job, we would try to persuade the boss to hire someone else. This practice continued into our adulthood. I would call Gilbert, or he would call me and we would try to get each other a job so that we could both bring some money home to our mother. We did manage to work together quite often, though we ended up having a fist fight at work more often than not.

Even the earliest memories I have of Gilbert are odd and kind of funny at the same time. I recall walking into the bathroom one day and finding him standing on a chair. He was in front of the mirror and he had a pair of pliers in his mouth. He was trying to shorten his buck teeth by clipping off the ends of his teeth using a set of pliers. I walked in and stopped in my tracks. I asked him what he was doing and he just hid the pliers behind his back. He said nothing. He just jumped off the chair, shoved me aside, and walked out. I do remember being confused but I don't think I ever mentioned it again. Thank God I walked in when I did. I don't know what he would have looked like as an adult with two crudely clipped teeth. He probably would have been angrier if he had to be funny looking as well.

Had I been a little older, I would have definitely gotten wise with Gilbert and earned myself a beating because I always used to go out of my way to fuck with him. This is what we did, being extremely poor and with no toys to speak of. We simply messed with each other to pass the time. I'd be minding my own business and Gilbert would piss in a glass and put it on ice, gloating how tasty his lemonade was. He insisted that I try it and I did. After one sip, I knew immediately that I had been had. Another time, I learned a neat little trick and decided to try it out on Gilbert. Don't try this at home kids, but I learned that if you take a metal wire hanger and continuously bend it at one of the joints, it will actually get hot enough to burn your skin. I enjoyed testing this on Gilbert's back and it did not disappoint. He actually had a nice small burn scar on his back from it, and occasionally he would remind me of what an asshole I was for burning him. But we had to entertain ourselves somehow.

Other kids at school were bragging about all the great stuff they were getting for Christmas and I was super excited that Gilbert had outgrown his pants, which meant that I now had a new addition to my wardrobe. We would be sitting around using anything in the house as a toy, including tools, kitchen utensils, or whatever we could get our hands on. Most of our toys came from broken toys that we would find in the street and put back together or merge with other broken toys to make it complete.

Once in a while, my mom would start to date someone, and the guy would come over the house as her "Friend" to meet everyone. When we met her friend Joey, Gilbert and I were sitting on the floor playing with our trucks. By trucks, I mean that Gilbert and I were using belts and dragging them all over the floor pretending they were tractor trailers. When we got really inventive, we would attach one belt to another and make a long train, pretending that we were conductors. Joey walked in and couldn't believe that we didn't have any cars or trucks to play with. He left, but he came back about a half hour later and gave us each a toy truck, with a trailer, that held about five or six cars behind it. We were beside ourselves, we were so happy.

Joey became an instant favorite of ours. He was actually good to us and he ended up being in and out of my mom's life for a long time. I found out when I got older that he was actually married, with a family of his own, which was strange considering how much time he had spent with us, but it was a forgivable offense. He was good to us and treated us like we were his kids as well, at least for a little while. Funny thing is that by the time I had reached high school, I was already taller than Joey and when I think about it now, he actually might have been a dwarf. This makes me laugh for some reason, when I think just how short he really was. It goes to show that just the smallest gesture or act of kindness could affect a child for the rest of his life. He didn't know us at all and within minutes he had given Gilbert and I more than we had.

Gilbert liked him too, and since he was my primary care giver, I followed whatever Gilbert did and said. My mother always left Gilbert in charge of me, which made me sure that she had it in for me. My brother would torture me, beat me to a pulp, and then clean me up before we got within my mother's sight. One particular Fourth of July, in what had to be about 1984 or so, was when I got my worst beating from my brother. It was well deserved on my part and I can freely admit that I had enjoyed every minute of it.

My mother bartended for many years at a little place called La Copa. Before she left to work that night, she instructed Gilbert to keep an eye on me. She also instructed Gilbert to make sure I didn't play with matches, but who knew that Gilbert was going to take these orders so seriously? The night was going by without incident as I ran around with my friend Hasim lighting fireworks, until my brother decided to be a dick and take away my matches. Well, first I have to explain Hasim to you. He was probably a year or two older than me, and he was a really nice kid. He was black, tall, and painfully thin. He also had a nervous condition that made his hair fall out in patches. It was a form of alopecia that only affected his hair when he was nervous or stressed. So he often wore hats and skull caps to hide his head. He didn't have a lot of friends because kids can be mean, I guess. Although I had never seen anyone make fun of Hasim or try to embarrass him about his condition, he told me that most people avoided him.

It was really a shame because he was such a nice guy. It really didn't matter to me that he was odd, because I had always been a bit of a misfit myself. I've never been one to fit into mainstream civilization. To this day, most of my friends in my life have come from the island of misfit toys. They're just my people.

Hasim and I were lighting our firecrackers and minding our own business when Gilbert came over and said, "Mom said she doesn't want you playing with matches."

Then he snatched the matches right out of my hand. I was pissed so I asked for the matches back and he refused. I tried my hand at asking nice and kissing his ass a bit but he wasn't going for that neither. I really think that he just ran out of matches and he didn't feel like finding more or buying some at the corner store. So he took mine. Hasim had a lighter but I didn't feel like I should be begging him to light all my fireworks for me, considering that I had my own matches just moments before.

Minutes later, there was Gilbert running around and having fun, lighting all his fireworks and having a good old time with my matches. I immediately began a plan of action for retribution.

I said to Hasim, "Give me the lighter."

He gave it to me without really putting much thought into what I was up to. I don't know if you are familiar with fireworks but one of them is called a "Jumping Jack". It's small and approximately the size of a firecracker. However, it doesn't have a big bang or explosion. You light it and throw it. It spins and the flame burns brightly, while changing colors and making a buzzing or whirling sound. This lasts about thirty-seconds and then it burns out. It's very entertaining when you're eleven years old, and I had one in my pocket.

I calmly walked over, stood behind Gilbert, and waited for my opportunity to strike. When he finally bent over to light another firecracker with my damn matches, I walked over and inserted the jumping jack into Gilbert's back pocket, leaving the fuse hanging out. I calmly lit it, walked right back over to Hasim, and handed him his lighter.

"Watch this," I said and waited for the show to start.

Hasim asked me "Watch what?" but I just smiled and told him to watch.

When the jumping jack lit up, the look of surprise on Gilbert's face made the whole thing worth it. He had no idea where the sound and bright lights were coming from. He had no idea what was burning his ass so much. All he could do was try to run. And run he did. Strangely enough, he had decided to wear white jeans that day.

29

Who wears white jeans? And when the flames started burning through his jeans, he was just a blur of movement. He was running down the street, smacking his backside, trying to put out the fire in his ass. All I could see was his white jeans running back and forth, the back of his pants turning red, orange, then yellow, and finally green. He was trying to outrun the fire and violently slapping at the back of his pants that was on him like glue.

We were in stitches. My friends and his friends were all hysterical at the sight of him running down the street with his ass on fire.

Hasim kept saying, "Oh my God, Oh my God."

I was laughing so hard that my asthma began to kick in. I was doubled over coughing because I could not catch my breath. Finally, the flames died down and Gilbert stopped running. He kept swatting at his jeans and there was smoke trailing up into the sky from his ass. He reached into his back pocket but it was no longer there. There was a gaping burnt hole in his pants and in his underwear, we could all see his red, singed behind. Then he found the jumping jack in what was left of the seam of his pocket, and he looked to be very angry to say the least. He glared back at all of us, and from the look on his face, you could tell that he wanted to kill somebody. He was staring daggers at all of us and his anger was building. He was trying to decide who he was going to kill, then he locked his eyes on me. It must have been the expression on my face because he knew it was me.

Somehow, he knew that I was the only one that was crazy enough to do something like that to him. His eyes had rage in them as he balled his fists very tightly and started walking towards me.

I heard Hasim utter "Oh shit." And he was right to feel that way.

I hadn't really thought this one out. Gilbert put his head down and started to run towards us. We were too terrified to even move but when I looked at Hasim, and was about to warn him that he should start running for his life, there were actually two piles of hair on either one of his shoulders. All of his hair had fallen out in one shot.

I exclaimed, "Hasim, your hair!" He smacked his hands on either side of his now cleanly bald head. I urged him to run and I think he did but I really can't say I am sure because I was laughing so hard. Hasim had turned towards me slowly, which his eyes big and wide, with two neat little piles of short curly hair on his shirt.

I tried to run but it was too late and Gilbert was on top of me in a flash. He proceeded to kick the shit out of me for what felt like an hour. I was on the ground and was doing my best to cover up as much as I could, but I still took the beating of my life. Let's be honest, I deserved it. I was laying on the ground for a while afterwards, a bloody and bruised pulp, but I was somehow laughing. All I could think of was just how ridiculous he had looked running down the street with flames shooting out of his ass like Wile E. Coyote. And how equally ridiculous he must have looked beating me up with his burnt ass hanging out of his pants. It was a win-win for me. It was just unforgettable.

Another evening, Gilbert and I both caught what we would always refer to as the "Kung-Fu Beat Down" from our mother. It was probably the funniest beating I ever received. My brother and I were obsessed with the karate movies they showed on television every Saturday at 3 o'clock. It was a double feature so we were good for about 4 hours of non-stop action. The only problem was that my mother usually worked until 4 or 5 am the night before and was usually sleeping at that time. She usually woke up around early evening, made dinner and then got ready for another night at the bar.

Usually there was a short break in between movies, and at this opportune time, Gilbert and I would work on all the karate moves we just learned from the movie we just saw. We were kicking, fighting back and forth and beating the shit out of each other, having ourselves a fun afternoon. Apparently, we were making too much noise and had awakened my mother who was none too pleased. She ripped the bedroom door open. (And when I say the bedroom door, it is because there was only one bedroom in the apartment) There were 5 of us living in that apartment. It had one bedroom and one other room that served as the living room/dining room/kitchenette. We all slept in the bedroom except for my oldest brother Indio who was only a part time resident there anyway.

My mother kicked the door completely ajar and started cursing at us in Spanish. We stared at her with bewildered amusement, as she seemed to be throwing karate kicks as she approached us. It all seemed incredibly comical until she kicked Gilbert in the stomach and when he doubled over, she punched him in the back of the head as he went down. I was frozen with amazement. She then turned to me and gave me a right cross that knocked me on my ass. As I was going down, I realize that my mom had made a Kung Fu noise when she hit me. Come to think of it, she had made a few noises too when she kicked and punched my brother.

She was yelling, "You want karate, I'll give you karate." She yelled, "whoo" and "whaa" as she was kicking the shit out of us.

I mean, really? Can you imagine your own mom giving you a beating, while making karate noises? This was pure hilarity, but I don't think she appreciated the amused grin on my face.

The last thing I remember was laying on the floor playing dead and watching her stepping on Gilbert's head and watching his eyes shut tight with every deadly blow she delivered. I think I passed out at this point, and it's unclear as to how long I was knocked out. I remember coming to and it was completely quiet in the apartment. Across the floor from me, identically laid out on the floor was Gilbert who was slowly coming around as well. I don't know how long we had been unconscious, but it had grown dark out. Gilbert and I made eye contact as we lay there. Neither one of us dared to move.

I said, "Hey Gil, did you hear the sounds she was making as she was hitting us?"

"Yeah," he said as he slowly rubbed his head. We made eye contact one more time and then we both burst into laughter.

We laughed for at least ten minutes straight. It didn't matter that we had just had our asses handed to us. It didn't matter that we had been viciously beaten and Gilbert had been bleeding from his nose. We were just hysterical that my mother had gotten out of bed in her "Bata" which is basically a nightgown/house dress in Puerto Rican culture, and kicked the shit out of both of us. She had done it while making all kinds of Kung-Fu noises, and simultaneously beating us up and cursing at us in Spanish. Then she simply went right back to bed and left us there. We were laughing so hard we had to shush each other because we were afraid to wake her up again. Then only God knows what language she would have kicked our ass in at that point. I still literally laugh out loud, wherever I am, when I think of that day.

But that's how Gilbert and I were. We never stayed mad and we never took it personal. Sure, my mother was probably a bit excessive in her dispensing of discipline but what the hell was she supposed to do. She was a single mom trying to raise five kids all on her own. My oldest sister had been born mentally handicapped, and my oldest brother was a drug dealing thief who respected nothing, so it was up to her to somehow get it all right. Raise us all and feed us, control us, teach us, and she had to do it all on her own. God dealt her one big shitty hand. She came here alone as a teenager, and it didn't get any better for her as she got older. She dated abusive men, worked shitty jobs, and didn't speak English. Let's just say that she wasn't getting any help, so she had to raise us all by herself. And to say that we were more than a handful is probably putting it lightly. So it was this violent love that made us the way we are.

Gilbert was stubborn though, as oppose to me, I always knew when to wave the white flag when my mother was concerned. She was going to have her way. And she was going to get her licks in, regardless of our attempts to flee or defend. On another occasion, Gilbert and I were up to no good again, and my mother caught us and threatened our lives if we didn't cut it out. We didn't stop and she came downstairs to dispense justice. She had a broomstick in her hand. We saw her coming and we tried to make a break for it. Well, let's be honest, Gilbert made a break for it and I just froze again. Out of the corner of my eye, I saw a broomstick flying in our direction. I don't know if she actually moved that fast and unscrewed the brush part of it off or if she came down with just the stick, but it was suddenly flying towards us like a javelin. I really believe she had set her radar vision to detect and lock on to movement, kind of like how a T-Rex's vision works.

The broomstick whizzed past my face and kept on flying down the block. Gilbert was running and it was on top of him quick. It hit him right at the base of his spine in his lower back and he went down like a ton of bricks. She had such precision when she attacked. She was absolutely surgical. The stick had hit him right where it couldn't cause any permanent damage but it just paralyzed him temporarily. He was on the ground, legs flailing about like a cockroach on his back. She walked right by me and she already had a slipper in her hand. She proceeded to beat him with the slipper for a few minutes, taking a break only to yell and curse at him. She then told us to get right upstairs. And when he could finally walk again, we did just that. Somehow I had avoided getting beat. I really think that the fact that he had the audacity to run from her somehow made her forget all about me. I don't remember what we talked about that evening but he was pissed that he had gotten the brunt of it. And it wasn't the last time.

When I was around twelve years old, I had developed an obsession with masturbation. I was all over myself and I just wasn't being coy or taking "No" for an answer. I abused myself so much that I had completely chafed myself and would have to take breaks for weeks at a time to heal. What does this have to do with Gilbert? Well, I'll explain.

I had little stashes of pornographic paraphernalia all over the house. Whether it was magazines or movies, or pictures, I was fully prepared. I didn't have my own bedroom so I had to be prepared for action wherever it may be that I happened to sleep that night. One awesome afternoon it was somewhere around 3 o'clock or so and my brother had just gotten home from wherever he was. My mother was waiting for him and pounced on him immediately. She started screaming at him in Spanish, and poor Gilbert had no clue what was going on. She had a magazine rolled up in her hand and she was waving the magazine back and forth, then smacked him in the face with it. I had no clue what was going on, at least not a first, but apparently she had found one of my magazines that I had hidden in Gilbert's closet. God knows what she was doing in Gilbert's closet because she never did laundry or folded clothes. Perhaps she had found the magazine accidentally but that didn't really matter now. From what I could overhear, she wanted to know what kind of sexual deviant he was and wondered how long he had been afflicted with this sexual disease of the mind. She was going on and on about how disgusting he was and how he was going to sign up for therapy if we wanted to live in this house with the normal people.

Gilbert had no clue what magazine she was ranting and raving about. At that point, I decided that it was probably as good a time as any to work on my jump shot at the park. I was getting dressed and lacing up my sneakers in record time. Then I heard Gilbert say that the magazine belonged to me. That rat bastard cheesed me out. But it didn't work, because she didn't buy it. I was already out of sight and on my way out the door, but if I were within three city blocks, I would have heard my mother clear as day. She went bananas. Now, years later, my mother can speak English perfectly. She has an accent when she wants to have one, but for the most part she communicates with one hundred percent proficiency in Spanish and English. However, when she gets pissed off English goes right out the window, and that day she was enraged.

She started berating him, Gilbert claiming his innocence the entire time, and she was just getting angrier with every word. The last thing I heard before I fled the scene was my mother screaming about how I was way too young to be involved with magazines of such graphic nature and that there was no way that the magazine could have been mine. She also stated that I was only 12 years old and how could I even come into possession of those sick publications. How dare he blame his mental deficiencies on his poor innocent little brother. That was my cue to exit. I snuck down the stairs and couldn't help laughing to myself as I could still hear my mother giving Gilbert the business.

I stayed out very late that night in the park. First, to make sure my mom had gotten it all out of her system and also to give Gilbert ample time to get over the fact that he had been persecuted for my deviance. When I came home, I went straight to the bathroom to take a shower. I hid in the living room all night and planned to sleep on the couch like I did most of the time. While I was laying down, Gilbert came out of his bedroom and was heading to the bathroom but he stopped to glare at me. I was going to pretend to be asleep but I figured I might as well get it over with. He was just standing there staring at me and I could feel the heat of his laser vision on my face. I returned the gaze and didn't say anything.

Gilbert leaned over and said, "You're a real fucking asshole, you know that?" I didn't say anything. I mean, how was I supposed to answer that? At the same time, I could not help but think of the hilarity of my mother yelling at him and calling him a pervert. A big smile started to develop on my face and before I knew it, I was covering my mouth so I wouldn't burst out laughing out loud. It also served to protect my teeth just in case Gilbert decided to punch me in the mouth.

I just couldn't help it. I started cracking up. Amazingly, Gilbert started laughing too. Not a hysterical laughter but a giggle at least, and then he walked away from me. I stuck my head under the blanket and laughed to myself for about five minutes.

When he finally came out of the bathroom, he walked right by me without stopping and said, "You owe me one."

I agreed and we left it at that. I wanted to say that I would take the train ride to the therapist with him but I didn't want to push it. I had really dodged a bullet and he had taken it for me. I don't think that we ever actually settled up or mentioned it again but even as I sit here remembering this and re-living that day, I still laugh thinking of my mother screaming at him.

Thoughts of Gilbert and our exploits always make me laugh. But It wasn't always fun and games. When we were younger, my family had been homeless for a while. My mother bounced us around from a friend's house to another friend's house and we weren't always all together. I don't recall where my other brothers and sisters were living but Gilbert and I ended up living with his god-mother for a few months. She was one of my mother's lifelong friends and her name was Lilly. She was probably the most violent and volatile woman I will ever meet in my life. I didn't like her one bit, never did. Upon our introduction, my mother had mentioned to her that I had a tooth that was loose and was ready to come out but I was scared to pull it out. She coaxed me into showing her my tooth and promised me that she wasn't going to touch it. I opened my mouth to show her and when I did so, she shoved her entire hand into my mouth and dug her nail into my gums. She ripped the tooth right out of my mouth. I heard it fall onto the ground and it must have slipped under the refrigerator because I never saw the tooth again. I just stood there, bleeding and in total shock. I started crying so she slapped me not so playfully and told me to stop being a baby. I ran into the bathroom and spit out blood for about an hour.

Needless to say, I hated her guts but I wasn't about to make her privy of my disdain for her. She was truly a scary person and a very violent woman, yet my mother never said a word. I really thought that she should have come to my defense in some way, but she never did. My mother had chosen this woman to be our guardian for the next few months, until she had gotten back on her feet. To say that it was a very hot and long summer was an understatement. I resented my mother for leaving us with this psycho but what was she supposed to do? We were dirt poor and homeless. I'm sure that any option would be better than all of us living in a shelter. Her hands were tied so she did what she had to do.

And so our summer began. Lilly had a few children of her own and they had all grown up on Knickerbocker Avenue in the Bushwick area of Brooklyn. They were all violent, and had been esteemed guests of the state prison system at one time or another. On my first night there I wanted to go home badly, as if there was a home to go to. I just wanted to be with my mother. I guess I had been crying a little too loudly in the bed because one of the elder brothers got pissed off, smacked me really hard on my ass, and told me to be quiet. He hit me so hard that it knocked me off the bed, and when I stood up and tried to scramble back onto the bunk bed I hit my head on the top bunk. I started crying even more and when he came closer to me, I got so scared that I pissed myself right on the spot. I waited for the next blow but it never came.

Next thing I felt was his hand rubbing my head. When I looked up, he was just standing there with a remorseful look on his face.

He continued to rub my head, then he said, "Sorry little man, I didn't mean to hit you so hard."

Then he noticed that I was standing there in a puddle of my own piss. As he looked down, and his face contorted, I waited for him to hit me again. But again, it never came. He kept apologizing for hitting me. I figure he felt like shit for literally knocking the piss out of me. Here I was a 6-year-old kid, so damn frightened that I had urinated on myself. I was also freshly homeless, so I guess he figured the last thing I needed on top of all that was another beating to add to my list of woes. He helped me change into clean clothes and told me to go to bed. He never hit me again, and he was always nice to me after that. He always called me "little man". I don't even remember his name but I can remember with amazing clarity what he said to me that night.

He said, "I'm sorry I hit you little man, but you gotta toughen up. Life is fucked up and the bullshit is going to get a lot worse than this. You can't go crying every time something gets fucked up. You just gotta man up and live with shit that God gives you. Trust me bro, it's gonna get worse. You understand what I'm saying?"

I nodded. And I wasn't just nodding so that I could get him out of my face. I think that I fully understood what he was getting at. Here I was a six-year old kid, and I already had a shit hand dealt to me. He understood that I understood. And he patted me on the head and told me to go to sleep. I did. I stopped crying and I went straight to bed. That was how my summer started. I had already learned one of life's lessons and I hadn't even had a chance to warm up my pillowcase.

Gilbert and I spent that summer in constant fear for our lives and also in curious amusement of how these people lived. Lilly's youngest son was a really nice kid who just didn't seem to fit in with that family at all. His name was Abel. He treated Gilbert and I like brothers. He was much closer to Gilbert because his mother had baptized Gilbert and he was also much closer to him in age. He also treated me well I must admit. But his mother, she must have confused him for a punching bag. She could find any reason, on any given day to beat him senseless. Whether it was the dishes, or his room, or the television being loud, she would punch him in his face like he was a grown man. She would insult him, beat him, and sometimes lock him in the bathroom, whatever she could do to demean him. And not once, ever did he cry. He never winced. He never even whimpered. He manned up.

That's when I understood precisely what his older brother had told me. I understood whatever Abel was going through, his older brother had most likely gone through exactly that, and there was no sense in crying about it. Life was just shitty sometimes. And for them, it was more often than not. Sometimes, the very person that gave you life, could be the one that made it so difficult to live. That's enough to fuck up any kid's head. It's no wonder they were all violent and constantly in and out of jail. What chance did they have? For some reason, she just didn't like to feed us. I have never figured out why. She would not feed us all day but one meal before bed. There was always a late dinner. Somewhere around nine or ten pm, she would cook rice and maybe a little something extra, like a fried egg. Even when she served us that one meal, the portions were so small that it never satisfied our hunger. You would think that since we didn't eat breakfast or lunch that she would perhaps make it up to us with a nice healthy portion of food. But no, it was always one scoop of rice. Sometimes it was yellow rice, sometimes white rice, but no more than one scoop.

The only time Gilbert complained she smacked him so hard he dropped his food. She had given him one scoop of rice and he asked for more. She told him no, and he complained. I don't think she was accustomed to having her rule questioned. She hit Gilbert so hard that his plate of rice went tumbling to the floor. I remember the look on Gilbert's face. He couldn't believe that he had just gotten hit for asking for more food. When he went to pick up the food, she pushed him away, and quickly swept the food away with the broom. She informed him that since he wasn't happy with his dinner, he wasn't going to have any. I am sure that Gilbert was so hungry that he was going to eat the food off the floor. When he tried to pick it up, she knew it too. She wanted to punish him further by taking that away as well. Abel, Gilbert, and I went into another room to eat. What we did was we split the food up into 3 servings. I ate some of my food. Abel ate some of his food. And we gave the rest to Gilbert. At first, he refused to eat our food. He kept telling me to eat. He claimed he would be fine and that he wasn't that hungry anyway, but we both knew he was starving. I started crying because I knew he wasn't going to eat and I was afraid that he was going to die of starvation. Finally, he relented and he ate just to shut me up. I know Gilbert. And I know he would have rather died than to admit he needed to eat. But being a kid, I was deathly afraid to be in this world without Gilbert. He was my Brother, my protector, and the only piece of family I had at this time. I now know that he certainly wouldn't have died from not eating one night but at the time, it seemed to be a life-threatening situation. But he loved me enough to put his stubborn nature aside. I remember him reassuringly patting me on my head and telling us not to worry. He was going to eat the food we had saved for him. He ate and I slept at ease, just a little hungrier, which was nothing new for us.

That was not, by far, the most interesting meal we had shared that summer. Lilly had a boyfriend who lived in the Redhook section of Brooklyn. It was a rough area in the 80's but has since changed to condo's and "waterfront" property and the kind of people that would like to hug their mugger and assure them that it's not their fault before handing over all of their cash and credit cards. He had a small apartment there in Redhook and we would spend the weekends there sometimes when he and Lilly were spending quality time together. He was a quiet guy, soft spoken and really didn't say much to us. He just kind of tolerated our presence. She would leave us locked up in his stifling apartment all day without anything to eat and just show up at some point and feed us in the night.

Funny thing is that we had a little bit of help from the neighbors. Since the apartment was always so hot and we were stuck in there for the whole day, we would spend a lot of time out on the fire escape. Before long, we had developed a friendship with the kids that lived next door. The oldest was the sister and she was absolutely gorgeous. She had 2 younger brothers and they would take turns talking to us through the window. The window that led to their fire escape had a gate on it so they could not come out and hang out with us but they would talk to us through the safety bars on their window. She was my first love. I think that this was the first time in my young life that I had some kind of romantic feelings towards a girl and I really wish that I could remember her name. We would talk for hours. Partly, because I loved her company and also because there was nothing else to do. In the morning, they would sneak us cereal and whatever food they had left over. They would have to wait until their parents went to work but we didn't care.

It was summer so we had nowhere to go. Sometimes they would go play outside and we weren't allowed out so we'd have to wait for them to come back in. One day one of the brothers came up the stairs and wanted to see where we lived. He knocked and after we inquired who it was, we let him in. He was amazed when he realized that there was hardly any furniture in the apartment. There were a few mattresses on the floor and a kitchen table. But there was no television, no couch, and definitely no food. He went through our fridge and cabinets and he was shocked that we were still alive. After he left, he ran straight upstairs and started to smuggle everything in his fridge to us. We told him we couldn't take it all because Lilly would know that were was foreign food in the house and we would have to explain where we got it. So the kids next door would give us a little bit of food at a time, and that's how we survived the daily hunger.

I remember sitting on the fire escape, even when it was late at night and we could see the elevated F train going by all the time. I believe it's the highest elevated train in the world, running across 9th street, past the Redhook area. We would fantasize about escaping. We would talk about how we were going to leave and walk to the train one day and just go home. But the truth was, there was no home. There was no place to go. We would all just sit and talk all day and night and we swore we saw everything from UFO's to shooting stars. It's really a wonder how the mind of a child works and how we would think of just about everything to distract us from the real things in our simple lives that had plagued us.

One day, right out of the blue, Lilly and her boyfriend came home with 3 pigeons. She told us that the pigeons were now our pets and we could give them names. So we each named one, and even though they were filthy pigeons, they were a welcome distraction. We played with them and chased them all over the apartment. Our only job was to clean up after them whenever they shit on the floor. We fed them little bits of dried up bread that they gave us to feed the birds. And we were also warned and threatened with bodily harm if we were to let the pigeons go so we had to keep the windows closed. It made the apartment dreadfully hot, and the smell of pigeon was just unbearable. One day, out of the blue again, the adults came home and told us to go outside and play. We were so happy to be getting fresh air that we didn't even tie our laces as we ran out of the door. We rang all the bells of the apartment house next door and sooner or later someone buzzed us in. Gilbert figured out where the kids next door lived and asked them to come outside and play. They were just as excited as we were so we all ran back downstairs, and the kids brought down a ball and bat, a football and whatever they could bring with them. I was running the streets playing football and baseball and I couldn't care less whatever else had happened that summer. We stayed out late that night. We had been locked up indoors all summer long so it was certainly a night to remember. Finally, we got called to come upstairs, and we were absolutely filthy and sweaty. We all said good night and swore that we would try to do it again the following day. We declared each other as best friends. We made grand plans to party the rest of the summer away. But the truth is, we never saw them again, not once.

When we got upstairs, the scene in the apartment was horrifying. There were feathers everywhere. And the birds were nowhere to be found. Lilly informed us that we were all to take showers, and then we could have some chicken soup before we went to bed. I was a little too young to immediately realize what had taken place but my brother and Abel figured it out right away. Gilbert's face changed to several shades of red and he was shaking, he was so angry. He said he wasn't hungry, and he wasn't going to eat any soup. I then realized what had happened, and I was hit with a sudden nausea that was too much to control. I threw up right there and covered my mouth as I ran into the bathroom. I vomited repeatedly and I was crying hysterically while she screamed at me that I better clean up or she was going to harm me in some way or another. Gilbert came into the bathroom and did his best to clean up after me as she called us ungrateful. Then again threatened us saying that this was the last time she would ever cook. Lilly warned us that we would be wise to eat but none of us did.

At one point, she hit Gilbert. She smacked his face loudly, and left the marks of her fingers on his cheek. And he just stood there defiantly. She told him to go to bed and when he came to lie down on the mattress we shared, I started crying. I knew that once again, he had taken the hit for me, and I just wanted to get the hell out of there. I told him that I wanted to be with mom, wherever she was. I just couldn't stand it any longer. I was nearing my breaking point. He told me not to worry and that we would be home soon. And it couldn't happen soon enough. The very next morning they packed us up and we went back to Bushwick. After a few terrifying months, my mother had sent word that she had found us a place to live, and we would be going home soon. On the day we were supposed to go home, we were driving home and Lilly's boyfriend got into an altercation in the street. We were all in the car and we hadn't even travelled two blocks before the fight erupted. Some guy on a ten-speed bicycle had crossed in front of the car without looking and words were passed. Seconds later the guy threw his bottle of beer straight into Lilly's boyfriends face. His face exploded in blood as the beer bottle opened a nasty crater on his face. We were sitting in the back of the car still when Lilly jumped out of the car and started fighting this man. Seconds later her oldest sons came running and they beat this man so badly that the ambulance took him first so that they wouldn't kill him.

We sat in the car the entire time and watched this whole war from beginning to end. They beat this man even after he was unconscious. They started picking up his body and slamming it down to the ground. Finally, people from the neighborhood stopped them before it was too late. They managed to drag them away before the cops arrived and arrested them, but the cops never even came. They also took the guys bicycle and wrapped it around a fire hydrant. One of Abel's brothers jumped in the car and drove us back to the house in Bushwick. Lilly's boyfriend went to the hospital along with his adversary. They came back from the hospital late that night and told us that we would have to wait to go home. It was eerily quiet that week.

Lilly was very busy caring for her man, and the older brothers went into hiding because they were being sought by the police for the merciless beating they had given that man. He had started the whole thing and he was the one who threw the bottle, but still you couldn't help but feel bad for guy as he was laying there in a pool of his own blood and they just kept right on stepping on his head. Lilly was somewhat pleasant for a while after that. She played the doting wife and cooked every day. She sent us out to play every morning because all the noise was causing her boyfriend a lot of pain and migraines.

Before the week was over, we managed to receive corporal punishment two more times. Gilbert had decided to steal a bit of milk from the refrigerator, which we were forbidden to touch, and Lilly noticed that someone had put his lips on the milk carton. Gilbert had thought that maybe he could do it stealthily enough to avoid being caught by her so he didn't dare use a glass. Lilly knew that it had to have been one of us, because her children would know better than to defy her rules. She made us kneel on raw rice for an hour, but she was unsuccessful in her plan to get one of us to snitch on the other. I had never known such pain could exist as each individual grain of rice dug deeper and deeper into my skin. I cried quietly the entire time while Gilbert remained stoic and defiant for as long as he could. He urged me not to cry, but he finally relented as a single tear ran down his face and hit the ground in front of us. That was all it took to break the dam of tears I had been unsuccessfully holding in. She had broken Gilbert, and at the point I knew my efforts not to cry were hopeless. It wasn't the first time she had done this to us, but it was by far the longest period of time she made us endure this method of discipline. My knees still stiffen and ache at the thought of it.

Finally, at the end of that last week, we were taken home. My mother had found an apartment and Lilly was tired of having us around. The drive to our new apartment felt like the sweet end of a long prison sentence. When we came out of the car, my mother noticed how skinny we were. I was always rather thin and sickly, but Gilbert had probably lost 15 to 20 pounds in those two months. My bones were sticking out of my shoulder and ribs, and my sister asked what the hell had happened to me. I hugged my mom tightly and told her I never wanted to be away from her again. She had tears in her eyes, which wasn't like my mother at all. My mom and Lilly chatted for about five minutes before they left. We said our goodbyes to Abel, and promised we would hang out again soon. We never saw him again either. After they drove away we told my mother what had transpired throughout the summer, and I don't know if she fully believed us. However, whenever she would go visit with Lilly we never went again. We always stayed home. And we begged my older sister Vilma to babysit us because we were afraid that my mother would leave us there again. It is sad that we never saw Abel again. My mother told me that he had gone to jail as a teenager. I guess he followed his brother's footsteps after all. Last thing my mom told me was that he had been ostracized from the family because it turned out that he was a homosexual. Apparently, Lilly could tolerate all the crimes her sons had committed, but Abel being gay was far too much for her to bear.

I was sad for him. I still am. He was a great kid, and he never had a chance simply because he was born into evil. Gilbert and I would speak of him often. Gilbert also talked about that girl all the time. He always said that one day he was going to go back to Redhook to find her, but he never did. I don't know how I would have survived that summer without Gilbert. Truth is, I probably wouldn't have. Gilbert was my hero, and he saved my ass on so many occasions. This was to be repeated throughout my entire life, even when I didn't need it.

When I was in the 7th grade, a group of my friends and I were all playing football in the schoolyard and somehow a playful fight broke out. We weren't really fighting. It was more like a mock brawl over a bad call or something. My friend Thomas and I were wrestling on the ground, and he probably outweighed me by fifty pounds. He quickly got the upper hand and while I was on my back, he stood up to put some kind of finishing move on me. Gilbert just happened to be walking by at exactly that moment and saw Thomas about to crush me. In a flash, Thomas was on the floor, screaming and writhing in pain. My brother had punched him in the back of his head and once in the ribs, instantly knocking Thomas down for the count. He couldn't breathe at all, and he was crying hysterically. I got up screaming at Gilbert, telling him he was a maniac, and told him that Thomas and I had just been fooling around. Gilbert didn't really seem like he felt too bad about it. He did say he was sorry and that he thought we were really fighting. Poor Thomas had two broken ribs and a lump on his head that resembled an egg.

Gilbert was just a strong kid, well beyond his years in terms of brute strength. He hardly even got sick. I think that I can remember him getting sick just twice in all our years. He got chicken pox when he was about ten years old, I think. Of course my mom made sure that I slept right beside him every night so that I could get it too, which really didn't make much sense to me. I did end up getting the pox, but I really lucked out. I got two little Pox on my arm. I had the fever and all but nothing more than those Pox-marks on my arms that faded as I got older and fattened up. Unlucky Gilbert was riddled.

As I mentioned earlier, Gilbert and I had different fathers, but you would never know it. We had the same love and sibling rivalry that every other set of brothers has. I once dumped a girl I was seeing for calling Gilbert my half-brother. I was eighteen years old at that point and was living on my own, and I had corrected her repeatedly and told her that he was my brother. I suggested that she not call him my half-brother ever again. She couldn't help herself I guess, because the next thing she said was that like it or not, we had different dads so technically we were always going to be just half-brothers. I kicked her out of my apartment and told her not to call me anymore. As I locked the door behind her, I could still hear her yelling at me through the door. It was muffled, but I could make out what she was saying. She was asking if I was seriously kicking her out, and if I was really mad. The doorbell rang a few times and I could hear her yelling through the window, asking me if I could call her a cab. I opened the window and asked her why she was still outside. She called me an asshole, and then she demanded that I call her a cab. So I did.

I looked her straight in the eyes and said, "You're a cab!" Then I calmly shut the window.

I never saw her again simply because I was serious about the bond that Gilbert and I shared. Back when I was twelve years old, I decided that I was going to find my father. I was pretty adamant about completing this task. I went to my mom and made a passionate and emotional plea to her, hoping that she could give me any information possible, to help me find my father. She listened very intently. I could see genuine sympathy and sadness on her face as she listened to the words of a heartbroken boy, trying desperately to find the trail to trace his bloodlines. Then, as

45

I was almost finished delivering my speech, she slowly began to shake her head. I was confused by her actions and I stopped to ask her why she was shaking her head. Was she really going to deny me the help I needed in order to find the man who made me? She continued to shake her head, with her lips pressed tightly and I started to get emotional.

I asked, "Mom, why are you shaking your head? Aren't you going to help me find my father?"

My mom looked at me and I could see the regret migrate across her face to her furrowed brow.

She looked me squarely and lovingly in the eye and said, "Baby, I really wish that you had said something sooner."

Now I was really confused. I asked, "Why mom?"

She said, "Because your father is dead!"

I was instantly crushed. I don't know how possible it is to mourn someone that you have never known, but at that instant I felt the sadness of someone who had just found and lost their father all in the same day.

With tears in my eyes I asked her, "When did he die?"

She answered me, "Just the other day."

I was rocked to my core. If only I had thought of this sooner, I might have had time to meet my father. But now, it was too late. And apparently, I had missed my opportunity by just days. It was deeply disheartening. I walked away from her because I didn't want my mom to see the tears in my eyes. This was somehow my fault for being completely aloof and disregarding my poor, apparently sick and dying father. So I cried. I went into the room and sat in a corner with the lights turned off. I sat there for a while, crying softly until Gilbert walked into the room and turned the lights on. He noticed me immediately, came right over to me, and started to pat my head. He asked me what was wrong and I told him the whole story. How I had been too late, how my father had just died, and now my dream of someday reuniting with him was now impossible.

He stroked my hair, and wiped my tears, and then he said, "Don't worry about it little bro, my dad died too."

I couldn't believe it. I said, "Oh my god, when did he die?"

Gilbert replied, "I don't know, but mom said he died just the other day."

So apparently my sweet mother was knocking off her all her baby daddy's like a serial killer. Maybe it was just easier to say that they were dead then to try to explain to a child that his father had left him when he was 6 months old. With a letter and fifty bucks, saying he'd come back one day. Hopefully the money would suffice for a while. That's all I got. Six months of diaper changing, and according to my mother, even though he hated even touching me when my diaper was dirty, he had afforded me a trust fund of fifty dollars to last me till now I suppose. That was more than 40 years ago. Maybe I was a hideous infant. Who knows? But telling a child that his father bailed out, never to be heard from again just leaves way too many questions unanswered. Kids always want to know why and will blame themselves half of the time. I guess telling us that they were dead was just a quick and fatal stab to any possible notion of a reunion.

The truth is our "Dads" wanted nothing to do with us. They didn't want to know us, love us, raise us, or even acknowledge that we were their children. You think she wanted to tell us that? So she whacked them. Killed them off neatly with the body never to be found, thus never to be seen or mentioned again. At first, I was angry at my mother for lying to me like that, but later I understood. Funny thing is Gilbert didn't get that she was being disingenuous about the passing of our fathers. He thought it was just a silly coincidence. But it was only many years later that I realized that my mother was just sheltering me from the truth in whatever manner she could. It was just her way. My oldest brother Indio, who was actually named William but no one ever called him that, was a real piece of work. My mother would constantly hide the truth about him in order to save face for the family. How I was given such a set of two very different brothers has always been a wonder to me. Gilbert and Indio locked horns repeatedly as they battled for my soul. Even though Gilbert was far younger, he refused to let Indio have his way. I honestly believe I wouldn't be here today if not for his protection.

Rumdog Vs. The Hell Hound

This is the part of the story where you will lean back and say, "Ok, Rumdog has finally flipped his lid." But I assure you that everything I am about to tell you is one hundred percent the truth. Whether or not you believe in God, or the afterlife, or if you believe we were brought here in pods by aliens a billion years ago, matters not to me. I know what I saw with complete certainty and at least my sister is still around to confirm exactly what happened that night. I was about 7 years old when this happened and it is something that I will never ever forget, be convinced otherwise, or feel the need to embellish about the series of events.

We were doing another one of our homeless stints for a few months and my mother was running out of options on where to put us. How many times can somebody bail you out when you're "in between homes?" My mother had to be desperate to put a roof over our head because we ended staying in war torn alphabet city, in the lower east side of Manhattan. I believe that the area is called SoHo these days and it's a lovely and trendy place to call home, but if you were to jump back in time to the early 1980's, it was a totally different animal. We were staying on Avenue A and East Third Street. It was another huge brick tenement walk up, with enough spray paint and human urine throughout its hallways to forcibly remind you that you were indeed living in a ghetto.

There were more than a few burned out buildings surrounding us, and for a rear view there was a huge pile of rubble where I presume a building had once stood. It had been overrun with bushes, junk, hypodermic needles, and basically it had become a place for people to do not so nice things to other people. Late at night, you would hear screams coming from the pile of rubble back there. One night, a woman was screaming her head off as some guy was raping her. She kept screaming for someone to call the police but I don't recall the police ever showing up. Another night some guy had gotten stabbed in his gut, netting the same lack of police response. He was yelling for help, screaming that he had been stabbed and needed an ambulance.

He kept pleading, "Please, somebody help."

It wasn't until early in the morning that the police and an ambulance did arrive. Gilbert and I watched as they carted him off on the gurney, and we were betting that there was no way that the guy was still alive. He had been bleeding for a few hours at the very least and had grown quiet as the late long hours crept into morning.

You might even ask yourself why it was that we didn't call for help ourselves, right? Well, there's an explanation for that as well. We were living with a woman named Maria, who my mom had known for some time. She had a cute little moniker, Maria La Loca, which directly translated meant Crazy Maria. I don't know that she would have my first choice to keep an eye on my kids, but as I stated earlier my mom must have been absolutely desperate to house us. Maria had lost her own children to the care of the state because she had tortured and burned them in hot water. She had some kind of mental breakdown, tortured her children and when the children were taken away from her, she had gotten very heavy into an alternative religion.

When my mom had brought us over to Maria's house, she was super sweet, and gave us cookies and ice cream, playing the loving doting mom. I had noticed that she paid particular attention to me. The four of us would be staying at her house, namely Indio, Vilma, Gilbert and myself, and she was showing my mom how big the apartment was. She reassured us that we would be having a lot of fun while we were staying there. For some reason she seemed to have genuine affection for me, because she kept petting my hair and straightening my shirt, making sure that I looked well kept. She had given us an inflatable ball and told us that we could play with the ball anytime we wanted as long as we behaved. It wasn't even fifteen minutes before Gilbert and I were punching the ball as hard as we could and running around the furniture like it was a baseball field.

At one point, Gilbert punched the ball and it fell behind a big recliner she had in the corner of her living room. I was trying to move the chair out of the way, but it was too big and heavy for me to move by myself, so I asked Gilbert to help me retrieve the ball once he had finished rounding the imaginary bases. He came over to help and I squeezed my little body behind the recliner until I could finally see the ball. I froze instantly. I thought that maybe I was going nuts and was seeing things. I had to be sure so I asked Gilbert to come look at what I had discovered behind the recliner.

He asked me what it was that I had found and I said, "Gil, you gotta come see this."

Reluctantly Gilbert stuck his head behind the recliner and the words just fell out of his mouth. He said, "What the fuck?"

It was probably the first time that I had heard my brother curse in all my seven years and I giggled nervously. Behind the recliner, I had found the inflatable ball sitting right on top of a big witches brewing pot. It was a black cauldron with bones on a string all around the outer rim. I looked at Gilbert and he was just staring at the pot completely wide-eyed. I asked him if this was a pot that witches used to make spells and he nodded slowly, but I'm sure he had no idea what to make of it. I reached out to touch the bones to see if they were real, but Gilbert grabbed my hand and told me not to. He then reached out carefully and touched the bones that were hanging off the pot.

He said, "I don't think they are real, they feel fake" as if he had any clue what real bones were supposed to feel like.

So I touched the bones too, and I expected them to be slimy or wet for some reason but they were dry. He grabbed the ball and warned me that we should probably not be touching this stuff. He also warned me that the ball would be staying behind the recliner permanently if it was to fall back there again.

He said, "Come on, don't touch it anymore."

I did as he said and we went back to playing with the ball. We decided to kick it instead so that it wouldn't get too much air under it, and during the soccer match, I mentioned to Gilbert that we should probably tell Vilma and Indio about the pot. Gilbert said that we would tell them later and that's where we left it. Later on, we had dinner and my mom left to wherever it was that she would be staying, promising to come see us within the week. We forgot all about the pot until the next day because Maria sent us directly to bed right after my mom had left. We sat up talking for a good while that night, and I was figuring that maybe this place wasn't going to be so bad after all. I could not have been more wrong if I had tried.

The next day, we were up early because Maria felt it necessary to wake us up first thing in the morning for no apparent reason. She got me dressed and took me shopping that first day. It was her and I alone. She left my brothers and sister at her house while she took me to buy clothes. She asked me if I wanted pizza, so I got pizza. She asked me if wanted ice cream so I got that too. She asked if I wanted to go church with her and I told her no because I had to use the bathroom and I wanted to go home. She suddenly bent down and grabbed my face in her hand, putting her face directly in front of mine. Her fingers felt like they were going to rip right through my skin. She told me that I was a bad boy if I didn't go to church to cleanse myself, I was going to go to hell. It wasn't the words that she said that bothered me, but more the fact that she had a tight grip on my face and she was speaking to me through clenched teeth. Moments earlier I was having a fine old day with this woman. Suddenly, she had become completely unhinged because I had to use the bathroom. My face was really starting to hurt and I told her that I would go to church with her tomorrow because my stomach was sick and I really had to use the bathroom. She smiled at me, then let go of my face and started to fix my hair.

All of sudden she seemed delighted. She took me to a few more stores, completely dismissing the fact that I needed to go, and then we went back to her apartment after being out all day. My stomach was killing me all day but there was no way I was going to ask her to stop. A few times during the day I felt like maybe I was going to have an accident, but I really believed that she would kill me on the spot had I done so. When I got to the apartment, I ran straight to the bathroom and as soon as I was done, I told my sister what had happened. I also told her about the witch pot behind the recliner, but when we went to see, it was gone. I swore to my sister that it had been there the day before, and I even called in Gilbert to testify on my behalf but I could tell that she didn't really believe us. I did make her promise that she wouldn't let Maria take me out alone again. I needed protection from this maniac, no matter how sweet and loving she was trying to be to me.

The oddest thing was that she could not give a shit about how anyone else was dressed or if their hair was out of place, but she would always dote on me. It was like she had some sick obsession with me. She had switched her routine as well. In the morning, I was the only one she would wake up. She would have my cereal and milk waiting for me on the table. But first, she would dress me and comb my hair like I was a doll. She would speak to me oddly, cooing at me like I was an infant.

Things were bad enough with the muggings and stabbings that would go on at night. Now I had to be awoken every morning at the crack of dawn so that this woman could play with me and comb my hair at least twenty times a day.

Things got worse. Maria decided that she was going to keep us. One morning, we woke up and she had changed the locks to the apartment. In the middle of the night, she had installed one of those locks that require you to have a key on both the inside and the outside. She had always had the police lock, with the big iron pole that leaned against the door to prevent break-ins and burglaries. But now, there was a new lock with a key hole on the inside of the apartment as well. You couldn't just open the door and let someone in without the key. Furthermore, she had begun to take the phone and the cord off the wall when she left the house so that we were unable to call my mom. We were actually kept in like prisoners in this apartment, and she had no intentions of giving us back to my mom. I remember one day my mom appeared out of the blue. We had no clue that she had been calling us every day to see how we were, but got nothing except endless ringing on her side of the phone. It wasn't ringing on our end because Crazy Maria, living up to her name, had made sure to dismantle the phone, making communication with my mom and the outside world impossible. When my mom came that day, she knocked on the door and Indio asked who it was. I could hear my mom on the other side of the door softly let out a breath of relief. She had no clue what happened to her children and didn't know what to expect when she got to us. She wanted to come in but we had to explain to her that it was locked on this side as well. I don't quite remember if my mom was crying but we all were on our side of the locked door. My mother slid a phone number under the door. She assured us that she was going to get us out of there and told Indio to call the number as soon as he had a chance. She promised us that she would come get us as soon as she could.

Indio whispered loudly through he door. He told my mother that Maria had taken the phone away as well but that he would find a way to call. He also said he would find a way to escape, take us all out of there and meet her somewhere. Before he did this, he would call her first to make sure my mother could come get us. I could hear the pain and uncertainty in my mom's voice as she told us that she loved us and would be back for us soon. It was all so surreal that we did all this through opposite sides of a door, but at least we had devised a plan to get us out of there. During the following week, there had been a few mishaps.

Vilma, Indio, and Gilbert had all found a bottle with clear liquid in it and decided to sniff its contents, one after another, for some strange reason. All three of them started to scream and writhe in pain as whatever was in the bottle assaulted their senses. They were screaming in pain in the bathroom, trying desperately to flush their eyes and face of whatever chemical they had been exposed to. I picked up the cap to the bottle, and moving as slow and careful as a bomb squad, I replaced the cap back onto the top of the bottle. I wanted nothing to do with whatever was in there and I held my breath as I screwed the cap back on. A few minutes later, my siblings all came out of the bathroom with their eyes completely bloodshot and tears streaming down their faces. We never found out what it was exactly, but the one thing we knew was that if we didn't get out of there soon, we weren't going to make it.

That night, Indio decided to break into Maria's bedroom. He found an extra key to the lock and the phone lines, which were needed to make the phone operable. We called my mother and told her that we had found a key and were ready to escape. My mother conferred with Indio, who was the oldest, and they decided that we would make our move in the morning. Indio would replace the phone cord back into her room so that she would not notice that we had used the phone. When morning came and Maria was out making her daily rounds buying religious candles and whatever else she bought at the boutiques, we would escape and meet my mother at the train station. We hung up quickly because we didn't want to get caught on the phone. Afterwards, we threw a little going away party for ourselves. We knew that in the morning, we would be leaving and we could not be happier.

We were singing and dancing in the living room, and for some reason, even though it was starting to get late, Maria was nowhere to be found. She would go to her "church" at least twice a day but she had never stayed out this late. We weren't really worried about her anymore as we sang and danced the night away, incorporating kitchen utensils as instruments. Gilbert was banging on a pot with a spoon and I was tapping a glass with a fork to the beat of our song. My sister and Indio were rapping in Spanish and we were having the time of our lives. Hope was near, and we could not contain our joy. And that's when it happened.

If you remember when I began to tell you this story, I warned you that at this point you were probably say that I had lost my mind. If you are naturally a skeptic, then feel free to believe what you want. But what happened, happened the way it did and that's just it. I wish it didn't, but you cannot just undo things. In the middle of our little celebration, Indio just completely froze and turned completely pale. The rest of us kept singing and dancing, oblivious to whatever it was that Indio had seen. I don't remember whether it was Vilma or Gilbert that was the next to notice that something was wrong, but they too fell silent. They were all paralyzed with fear, leaving me as the only one making a ruckus in the apartment. Eventually I stopped banging my fork on the glass and when I turned to see why they had stopped singing and dancing, I saw was something out of a horror film.

All four of us were frozen in place, staring out at the window, in complete shock. Staring right back at us, through the fourth floor window, was a huge dog like creature with blood red eyes. They weren't eyes like that of a normal creature, but they were more like dim red lights coming from within the dog like entity in the window. I'm not sure how long we all stayed frozen in place but slowly the dog thing began to survey the room, seemingly appraising us, until it finally locked eyes with me. It cocked its head and its eyes narrowed.

All of a sudden, Indio began to yell "We believe in God, we don't want you here, get out of here."

Vilma chimed in "Go back to where you belong, we believe in Jesus Christ, you don't belong here."

Just like any sensible kids should, Gilbert and I ran. I was so scared that I jumped right onto the refrigerator. Not the side, or up the door but I jumped clear to the top of the refrigerator in my panic. I looked down and saw Gilbert running in circles trying to find a place to hide in the kitchen, but couldn't seem to make up his mind in his frightened state.

I looked back at the living room, completely expecting to see the evil hound devouring my brother and sister, but it was still sitting at the window as Indio and Vilma recited prayer after prayer, trying to drive the monster away. Then the fucking thing blinked. Its red eyes open and closed momentarily. I suppose that was what gave Indio the strength and courage to do what he did next. He walked right up to the window, still praying, and stood face to face with the creature as he slammed the window down as hard as he could. He never stopped praying but he grabbed my sister's hand and they both started to back away from the window being very careful not to turn their back on it. The hound remained at the window, turning its head to follow their movements but made no other move. Gilbert ran over and held onto to Indio's waist as Vilma was trying to get me to go to her.

I don't think she knew that I was hiding on top of the fridge because she put her hand behind her, hoping that I would take her hand. When I didn't come right away, I remember her distinctly snapping her fingers twice and put her hand out again. I took the cue, hopped down from my perch, and ran over to grab her hand. We all walked backwards to the bedroom, and quickly shut the door behind us and ran to the bed. All four of us lay down together and prayed that whatever it was in the window would go away. We prayed for hours.

Eventually we all fell asleep, but we woke up when we heard the door slam as Maria came home. We had left all the lights on, and when she came in, she decided to check in on us, something else that she had never done before. She stuck her head inside the door and asked us how our night had gone. She had a strange smile on her face. It was the smile of someone who already knew the answer to the question, but asked nonetheless to obtain further enjoyment. I'm pretty sure that we all knew that we were dealing with someone who was the very definition of evil. I don't know how we slept that night at all, but we somehow made it, not forgetting that we were plotting our escape the minute she left in the morning.

Now if you don't think this story is weird enough, I'll give you a little more before it's finished. In the morning, the entire window was covered in shit. Not smeared on the window, or a few lumps on the window sill, but halfway up the window was nothing but shit. We waited patiently until Maria got dressed and ready to go that morning, and if she had noticed the wall of shit on her window, she certainly didn't seem alarmed by it. She was oddly in a good mood again, and on her way out. She smiled at us again and told us to be good boys and girls, like the real psycho that she was. We waited ten minutes, packed all our belongings, and waited by the door as Indio broke into her bedroom again to get the extra key, praying that it was still there. Thankfully, it was and we high tailed it out of there as soon as we checked outside to make sure the Maria was not out there somewhere, waiting to jump on us. We ran to the subway, and met up with my mom. I have little recollection of a tearful reunion or any exaggerated hugs being exchanged by us but I do remember that we told my mom the whole story. Of course, she didn't believe us.

I'm glad that I have someone that will vouch for that story because it certainly can be viewed as a fantasy or more likely a nightmare, though I honestly wish it was just that. Only God knows what that thing was that night, but whatever it was, it was there for us. Moreover, I think it was there for me. I explained this to Vilma years later and when I did, it seemed like she had been looking for answers since the evening of the event and I had just wrapped it into a neat little box for her. Here's what I told her;

Maria had always been a creature of absolute obsessive habit. She woke up every single day at the crack of dawn. She made us eat the same breakfast every single day. She would go to her church twice a day always at the same time. She came home every night right around 9 pm and whisked us into bed right away. Lights out, no talking, no getting up to use the bathroom or get yourself a drink of water, it was all forbidden. So to say that she was structured is perhaps a bit of an understatement. But on the night that it happened, she was mysteriously late in coming home. She didn't arrive home until hours later than her usual routine, and when she did, she was smiling. There was also a reason why she obsessed over me so much.

She was grooming me, and making sure I was an appetizing little package for whatever it was that came for me that night. That's why she paid no attention to the other children, but dressed me and combed my hair every two minutes to make sure that I looked presentable. I was to be her sacrifice and it had come to collect. Why else would she lock us in that apartment, and made sure that we had no contact with the outside world, with no possible way to call for help. I also explained to my sister that when the creature gave everyone in the room the once over, it had locked its eyes on me, and cocked his head to the side. Almost like there was some sort of recognition that it had found the one that it was there for. After we all broke out in prayer, I do believe that it was thrown for a loop.

It hadn't expected any opposition from a bunch of helpless kids. When Indio began to pray and in a sense rebuking the hound, it had blinked. Even if that was one of the few good things that Indio had achieved in his life, it was probably the most important thing he had ever done. Many years later, when Vilma and I had this conversation, she nodded her head and was almost speechless, but she agreed that it all made sense. The last thing I said to her about it was that even though it hadn't gotten us, it had touched us somehow. Maybe that was what all the shit all over the window was about. While it hadn't been able to sink its teeth into us and claim us, we didn't get out without a scratch. It had marked us. And we suffered for it. No one escaped without blemish.

Here's what I take from that night. Again, I'll emphasize that I am no zealot. I do have a strong belief in God, and that's my prerogative to do so. I am no converter or soul saver by any means, and I think everyone's belief or non-belief for that matter is their own business. It's puzzling to me that God is mentioned every day, just about everywhere, on our money, in our courts, or simply for the reason that someone has won an award or some sort of honor. Yet, if you claim that you saw God, people would be ready to tie you up in a straight-jacket and send you to the funny farm. Why would people think that you are crazy if you saw something that we all claim to believe in? It is kind of odd, isn't it? I make no such claim, but for me, what happened to us simplified the notion to believe or not.

This world is made up of contrasts, and opposing forces. There is no dark without light. There is no cold without heat. And there is no good without evil. Everything in this world has its' own polar opposite no matter what it is, hence my rationale. Whatever happened that night in Alphabet City, it cemented the fact that there is a force among us that is pure evil. Whether it was Satan, or your everyday run-of-the mill demon, it was right before our eyes in the flesh. It was real. I have no doubt about that. That is what leads me to believe, without a doubt that God and pure good is real. I've never seen God. I've never seen an angel, or anything that gives me proof that there is such a thing. However, I did see its complete opposite, and one simply cannot exist without the other. I am in no rush to see the other side. I have been asked if it really helps to think that there is a God, or a supreme being that we will all meet at the end of our journey. I think it certainly can't hurt.

Indio

Of my oldest brother William, I have little else to say except that he was just no good. Gilbert had saved me from him and his destructive ways many times. After we got older, I'd estimate that Gilbert was probably about sixteen years old when he finally got the best of him in a fight, but still there were a good many years in between of abuse and torture. William, who was called "Indio" by everyone on the street, was a junkie, a bully, and a thief that would kick the shit out of Gilbert and me on a weekly basis. It probably could have been a daily occurrence but he just wasn't around that much. But when he was, believe you me, we were getting smacked around.

He would go out, get high as a kite, and in the process steal something and bring it home to hide. Then, after he would sell said stolen item to another one of his junkie friends, he would go out and buy more drugs. In the morning, he would wake up, forget all about selling the stolen items, and start to interrogate us about where we had put it. He'd smack us around one at a time, calling us liars, and threatening our lives until he found out what had happened to his loot. Sometimes we were lucky and we recognized the person that he had sold the items to. He'd start with the smacking and accusing, and we would plead with him to call the guy that we knew was with him the night before. He'd scream and yell, saying that he didn't sell anybody anything, until he finally cracked and picked up the phone after getting tired of fruitlessly beating on us. When his friend would confirm that he had indeed been at the apartment and bought something off of Indio, the focus of his investigation would then change to his friend, who he would then accuse of stealing because he couldn't remember receiving any money.

Not once did he apologize. Never did he say, "Hey, sorry for leaving that four fingered welt on your face."

He had no remorse. He had no conscious whatsoever. I don't think that he would have literally killed me but I do believe that if not for Gilbert, Indio could have completely destroyed what was left of my childhood spirit, and by then I honestly didn't have much to spare. When Indio would start in on me, Gilbert would stand up to him and take a beating. He'd take my beating. And never once did Gilbert ask for a thank-you or bring it up.

I committed a burglary at eight years old because of Indio. It was a normal summer day of him waking up late in the afternoon and immediately plotting to commit some crime in order to score some money. Our neighbors in the rear apartment were friends of my mother, and had very recently suffered a death in the family. On the day of the funeral, they had all gotten dressed up and left their apartment, which was sure to be empty for a few hours at the very least. Indio, seeing his opportunity to fill his pockets, quickly started in on Gilbert to climb up from the yard into the window and go into the apartment, so that he could then break in. This was something that he could normally do himself.

Burglary was old hat for Indio, but the family also had a huge German shepherd. The dog also liked to bite people, especially strangers. But we were friends with the people next door and we played with the children often so the dog recognized us. He instructed Gilbert to climb in through the kitchen window, take the dog and lock it in the bathroom, and then open the front door to let Indio in. Gilbert refused and Indio started to hit him. He started with smacking him in the face and when that didn't work, he started to punch Gilbert. He busted Gilbert's lip and then punched him in the stomach, knocking my mighty Gilbert down to his knees. Gilbert gasped from the force of the blow to his mid-section and gagged as he stifled the need to vomit. Still, he refused. Indio was about to hit him again, while Gilbert was down on his knees, when I jumped up and told him that I would go. I told him I could climb up and do it. Gilbert told me to shut up, that I had better go back to the room, but he was silenced by another one of Indio's blows. This time Indio hit him on the side of his face, by his ear. I saw the pain on Gilbert's face and I knew that I could not watch him be hit again.

I had tears in my eyes but I took both of Indio's hands in mine and said, "Stop, I'll do it." I figured he couldn't hit Gilbert anymore if I held both his hands tightly, and did my best to distract him.

"Come on, follow me," I said.

We went out into the hallway and I pointed out where I could climb up. Although I was devastatingly short, I could climb into the window quite easily. He forgot all about Gilbert as I told him to wait for me by the apartment door. I went out through the basement, climbing up the side of the building in the yard, and I got into the kitchen window with relative ease. The dog was barking but stopped when he saw it was me. I was nervous for a minute, thinking that this dog was going to tear me to pieces at any moment. I noticed the dog biscuits on the kitchen counter and I gave the dog one just to get his attention. I grabbed another biscuit and had the dog follow me through the apartment. That's when I heard the dog growl behind me and I was pretty close to soiling my pants.

If this was the way I was going to die after eight long eventful years on this earth then so be it, but I had to do everything in my power to stop the senseless thumping Gilbert was taking just a few minutes earlier. I turned around slowly, and saw that the dog was growling at the door. He must have smelled or sensed that Indio was standing there and it was in full attack mode. I called him over a few times but the dog wouldn't budge. He was staring intently at the door and waiting to tear apart whoever was on the other side. I spoke in a loud whisper through the door and told Indio to get away from the door until I could get the dog into the bathroom.

He replied in the same loud whisper "Oh, ok."

I realized something when he spoke. There was something about the tone of his voice that I had not heard before. He was happy. Could you believe that? Here he was beating one of his little brothers senseless, and forcing his even younger brother to burglarize the home of a family that was just a little busy burying one of their own on this day. Yet, he was perfectly happy. I heard him make little noises with his mouth as he scurried away and moved further down the hall.

I heard him say in the same loud whisper, "Ok, how about now?"

I called the dog into the bathroom and lay the biscuit on the toilet seat, hoping the dog would go in.

For what seemed like an eternity, the dog continued to stare at the door, but as all dogs usually succumb to their hunger, he went into the bathroom to retrieve his biscuit. I closed the door behind him and the dog didn't make a sound. I made sure the bathroom door was shut tight and I opened the front door to the apartment. Indio came sprinting over and tussled my hair, telling me I did a good job. It was like I had hit a home run in a little league game. I walked into our apartment and I watched as he carried stuff out of the apartment, and up the stairs to the roof. He had another junkie friend a few buildings down and the roofs were all connected, so I gather that's where all the stuff he stole went to. Up the stairs and onto the roof, where we would then walk down a few buildings and take it down the steps of another building, never to be seen by the public eye.

When I peeked back inside, Gilbert was putting ice on his lips to bring down the swelling and the look on his face was not one that I will ever forget. Whatever relief I felt that Gilbert was ok was certainly not shared by him.

He just shook his head at me and said, "You shouldn't have done it."

"He stopped hitting you right?" I said to him.

Gilbert replied, "So, it's still not right."

And then I said something that no child has any business saying. I said, "Yeah, well you're not in pain anymore. Now it's their pain, not ours anymore, and that's not our fucking problem, is it?"

I walked out. I left the apartment and I walked up to the abandoned train station right around the block that ran over Fort Hamilton Parkway. I climbed up the dilapidated stairs and sat up there for some time. I cried nervously for some time, thinking I was going to be arrested the minute I got back to the building. I also kept replaying the sickening thuds of the blows that Indio was hitting Gilbert with and it actually made me vomit. I kept hearing Gilbert gasp for air when he had been punched in his stomach and the stinging slap of the hand on his face. I then came to realize that through the whole thing, Gilbert had not once made a sound of protest or cried out in pain. I think that maybe it had made Indio angrier, that he couldn't hurt Gilbert, much less break him. But I couldn't take it anymore.

I wasn't and have never been as tough as my brother Gil, so I did what Indio wanted. I eventually coaxed myself into facing the music and decided to walk back home, but not before I peeked down the block to see just how many swat teams were waiting to pounce on me upon my return. I saw nothing out of the ordinary. Truth is, nobody cared. I walked back into our little two roomed Shangri-La and nothing was amidst. The cops had come and gone and taken a report, but as usual, nobody saw a damn thing. I was way too young to be a suspect, and Indio was nowhere to be found. The people next door just got screwed on what had to be the worst day of their life. I mean, the phrase "When it rains, it pours," still didn't quite grasp what these poor people had just gone through. But for us it wasn't just one day. It was a life sentence. Indio would come and go, in and out of our lives and once in the blue moon, he would buy some Chinese food or give my mom a few bucks, but it was rare.

When we were living on Church Avenue, it was even worse. We lived on the first floor of a two story house that had been condemned many years before we happened upon it. The house did not have one window that was completely intact. Every window was broken and covered in plastic to keep the elements out. None of the windows actually went up or down and if there happened to be a little bit of glass left on the frame, it was completely taped up to make sure that the window couldn't move, preserving whatever little glass there was left. We had no electricity. We had no hot water. Ready for this? We had half of a bathroom floor. In the bathroom there was a sink, a toilet bowl, and a huge hole where the bathtub was supposed to be. If you were lucky enough to take a shit while someone was in the basement, you could totally make eye contact and have a full conversation.

Where was the tub you ask? Why, it was in the kitchen of course. To wash ourselves we had to run a hose from the kitchen sink into the tub, and then fill up pots of water and boil it on the stove to try and have a hot bath. Of course there was no wall separating the kitchen and living room so we had to hang a huge curtain in between the tub and the sink in order to provide Vilma with a tiny bit of privacy whenever she bathed. Whatever electricity we got, came from a garage that was about 50 feet in front of the house. They fixed and painted cars in the garage, and they had somehow come to some arrangement with the owner of this luxurious property to run a whole bunch of extension cords from the back of the auto mechanic shop into the house. Half of the wires supplied our apartment and the other extension cords were run up to the second floor where no fewer than twelve Mexicans lived.

I can still remember all the loud music and the smell of beer coming down from the apartment upstairs. You would think that is was really a miracle that nothing happened to my sister or my mother while we were living in that house, but those

Mexicans were all hard working guys who busted their ass all week. On Saturday nights, they would drink like pirates and play Spanish music all night. I think maybe one or two of them had gotten drunk and made a fresh remark or two towards my sister, but that was the worst of it. It really could have been worse. Besides, we had bigger problems to worry about. We had two extension cords running into the bedroom, two more running into the living room and kitchen, and one last cord running into our half a bathroom. There were about two or three trees surrounding the property, so once in a while there was a fire that was started by the dead dry leaves getting set ablaze by an electrical spark from one of the cords. Sometimes it rained so hard that the front of the house flooded, so if you really wanted to have fun, you could try running electrical cords under water. Those were good times, I tell you. On those days, we had no power. It was way too dangerous to have an electrified puddle sitting in front of the house so we sat in the dark and burned candles, but I kid you not, we had fun.

We made life interesting with the little we had. Believe it or not, rainy days weren't the hardest times. There was nothing worse than living there in the winter. I am not exaggerating when I say that the house was condemned. It was simply uninhabitable, yet inhabited. The house leaned to the left and had only remained upright because it was supported by a huge cinder block wall on the property line right alongside a school bus garage and depot. Again, the windows were non-existent and the outer and inners walls were Swiss cheese. Over the years, I have brought this place up to a few friends of mine and I just cannot accurately describe how awful it was living there. I really do wish that I had the foresight to take pictures of this house just to show that I am not exaggerating about the shape that it was in. When we would walk home with some of the kids we went to school with, Gilbert and I would walk past the house and up the side street until we were out of sight. Once we were convinced that nobody was watching, we would then scurry back up the avenue and into the walkway past the auto body shop.

Eventually, the whole neighborhood caught on that we were living there and it just wasn't a big deal anymore. The kids used to call it the cardboard box and it kind of made sense. It was exactly like being homeless, but living in a pretty sturdy cardboard box. We had four walls and a roof over our heads, but that's where the amenities ended. Just like a cardboard box, there was no way to keep it warm. It used to get so cold in the house that my mother would walk around in a fake fur coat. She probably had three or four layers of clothes on, and a huge faux fur coat in the house. This thing was huge, from her shoulders to her feet, and she wore it all day and night. We had gotten our hands on kerosene heaters and that's how we kept warm. I take that back. I should never say that we were warm.

That's how we lived, barely surviving. If you remember the eighties, there were some really brutal winters back then, and we were stuck inside our little condemned igloo with kerosene heaters trying to get to the next day. On the days my mother didn't have any money to buy fuel for the heaters, we all just slept together. To say that we suffered doesn't quite tell it. I was forced to find a way to help my family survive the cold. One early evening during the winter, I ventured out to go find a job. My mom had no money and we were sure to freeze another night without the heaters. My mother would run the burners on the stove sometimes but with the house being so porous, all the heat would just escape through the walls and the missing bathroom floor into the basement. I figured that if I went to the local supermarket and packed bags, loaded groceries into cars at least, I could maybe make five dollars in tips. That would allow me to buy at least one small container of kerosene. I told Gilbert where I was going and asked him to join me so that maybe we could make enough to buy two bottles, but he didn't share my enthusiasm. He was always tougher than me anyway so to him it was just another cold night. But I just didn't feel like freezing my ass off again.

I went out to the supermarket and I packed groceries until I had about ten bucks in my pocket. To me that was a windfall. I bought a few cheap thin pepper steaks for about four dollars and then I hit the local Benjamin Moore paint store to buy the kerosene. Here I was, barely out of elementary school and those were the things that were running through my mind. Feed my family and provide them with warmth. Again, things no child should ever have to worry about. Nonetheless, I did well that night and as I was walking home, I saw Indio doing a quick little drug deal right around the corner from the house. He gave a guy a handful of small, clear envelopes and the guy gave my brother a wad of bills. Probably not a major drug deal but to my eleven-year-old eyes, a wad of bills could have been a million dollars. I hid behind a car just to give Indio time to get back into the house and I walked in two minutes later with the steaks and kerosene.

My mom was so happy that her eyes lit up when she saw the kerosene bottle. She was surprised that they had sold me the flammable substance being that I was a child and alone, but the guy had recognized me from the other countless kerosene runs I had made with my mom and Vilma. Nobody even cared about the cheap little steaks I bought because we were going to sleep warmly that night. The heaters would usually burn until five or six in the morning but that was good enough. A very little bit of heat would still remain in the morning while we got dressed for school, and only my mom would stay in the house, wearing her coat all day.

But that evening as my mom poured the fuel into the heater, I watched as Indio hid something in his bedroom. It had to be the money he had just gotten. After the mini celebration, my mom got right to cooking and we might have even dared to feel like a normal family that night. Indio seemed to be in a good mood too, so I pressed my luck a little.

I took a chance and asked, "Hey, I don't know if you have any money but maybe you can buy another bottle of kerosene and we can warm up the whole house tonight."

He just laughed at me. He made some excuse about not having any money and went back into his room, only coming out once to eat the steak and rice that I had provided without as much as a thanks. I watched him intently that night, and it was then that I hatched my little plot. Now I abhor stealing. I won't take as much as a nickel that doesn't belong to me, it's just my way. But on that night, I told Gilbert that I had seen Indio dealing drugs outside and that he had some money. Gilbert told me to forget about it, and advised me that if Indio did have money hidden in his room, he certainly didn't intend on sharing or helping out mom so we might as well forget about him pitching in. I told Gilbert, with as serious a face as I could muster, that Indio was definitely going to pitch in. He just wasn't going to do it voluntarily. Gilbert told me I was crazy and that I was asking to get my head kicked in, but by that point, I was getting used to taking a beating so it was par for the course. And so it began.

The very next day I waited for Indio to leave the house and had to move fast because he was never gone for too long those days. It was freezing out and he would only go out to do a quick deal or run to the store to buy cigarettes. When he ran out, I sprang into action. I went into his room and started searching where I had seen him stash something the night before, which was right over the door way. At first, I didn't find anything, but then I noticed a crease between the wall and the doorframe. In that crease, there was an envelope, and in that envelope there was a lot of money. How much money? I couldn't believe my eyes. I was temporarily distracted by all the cash and had forgotten my plan of getting in and out as quickly as possible. I had never seen so much money in my life and I couldn't help but to count it. He had four thousand dollars hidden in the doorframe. We were freezing every single night. We barely had enough to eat and we were actually living in an abandoned house like squatters. Meanwhile, Indio was sitting on four grand.

As I said before, my brother was not a very nice guy. I didn't know how much to take at first, and then I thought maybe I should just take a little so that he wouldn't notice it. I grabbed 20 dollars. That was all. I stuffed it into my pocket, replaced the envelope back behind the door frame, and made my way out of the house. I went straight to the supermarket and started packing bags in order to establish my alibi. I only made a few bucks that day but that was enough. I put ten dollars aside and I bought some chicken, some bread, and some cold cuts to last the week. Then I went to get the kerosene again, but this time I bought two bottles.

This was kind of heavy for me but I managed and when I got home there was another celebration. I told my mom what a good day I had at the supermarket and that I even went on a few deliveries. We slept warm, we ate well, and my mom even had some cold cuts so that she could make herself a sandwich the next day while we were at school. For a few days, life was good. Then Indio slowly started to catch on that I was stealing from his bundle. Well, he didn't know it was me, but he knew he was short 20 dollars every day. He started to move the money round his room, but there are only so many places that you can hide something in a room and I found it every time. I took a few smacks in the mouth and he twisted my arm and fingers about once a week trying to get me to talk, but it was to no avail. Gilbert even got in on it sometimes, and he'd take a smack or two for me when my mother and sister weren't watching. That was just the way it was. If I wanted to sleep warmly, there was a price to pay. When I wanted to get enough kerosene to make sure the whole family slept warmly, the price was just a little higher. Nothing was free. Nothing was easy, especially life with Indio.

It still shocks me to know that my older brother Indio was hiding all that money. Enough money to get us all out of there and into a decent place to live. It's hard to believe that he could sit there and watch us go through so much heartache without once offering to help. But that's the kind of person that he was. He would disappear for months at a time, and then re-appear like he'd never been gone. It usually coincided with when he was in need.

Nowadays, when for some reason my landlord forgets to put oil in the heater and my apartment gets cold at night, I get transported back to 30 years ago. I'm fine one moment and without warning, I'm suddenly back in that house freezing under four blankets, trying to find warmth against my brother's body. It keeps me up at night thinking of how we all suffered so much. After all, we were just trying to earn the right to wake up the next day, and to suffer a bit more. I think about Gilbert and how he took many beatings for me, knowing full well that it was me that was stealing from Indio. He never once said anything about it nor did he ever rat me out. I think about my poor Ma, shuffling us off to school every morning, comforted by the knowledge that we would be warm at school and that we would be fed, yet knowing full well that she would not enjoy any of those perks. She would be home alone, all day wearing the ridiculous faux fur. These are the thoughts and memories that both drive me and pull me down to depths I care not to revisit. This went on for many years, us living in poverty and barely scraping by.

Handcuffs

I've never been a fan of being bound. Yet, it seemed that try as I might to avoid it, I was always getting myself into trouble. This led to being restrained more times than I'd like to admit. It was always some bullshit or another, and very rarely did the police have anything solid to hold me on, but once they know your face, you might as well get used to the idea of being thrown up against the wall. I don't think I was a bad kid, but I got along just as well with the criminal element, as I did with the geeks and the "good kids".

Once in a while, I'd get chased and got away. Every now and then, I got caught by the cops and took a beating. I always kept my mouth shut, and that was something that I had learned from my oldest brother. The police had come to the house on more than a few occasions looking for Indio and some answers, and he never knew nothing. He played dumb and stuck to it. I wasn't quite as bright as he. I would completely stop talking. I knew what was coming, and I had taken so many beatings by then that it really didn't matter much. The one thing I knew for sure, was that I could take more than a few knocks to my head. Pain and physical abuse was just something bigger people did to smaller people. I was in the latter group so it didn't take too much brain power to know the score.

There was one day in particular that stood out from the rest. We all like to blame other people around us but in truth, it is usually nobody's fault but your own when you get yourself in hot water. I had many chances that day to fold up my tents and go home, but I decided to push the envelope for some reason. I was standing at the bus stop, ready to throw in whatever change I had to pay my fare, but as the bus came to a stop in front of me, I walked away from it. I wasn't ready to throw it in the change collector just yet.

I hooked up with a few kids that I had known from the neighborhood, and we parlayed our money. We had enough to get a few big bottles of beer, and that would be enough to get us started. Once we finished drinking the beers, we were still gunning for more, so we decided to start collecting bottles to collect the five-cent refund on each. We were certainly very resourceful when we put our minds to it. Before long we had a couple of hundred bottles and cans in a cart, then went from store to store to collect our loot. Back then you could buy a bottle of liquor at just about any corner store, even though it was illegal. The store owner couldn't even complain about us being underage because what they were selling was illegal anyway. When we asked for the bottle of rum, they really had no choice but to give it to us. We drank a lot that night, and we drank it straight. The three of us put away most of the bottle, before our hunger started to rumble in our empty stomachs. We had spent all of our money on the rum, so it wasn't like we had many options.

One of the boys, Tommy suggested we go for pizza and run like hell after they served us the slices. We didn't care much for that idea. Another brilliant idea was to go to a local fast foot restaurant, and hang out by the drive-thru. We could listen to the customers as they made their orders, and if someone made a big enough order, we could run and swipe the bag when the food was being passed from the window to the car. We had actually done that before but it ended up being a bad idea. The customer had given chase in his car, and we had dropped most of the food trying to get away. I was never particularly fast anyway and being drunk off my ass wasn't going to make for a quick getaway. We couldn't come up with a viable solution to ease our hunger, so we decided to roam the neighborhood until something came up.

We had strayed from our usually stomping grounds and ended up in the Sunset section of Brooklyn. This wasn't our territory, and since we had been in a few fights with some kids from this side of town, we were being careful by darting back and forth in the darkest of places. If we were to run into trouble tonight, we would be grossly outnumbered and completely weaponless. It wasn't like me not to carry some sort of box-cutter or knife, but this was a total impromptu adventure. We walked quietly and quickly until we were out of the more populated residential areas. We were walking along the border of the waterfront along the shipyards, and decided to pass by the factories, which would all be shuttered at this time of night. We passed an old diner and kept walking when Juan, the eldest of us, stopped in his tracks and looked back over his shoulder at the dark and obviously closed eatery. He seemed to be lost in thought as both Tommy and I stopped walking as well.

After a few moments, my curiosity peeked. I asked Juan, "What are you looking at?"

Juan had a gleam in his eye and a funny little smile on his face.

He asked, "What are the odds that a place like that has an alarm system?"

I looked at the old beat up diner, with the front gate completely covered in graffiti, and thought that it probably didn't, but I really didn't see where Juan was going with it.

69

I looked at him and said, "Probably not, what's your point?"

His grin grew into a full smile bearing his crooked and prematurely yellowing teeth. As a matter of fact, it was one of the rare moments when Juan wasn't holding a cigarette or asking if anyone could spare one.

He said, "Let's see if we can get in there somehow."

Tommy and I looked at each other and without saying a word, a collective shrug of our shoulders confirmed the fact that we really didn't have anything better to do. We all seemed to start walking towards the diner at the same time, without giving it much question afterward. We hopped over a short fence around the side of the diner when I stopped suddenly in my tracks. I came face to face with a big German Shepherd that was equally surprised to see me as well. I didn't move an inch as the big dog began to growl and bared his teeth in preparation for his attack. He crouched down just a bit to begin his attack when a huge puff of white smoke caught us both by surprise. I lost sight of the dog in the smoke, and began to back up against the fence. I was also trying to find the biggest stick possible to protect myself with after all the smoke cleared. I had no idea where the smoke was coming from nor did I recognize the sound that kept resonating over and over in my ears. Finally, I heard Juan laughing like a child and realized that the smoke was coming from a fire extinguisher he had found somewhere in the backyard of the diner. The noisy cloud had surprised both the dog and me, so we had simultaneously retreated to safer confines. I only saw the dog one more time as Juan sprayed the dog again with whatever was in that extinguisher and he yelped before he disappeared out of sight.

Juan couldn't stop laughing. If he didn't know about my aversion to dogs, he certainly found out that night. I still wear a scar on my face and mouth thanks to a nice friendly dog, and I had my fill of four legged creatures. I was standing in the corner of the yard with my back neatly tucked against the fence, giving the animal only one possible angle in which to attack me, and when the smoke cleared, I was still in attack mode. He was holding his side from laughing so hard, and when I finally relaxed and dropped my makeshift weapons, I thanked him through clenched teeth. I suggested that we leave, but Tommy and Juan were completely against that notion. They had also decided that the best probably entry into the diner would be through the roof, especially with that crazy hound running around. I concurred, and up to the roof we went.

The diner had an old ventilation system with a huge fan that was bigger than all of us. Juan bent one of the blades back and immediately gained entry into the airshaft. He was almost twice my size so I knew that I could fit quite easily as well. I went in right behind him and we crawled through the airshaft until we came to a turn in the ductwork. We all navigated our way through the shaft without incident when we came to a sudden drop with a grated panel. Beyond the panel, we could actually see the floor of the diner. This was going to be much easier than we thought. Juan kicked the panel down and one by one, we hung down from the airshaft and let go. The drop was probably four to five feet at the most which was easy to handle. After Tommy jumped down, and we were all inside the diner, we decided to do a little walk around to make sure there wasn't a security guard or anyone else lurking in the establishment. We had decided to break into the place and had actually gained entry in minutes so we thought it was probably a good idea to look around before we started to do whatever it was we wanted to do there. We hadn't really thought it out at all, had we? After we knew that we were alone for sure, we went looking for a refrigerator, hopefully one fully stocked with beer. The first icebox I found was full of frozen meat. There were boxes labeled Burgers, Hot Dogs, Steaks, and huge bags of frozen cut potatoes. I closed the freezer door and started to walk around the diner when I saw what I was looking for. Right by the entrance to the diner, was a huge refrigerator with glass sliding doors. It was fully stocked with all different types of sodas but right on the top shelf was what I wanted. There wasn't a great selection, only two types of beers, but in a pinch it would do just fine. I walked over and slid opened the doors, and even though I had to tip toe to reach the top shelf, I managed to grab three beers and brought them back to the boys.

Juan was busy spraying ketchup all over the place and breaking open the sugar dispensers for some reason. His plan was to wreck the joint but I had a better idea. I went over to the kitchen and checked the grill to see if the burner pilots were still lit and they were. I looked at Tommy and Juan, who were having an egg fight in the back of the diner, and asked if they were hungry. After I managed to dodge a few eggs that whizzed past my head, I told them to stop being asshole's for one moment and listen. They decided to stop the destruction momentarily to hear me out.

I asked again, "Are you asshole's hungry?"

Juan flashed his smile one more time. He asked, "Can you cook?"

I replied, "Oh yeah, I can cook. What's it going to be, Burgers or Steaks?"

Juan said, "Both!" and so it began.

I started off by grilling a few steaks. The aristocrat I am prefers his steaks medium to medium rare. The trick is to get the grill as hot as possible so that the steak sears, trapping the juices in the minute it hits the heat. A little bit of salt and pepper is all you really need to make yourself a delicious steak providing it's a decent cut of meat. The savages I kept company with both preferred their meat very well done. You might as well take a knife and fork to your own sneaker if you ask me but who was I to tell them how to eat. I had actually finished my steak when I went back into the freezer to fetch some burgers. After those were on the grill, I took the steaks off and put them in plates for my boys to eat. They were eating the steaks like they hadn't eaten in weeks. I sat cross-legged on the counter and sipped on my second beer, taking in the scene before me. I was never really a beer drinker and I'm still not, but I have to say that I was enjoying myself a nice cold one. Suddenly, I came up with a great idea! I hopped off the counter and started to walk into the rear of the restaurant. I love fried eggs on my burgers and I knew there were plenty of eggs in the back, hoping that the two retards I was with didn't break them all in the egg fight. Luckily, there was still an entire crate left in a smaller refrigerator, so I scooped three eggs out of the container and went back into the kitchen. That is when, as they say in the old proverb, the shit hit the fan.

The entire front of the diner was lit up in blue and red. Juan and Tommy started yelling and running for cover but as always, I didn't move much. Outside I could a sea of cops surrounding the place with guns drawn, so we were nothing more than trapped rats. My two accomplices decided to try to escape back up into the airshaft and out onto the roof but the police had that covered. I heard the ruckus of footsteps and bodies being slammed down. Right over my head on the roof, I could hear the usual commands, "Freeze or I'll shoot…I'll blow your fucking head off" …and all the other usual threats the police like to make. I still didn't move. Finally, I decided that I should probably do something before they shot me dead. I noticed that Juan had dropped his cigarettes in his rush to escape, so I bent over to scoop them up. There was one cigarette left in the pack. I went over to the huge commercial stove and shut off all the burners except one. Unless the police were especially hungry, the burgers would go without audience tonight. I bent over slightly and lit the cigarette, then shut the last burner of the stove. I jumped up onto the counter, and once again sat cross-legged as I watched more and more cops approach the front gate of the diner with their guns out and ready to fire. Everything outside was a giant swirl of blue and red activity, yet all I could do was sit on the counter, finish my beer, and take the last few pulls from my cigarette.

I felt like I was watching a movie. Except I was the star in this one. I was scared. No, lets be honest. I was terrified. I knew that tonight was going to be bad. I don't know how I had known what was coming, but as I have said before, I have always had the ability to see things in advance. Hours earlier, when I had walked away from the bus stop, I knew right there and then that I was going to get myself into trouble. It mattered not. As I sat there on the counter, contemplating my fate, I heard one of the officers call out my name. It shocked me at first but then I figured that they must have asked the other two if there was anyone else inside and they had answered in the affirmative. Not that they ratted me out or anything because I was sitting there in the plain sight of all the other cops smoking a cigarette seemingly without a care in the world. That couldn't be further from the truth. I knew something bad was coming. I figured I might as well enjoy my last drink and smoke before I got my due. The cops called out my name again, and repeated that they would shoot me if I didn't come out with my hands in plain view.

I finally answered. I said, "Yeah, I'm coming" in the same tone you would answer a parent who was rushing you to the dinner table.

When I got to the airshaft, I realized that I was too short and would probably need to climb up on something to reach it. I dragged a few chairs over jumped up, barely locking my fingers onto the entrance we had made in the duct work. I pulled myself up and after I climbed a few feet, I was blinded by flashlights. That was the easy part. The next thing I felt was blinding pain. I was hit with a flashlight on the back on my neck and thrown down face first onto the roof. I had a knee deeply dug into my back and I opened my eyes to see that I was face to face with Tommy. He had some swelling on his face but looked ok otherwise. We made eye contact, and he said the funniest thing.

He said, "Don't worry, everything is going to be ok. We're minors, they can't touch us."

I managed to utter "Yeah right" before I felt a huge hand on the back of my head. One of the officers picked me up, using only my hair, and dragged me to the edge of the roof. I really couldn't see because all of the blue and red lights flashing in front of my eyes, and because I had little pieces of gravel and rock from the rooftop

73

stuck in my face. I knew two things. The cop that had me by the back of the hair was white, with a thick Brooklyn Italian accent. I also knew that I wasn't the only one that had been drinking tonight. I couldn't see his face, but I had bigger things to worry about. I was standing on the edge of the roof, with my hands tightly handcuffed behind me.

The cop was talking shit into my ear. He kept saying, "You like to hide you little fuck? You like hiding?"

I replied, "I wasn't hiding, I was finishing my cigarette."

Apparently, that was the wrong thing to say. He lifted me off my feet, again using a handful of hair to get me up as I felt the tiny strands of hair breaking off one by one. I thought he was going to throw me off the roof but instead he tried to lower me onto a freestanding phone booth in front of the diner where a few other cops were waiting. Whatever hair didn't tear off my head slipped through his fingers and I fell about ten feet onto the phone booth, bouncing off it and landed on the street face on my shoulder and chest. I felt my breath leaving me as I struggled to take in the slightest bit of air. I heard the cop say, "Whoops" and a few of them started laughing. Yeah, this was going to be bad.

They scraped me off the sidewalk and tucked me into the backseat of one of the patrol cars. I was barely conscious but I remember how much the cuffs hurt my wrists as the car bounced up and down the cobble stone lined street. It wasn't a long ride, but it felt like an eternity with the pain I was in, still I didn't say a word. I had gotten dropped off the rooftop for telling the cop that I wasn't hiding so I thought I should probably keep my mouth shut for as long as this ordeal was going to last.

When we got to the precinct, I gave them my name and home phone number, and really didn't say much else. Juan was a little older than me and by then he was already a seasoned veteran when it came to the police. He was cursing at them and spitting at them like a maniac. He called them a bunch of pussies and laughed when they threatened to kick the shit out of him. All three of us were sitting in chairs, with one of our hands cuffed to the wall. They went over to take the handcuffs off of Juan and he started kicking at them with his legs being his only possible defense. After a brief struggle, they finally got the cuffs off of him and took him into an adjoining room, which was out of our sight. We could hear the thuds as they were men of their word, and began to beat him down. He was still screaming and cursing at their mothers throughout the beating. When they brought him back in, he didn't look too bad but it was obvious that hands had been laid upon him. He was certainly quieter now. Still, defiant and stirring like a wounded animal, but he decided against another outburst.

I couldn't believe what happened next, of all things. They had an officer come with the K-9 unit. What was it with this night and all these damn dogs? I couldn't get away from these animals. They started fucking with me by putting the snarling dog inches away from my face. I turned my face away from it. I could smell the dog's foul breath as he barked over and over and sprayed dog spittle all over my face. That's how close this dog was to me. After having my own face bitten as a child, I wouldn't wish that on anyone. I was sure that I was just about to get another piece of my face ripped off but thankfully, the dog seemed to be well trained. It continued to bark and spit on me until they decided I had had enough.

Then they moved on to Tommy. He didn't seem to be as fearful of the dog as I was, but he certainly wasn't comfortable as he too turned his face away from the dog and closed his eyes.

I turned my face away from Tommy because I didn't want to see it if the dog lost control and bit him. I heard the dog barking incessantly and I figured as long as he was doing so, that meant he wasn't busy chewing on Tommy.

Then my old friend from the rooftop walked into the room and walked straight over to me. He unlocked the handcuffs and removed my hand from the wall I had been shackled to. He bent over, grabbed my face in his hand, and turned my head upward to face him.

He said, "You ever get arrested before scumbag?"

I shook my head no. I was done talking.

He nodded his head and said, "Well we're gonna find out right now cause its fingerprint time, so follow me."

I hadn't been a saint but for some reason I was thinking that my fingerprints were going to pop up at murder scenes and bank robberies. The burglar I had committed with Indio a few years earlier also popped into my head. No one would believe that I had done it to save my brother. I was sure that after the prints were run through the criminal justice computer system, I was headed straight to prison for life. I was stiff and nervous as he took my fingerprints and tried to get my fingers rolled properly on the paper. The first set turned out a blurry mess. Mr. Italian Officer was not a patient man.

He got a fresh sheet of paper, and said, "You better relax kid, cause if I have to do this again, I'm gonna break your fucking hand. So make sure you stay still."

I figured I'd better concentrate and get it right this time. Thankfully, I managed a decent set of prints, and then he took me to the bathroom to wash my hands. I thought the worst of it was over, but I couldn't be more wrong.

He instructed me to stand in front of the sink, and then told me to wash the ink from my hands. He insisted that I use the soap that was in a receptacle, which felt kind of odd since it had little hard rock like pieces in it. It wasn't like any soap I had ever used before but it was certainly effective in removing the ink. The officer was standing right behind me, and I could feel him right on top of me. He was actually standing against me, and it started to make me very uncomfortable. I looked up at him through the mirror and saw that his last name was Devino. I knew he was a fucking Italian. The name ending in a vowel always gave it away. He noticed me looking at him and gave me a rap on the head with his nightstick.

"Mind your own fucking business," he said.

I saw the stars as that knock on the head shook me up badly. My legs actually buckled a bit. I stood up again, and once again made eye contact with him through the mirror. He hit me harder this time, and again I buckled but refused to go down. I felt the swelling immediately as the lumps on my head quickly developed a pulse of their own. I stood up again, and continued to wash my hands, but I could not help myself to once again, eye him up in the mirror. He bent me over the sink and gave me a good wallop on the back of my head, almost knocking me unconscious. I felt the warm trickle of blood start to ebb as it began to flow down the back of my neck, and it was probably the only thing that actually kept me conscious. He noticed something jutting from the back of my pants. Nobody had bothered to search me when I had been arrested, and when he had bent me over to crack me over the head, he noticed the big and obvious bulge behind me.

He asked, "What do you have there?"

He gave the bulge a light tap with his nightstick and the sound echoed throughout the bathroom. I still had the unfinished bottle of rum. Somehow and miraculously, it had survived the fall from the rooftop and car ride to the precinct. He kept me bent over with my forehead scraping against the water spout of the sink as he removed the bottle from the back of my pants.

He started laughing quite heartily as he discovered my stash of unfinished booze.

He let me go and opened the bottle to take a sniff and inspect what was in the bottle. It was exactly what he thought it was. I had been able to stand up when he was distracted by the bottle and had taken a swipe of the back of my head to inspect the damage. I was in fact bleeding, but not as much as I had expected. Head wounds tend to bleed profusely. I washed the blood off my hands and when I looked back up in the mirror, he was putting the bottle away into his jacket pocket. That was hard to swallow. A beating I could take, but taking another man's hooch is just bad business. He realized I was watching him again, and his face contorted to anger. He took the nightstick and placed it against the side of my face, along my jawline. He was still standing right behind me so I had no place to go.

He asked menacingly, "Didn't I tell you to mind your business?"

I didn't say a word, but instead kept my eyes on him and the looming threat that was the long piece of wood right against my head. He started to laugh.

He said, "You're a tough little fucker aren't you?" in between his laughter. I still didn't say a word. Then he said, "And you're quite the little boozer too. How old are you kid?"

"I'm twelve," I said. It was the last thing I would say that day.

"Twelve years old?" he replied. "And already you're a little Rumdog. That bottle is bigger than you kid. What are you doing drinking all that?"

I didn't answer him. Not because I was trying to be defiant, but because I was absorbing and processing what he had just said. "Rumdog", I kinda liked that. I didn't break eye contact with him through the mirror, and I didn't know what was coming next. I figured I was going to take some more punishment for refusing to put my head back down.

Suddenly he said, "Finish washing your hands you little spic, before I break your face."

I supposed our little moment of bonding was over. I put my hands back in the running water but for some reason or another, I could not stop watching him. The stick was still on the side of my face, and it felt cold and menacing against my ear. The bathroom door swung open, and another officer poked his head in. He seemed taken aback by the sight of me standing in front of the sink with a nightstick against my head. After a moment the officer said, "Jimmy, what are you doing? Let's go."

Devino said, "Hey, look what I found on this little fuck."

He tucked the nightstick under his arm and reached into his pocket, pulling out the bottle of rum. He showed it to the other officer, seemingly very proud of his little find. The other officer wasn't quite as moved by the discovery.

He said, "Ok, well his mother is on his way to pick him, so let's make sure he's in one piece. Ok?"

Officer Devino, known as "Jimmy" to his cohorts apparently, nodded his acknowledgment. I finally stopped watching him. I proceeded to wash the ink off my hands, and do my best to clean up my head and face.

"Lets go!", said officer Devino, and he escorted me back to my awaiting chair from where he had gotten me earlier.

Juan and Tommy were fast asleep by then. I already knew that I would never mention any of this to anyone, especially my family. It's funny how the mere mention of my mother was enough to assure me that I was going to survive this encounter. After I washed as well as possible, I grabbed a wad of paper towels, dried my face and soaked head, barely very careful not to agitate the several lumps on my head, one which had a small but deep cut. I didn't want my mother to walk in and see me a bloody, wounded mess. I wanted to show her that this was no big deal. I knew that my punishment would not be over just because my mother was coming. I suspected, quite correctly, that I was going to get more than a handful of lumps from my mother as well. I also knew that she would only go so far.

My mother finally arrived at 4 am, and by then I was half asleep and still handcuffed to the wall. She let out one single embarrassed tear when she had arrived and saw me handcuffed to the wall, but she had no clue of the beating that I had endured. She silently signed all the paperwork accepting custody of me. She smacked me several times on the subway while we were going home, but that was just the appetizer.

After we had gotten home, she instructed me to take off all of my filthy clothes and to put them in a plastic bag, which I did without question. Whatever I was wearing was covered in mud, roof tar, dirt, ink, and several blotches on the back that unknown to her was my blood. I am not of fan of very hot water, but that morning in the shower, it felt medically necessary to use as much hot water as I could to soothe the extreme pain and soreness all over my body. I had never been in that much pain, no matter how many beatings I had taken. I closed my eyes momentarily and let the water do its work when I heard the bathroom door open. I thought to myself, "Here it comes" and it did.

My mother yanked the shower curtain open and started to beat me with a leather belt while I was standing there naked and wet. I did nothing to defend myself. I took as many blows as I could, before the pain began to overwhelm me. I knelt down and covered up whatever vital body parts I could, and hoped she would tire of swinging the belt. Eventually she did, and she yelled at me to finish up and go right to bed. She told me that this better be the last time that I embarrassed her and the family. I waited for her to leave, and when she did, I finally felt like it was safe to let out my emotion. I cried silently while sitting there in the tub, trying to keep the sound of my sobs as quiet as possible. I didn't need to get hit again. I was done.

I knew that whatever had happened that night, I had done to myself. I had put myself in real danger for no reason whatsoever. While I was sitting on the counter, and watched as all the cops encircled us with their guns drawn, I felt dangerous. I felt notorious and powerful. I was also rightly afraid and aware that they could end my life and tortured little existence right then. I pondered this and it did not seem like a terrible option. Oh, but what about my poor mother? I think that's why I decided to give myself up without incident. We weren't there to steal, or to be criminal masterminds. The whole time in the diner, we had never even looked at the cash register. We were stupid, foolish and completely unaware of the real danger we had put ourselves as well as the police in. The only thought in my head was how much my mother would cry if I were to be killed in that diner. That meant the shabby little boy I was might actually be loved. Everything happens for a reason. Now, I was the newly christened "Rumdog" and I had liked that very much. I had things to do. In my mind that meant that maybe, I mattered. As impossible as that may seem to me.

The Silver Lining

The more that I heard Rumdog speak, it became apparent that he had become a lunatic, or perhaps he had a completely unorthodox method of dealing with immeasurable disappointment. With the things he saw and experienced before the age of twelve, he really should have grown up to be a different person. He should probably be a resident of some correctional facility, or resting comfortably in a psych ward, yet there he stood in front of me, of seemingly sound mind and looking at me straight in the eyes waiting for me to make myself ready to record his next stroll through memory lane. They say that the eyes are the windows to the soul, but Rumdog, with his dark watchful eyes don't appear to be holding any secrets behind his veiled gaze. The truth is, while I'm becoming accustomed to his constant yet unobtrusive appraisal, it's a little bit un-nerving to know that I am not being measured not by what I say, but by my reactions. Sometimes, during our interaction, our eyes would happen to meet, and while I knew he was looking at my eyes, he was watching my hands, my posture, and even the way I was breathing. What I really felt, while I was looking at my own reflection in his eyes, was that I was looking into a two-way mirror like the ones that are used in an interrogation room. You can see a perfect reflection of yourself, and at the same time, you know there's an unknown amount of eyeballs fixed on you and measuring your responses.

I had a sinking feeling that at any given point, because it was vitally important to him that I believe and understand his plight, he would decide to stop talking, leaving me with an incomplete story. I felt that at any point he was going to shake my hand, and tell me that it just wasn't going to work.

Knowing him and his manner now, I'm sure that he would tell me not to take it personally and buy me a drink whenever I was to see him next. I knew that it was just his way. Thankfully, that moment had never come, and I can honestly say that I believed everything he revealed to me. He never seemed any different to me than any of the other neighborhood kids, but I now saw that I had misunderstood and under-estimated everything about him. It also became very clear that I didn't know much about him at all. I had no clue what he did for work, he obviously did ok for himself financially. His apartments furnishing was sparse, but nothing about it seemed cheap. The apartment itself was certainly out of my price range. There were just things he never talked about. Until now, we had never spoken about his life and upbringing. I had not known how poor he really was. He tends to speak in run-on sentences, and jumps from year to year somewhat unpredictably, but I think that I have managed to follow his unorthodox method of communication.

He went on to tell me that he had no clue how different his life was until he started to befriend kids at school and he witnessed what a normal family life was supposed to look like. He didn't realize that he was poor until he saw the great meals other kids his age would push to the side in disapproval. He would attend sleepovers and would ask to stay again, trying to have at least one more night of normalcy in his hectic and unconventional life. And this is where and how he began to learn what life for a kid was supposed to be like. I think that Rumdog has both a curse and a gift to carefully watch his surroundings at every given moment, and is unable to shut down the radar that is constantly monitoring all that he sees. He may not seem like he is keeping a vigilant orb on you, yet he notices every unspoken hint by your gestures, your hands or whatever "tell" you may exhibit.

This is most likely a by-product of his childhood, when he was always watching what was going to happen next. This stayed with him throughout his life, as a child, a teen, and later on into adulthood. He might sleep the night away, or he might wake up to violence as his oldest brother tore apart the house. He could never tell what his night was going to be like as he lay down to sleep, subsequently leading of course to his severe bouts with insomnia. This came in handy at times, when he was sober enough to hold on to a job. He would do overnight shifts, or for when he was able to party for thirty-six hours straight. Sometimes during his overnights, he would do the shifts of all his coworkers, just because he knew that there was no way he was going to sleep at all that night. Everyone would wake up completely refreshed after a good night's sleep and he would then head home, and still not be able to get a wink. Of course, after self-medicating with rum and through utter exhaustion, he would finally find his slumber. It was never thoroughly restful.

He hadn't learned yet how to turn it off, his mind. His method of self-defense, though undeniably reliable, also took a toll on him as it refused to defuse. It was always on, even as he slept, giving him fitful hours of bad dreams of past scenarios, and on many occasions, warning of unwanted scenarios to come. He had this gift, which I stated earlier also doubled as an affliction, to wake up and have 100% recall of his dreams, that weren't really dreams at all. They were warnings that his subconscious stubbornly insisted on delivering, even as he lay unconscious. It had been that way for more years than he could remember, ever since he was a boy. Although he had no choice in the matter, he did pay attention to detail.

He had no father to speak of, so he took watch of all his friend's dads. Right around his twelfth birthday is when life began to change for him, beginning with the day he met a man named Henry. While his life would continue to have its ups and downs, meeting Henry and his family was one of the few bright spots in his young life. It showed him that there was hope. It showed him that maybe, just maybe, one day he was going to be able to shed his paupers clothing and have a chance at a decent life. Of course, he had no idea just how many highs and lows he was going to experience, but the fact that these people had brought him into their home and loved him was a foreign gesture to him, and he became instantly attached. It wasn't that he didn't feel loved by his family, because he certainly did. To him, it felt like perhaps the traditional structure of family and home was the one thing he was missing. It also wasn't the fact that Henry's family would all sit together at the table to eat dinner and share conversation, but it was more that his own family didn't have a dinner table. So, while he was enjoying every night and every meal he shared with this family, he was, as always, paying close attention to how it was supposed to be.

Now, that he had his own kids, they could have dinner at the table and share how their day went. Once in a while, he may allow them to eat in the living room in front of the TV, perhaps when they have their friends or cousins over, but for the most part, dinner is a shared block of time for the family. The TV goes off, no hats, cell phones, or headphones at the dinner table, and they talk like a family should. Thirty years later after he met Henry and his family, he could still remember their example.

Rumdog has a habit of popping in and out of the room quietly and without a sound. I hadn't noticed when he left the room but I did notice when he was back and sitting comfortably in his reclining chair. He never actually reclined it, but *more so, he would sit upright in the chair while rocking by shifting his weigh back and forth. When he would begin to talk again, he would look at the wall, and you could certainly tell he was not only trying to remember the important details, but that re-living these memories still took a toll on him. He began to tell me the tale of the men he had adopted as his own. It all started on his twelfth birthday, the day that he recalls and refers to himself, as the silver lining. This is what he said;*

Sometimes, I'm about to fall asleep, and right before I'm about to shut it down for the night, my brain goes into recall. Truthfully, sleep evades me for as long as possible on many nights. And my brain has to go into rewind and recall until it decides to shut down. This can take many hours. My recollections are usually things from my childhood. Things that I look back on which saved my life and well-being. I have my "Fathers" as I like to refer to them. People that happened to be prominent figures at different junctures in my life raised me unintentionally. These men shaped me, molded me and whenever something in life challenges me, I revert to the experiences of these men. And I try to remember their advice, the way they handled situations, and how they kept their family together. I admire these men, and I will always hold a place in my heart for them as my pseudo fathers.

I never had a dad, my mom being the sole provider for all five of us. It's not an uncommon story, but me having the opportunity to listen and learn from different men is what makes my story a fortunate and eventful tale. It all figures into my parenting. I do what they did. I listened when they spoke to their children and pretended that they were addressing me as well. And maybe they were. Maybe they were kind enough to spread knowledge to the unintended, just for the sake of casting a few crumbs of wisdom to the fatherless poor kid from down the street. Either way, I was listening. I stored. And when they were busy going off on their kids, I was all ears. Their own kids would roll their eyes, and yawn during these lessons while I would sit there, silent.

Have you ever noticed that listen and silent use that exact set of letters? I never thought that to be a coincidence. My friends were spoiled and probably couldn't wait for their Dad's to just shut the hell up so that they can go back to whatever it was they were doing. Well, not me. I never had this in my life so I was going to appreciate whatever it is they were offering in the sense of fatherhood. They were a real family. They had real homes. They ate real food every night for dinner and I couldn't believe they had meat every day as a side course.

My first outside influence other than my brother Gilbert was a great man by the name of Henry. Meeting Henry changed my life in countless ways. He was truly the first real father of my life. I met Henry on my twelfth birthday. I knocked on the door to pick up his gigantic son Rick, while on my way to school. Now that he's an adult, he's really not that big at all, slightly larger than the average man but Rick had been pretty much full grown by the time he had reached middle school age. When I knocked on the door, Rick's younger brother Steven greeted me at the door. He had no clue who I was or I he, but I met Rick just the day before and we had walked home together from school. He told me to come by early in the morning so that we could walk to school together and I figured why they hell not. Never hurt to have a little muscle around being that I was almost a dwarf till halfway through High school.

So there I was, and after Steven gave me a quick up and down, he decided I was cool and told me to come on up. I went up the stairs, met the whole family including their German shepherd mix Rocky. Little did I know, I would go on to walk Rocky a thousand times throughout the years to follow. He was actually a great dog. Other than the one time he bit me on the knee, due to my trying to be a peacekeeper while he was busy brawling with some other dog that had crossed our path, Rocky and I got along fine. But he too had to assess the little drably dressed stranger that came to the door. I had no clue just how attached I would become to this family and how important a role they would play in the future.

Gilbert was my primary father. So I suppose you can label him father number one. Yes, he was just two years older than me, but no one protected or gave me more than Gil. He fought for me. He fought alongside me. He would never let harm come to me, unless it was his huge hand knocking me around of course. But the day that I met Henry and the rest of Rick's family was really the first time in my life that something had changed, and I was paying attention enough to realize that it had happened.

Steven and I hit it off immediately. Reason being, it was also his twelfth birthday. We were about halfway to school when we made that discovery, and when we got to school, I introduced Rick and Steven to just about everyone at school. For some reason or another, Gilbert and I were pretty popular and well known. Nobody really messed with us. We were probably respected more because of Gilbert's fierce fighting skills and less because of my natural charm. It only took about a week for all of us to become as thick as thieves and we were doing sleepovers and playing sports every day after school.

At first, Henry would hardly speak to me. He would come home from work in a raggedy beat up van, completely covered in black soot, and head straight to the shower. I thought he looked like a coal miner. However, he was actually a boiler cleaner. He would toil from early in the morning to quitting time in filthy, smoky, boilers in Queens and Chinatown in the city. He ate lunch at the same spot just about every day, getting a two-dollar plate of rice and pork, and went on with his work day. He took me to work sometimes after he got to know me a little better, and he paid me twenty bucks a day to roll around in soot for the entire day. And with the smaller boilers, my diminutive size would come in handy to get into the tight spots. Sure, he was violating several child labor laws, but I was twelve and making a hundred dollars for the week. What other kid could say he had that kind of dough. For me, it was a big deal.

I had grown up dirt poor, as you already know, so this was like hitting the lottery for me. Rick and Steven hated going to work with Henry and would look for any excuse to get out of it. They had the spoils. They had a nice house. They had the comforts that I did not so they didn't quite understand my eagerness to go out, get dirty, and make some money. Henry would even take us to his property upstate and we would chop down trees all summer, clearing the land for the house that they planned to build. Again, his child labor force was put to work and for that he didn't pay me. He didn't have to because I would have stayed there, and chopped down trees all year, just not to go back home to my condemned house in Brooklyn. We camped, and I saw deer for the first time in my life. I saw several black bears and whatever wildlife was in those woods. I was absolutely having the time of my life.

It's funny, how two people could be doing the very same thing and have the opposite point of view. Henry's kids hated it. I loved every minute. For that summer, I wasn't poor. I didn't go hungry. I felt like I was one of them. Moreover,

Rick and Steven treated me like I was their brother. We shared everything. I remember Henry taking the kids clothes shopping for the new upcoming school year and maybe he saw something in my face, because Henry and his wonderful wife Elsie bought me a brand new outfit to wear the first day of school. It took all my will power not to cry that day. I felt so humbled and so thankful that I could not even speak. If I had said those two words, "Thank You" my voice would have betrayed me by cracking. I smiled as they told me to pick something out. I took a long time because I was trying to pick the cheapest clothes possible. Elsie then came over, she showed me a really nice white button down shirt and blue jeans. It was nicer and more expensive than anything that I had ever owned. I smiled and nodded, trying to say thank you, but again, I could not find the words that were stuck behind the lump in my throat called appreciation.

They always did things like that for me. I was just another one of their children. I'm sure they felt bad for me, but I never felt like they pitied me. They loved me. I decided then, that when I grew up, I was going to love my children the way they loved their children and me. We would turn the house upside down, and they never complained. We would beat up and torture Susan, who was the youngest sister, and hang all her dolls from the ceiling fans and they would just shrug it off. In my house, that would have been the broom or the belt, but Henry and Elsie's parenting was so much different. It was more love, than rule.

My ex-wife could never understand how I could just sit there and listen to the racket my kids were causing without it bothering me one bit. I tried to explain to her that one day, the house would be silent without any kids running around. There will be no more of the gleeful screams and laughter coming from our children. At that point, you will miss it and wish that you had encouraged them to do it more often. Every once in a while I reach out to Henry and Elsie just to thank them for teaching me patience, love and acceptance, for trying to me a better person, and for making me a better dad. Spending time with that family was truly some of the best times in my life.

When they moved upstate, they offered to let me live with them. One of their friends named Nathan and his family offered to let me live with them as well. Nathan played football for Eldred High school and they had some sort of football program they thought I would do well in. I was small, but I was quite athletic. I was fast and I had hands like glue. I though that maybe this was my chance at finally having a normal life, but at the end of the summer, my mother insisted that I come back home to Brooklyn. My dream was over and I was forced to return to Brooklyn completely broken hearted. Sadly, Nathan was killed in a car accident some time later while driving home from a party. God knows if it was fate that kept me from moving upstate, but all I knew at the time was that I was truly saddened that they had moved so far. I had other friends in NY but when Henry finally finished building the house and moved the entire family upstate, I had no one to replace them. He would come to Brooklyn just to pick me up sometimes on the weekends.

He would work all week and then stop to pick me to take me upstate. He would drop me back home on Monday mornings then head to work. That's the kind of man he was. He would come home looking like he rolled around in a chimney all day, completely black and soot covered, his eyes being the only thing you could make out. He would come home like this each and every day, go straight into the shower and cough up the past ten hours of soot, out of his lungs, out of his nose, out of his mouth, until it was mostly out. Then he would come out of the shower, and yell out to his wife "Hey Elsie, what's for dinner?" She would yell something back from the kitchen and he would have the same reply.

"Oh, ok. It smells good!" Even now, I can hear his voice bellowing throughout the house.

When Henry came home from work, it was always my favorite part of the day. He would always tell us a stupid joke, or tell us a hilarious story. And the stories were always laden with curses to our delight.

Then he'd warn us, "Don't tell Elsie I told you this" or "don't repeat what you just heard or be smart, use your head."

More often than not, we wouldn't believe his outrageous stories and he would say, "You don't believe me? Go ahead ask anybody, ask your friends."

But no way were we going to ask around about anything he told us. Half the time he was fucking with us but many times his stories had some kind of lesson in it.

The lesson usually was "Don't be a dumb fuck." You would think that maybe he wasn't the best influence, right? It was just the opposite. He was preparing us for the real world.

While you were at school and they were teaching you that Columbus was actually some kind of hero, Henry was teaching us that life is hard. He taught me that most of our friends weren't worth shit. He warned all of us about the pressures that our so-called friends were going to put on us, and how most of them had their own intentions and not our own safety on their agenda. He spoke plainly, and he always made sense. He was a great man for the simple reason that he worked hard every single day and came home to his wife every single night. He had also decided that he was going to raise all of Elsie's children as his own. It takes a special kind of man to do that. It really amazes me that a man can make children, bring them into this world, and feel no bond or obligation to raise the child. A man that abandons his children is truly not a man. If you refuse to raise and support your own offspring, well then there's just something fundamentally wrong with you. But a man that decides to take that responsibility for children that he had no part in making. Well, that's just a super hero. He was an influence and example that I desperately needed to affirm that life was just not one tragedy after another. He has been with those kids since before I knew them and I've known them for 30 years now. I love that family with all my heart, yet I don't see them as much as I should. I try to keep in touch with them but I really should do better by them. I promise to see them and visit but I'm always busy doing mindless things and boozing. It's really no excuse considering that I owe them so much. Maybe one day I can somehow repay that debt.

I'd love for my children to know them, and to understand and appreciate that Henry and his family are the primary reason that I always tried to be a Dad, no matter the circumstances, and no matter how inadequate I might have felt. I will never be able to express the words that are needed to show them the level or respect, admiration, and appreciation that I have for them. This is the best I can do. Still, I believe that it's not enough but I don't know what kind of grand gesture I would have to make to let them know just how much they rescued me, and just how much Henry and his loving family saved my soul and spirit.

Then there's Chris the Bear.

Chris is actually the Godfather of one of old lifelong friends. He was one the nicest guys I have ever met. He was funny, charming, easy going, and a deeply religious man. He also had the ability to tear off one of your arms and beat you over the head with it. He was a big man to say the least. He was also heavily muscled, tattooed, and had achieved God knows how many levels of black belts. He could bench press 500 pounds and throw a flying kick to your head and punt it 40 yards. He was a big strong scary man to say the least. Yet, he was also the most righteous man I would ever meet. His physical abilities were in stark contrast with his demeanor and I loved that fact that he was incredibly powerful yet innately gentle. He was the first person that I ever met that taught me that you can be a man of God, and be a bad motherfucker at the same time.

For some time in my life, I had lost my sense of religion and God. I'm no zealot, and I certainly don't throw bibles at my people from atop a soapbox on a street corner, but I do have a strong sense of spirituality and God. At one point of my life, I had just given up on the notion of something bigger than all of us. I was drinking at a very dangerous pace, and I figured that my life was going to end exactly that way. I would drink myself blind every night until I would never again remember the things I had survived. I was having it out with everyone, and for some reason I began attacking cab drivers that were unlucky enough to have to drive me home from the bar. I was attacking my family members and denouncing that they had ever been kin to me. Every woman I dated walked away from me in tears and in fear.

I would destroy every single piece of furniture in my house when I would be at my worst. There was a rage in me that would only manifest when I tried to use the content of a bottle to fill the void that was within me. Drinkers like me know exactly what I'm talking about. You wake up most of the time feeling as empty. Your everyday life becomes pointless and without direction or purpose. One day seems to bleed into the next. You wake up with a headache almost every day, and now you have to fill your day with people you don't want to see and talk to people you stopped having anything to say to long ago. While most people live from paycheck to paycheck, crazy little drunks like me live from hangover to hangover, filling the middle with useless day-to-day shit. Yet the void remains. What I tried to explain to Chris is that I was struggling to remain spiritually and emotionally cohesive. I felt empty.

I would take the first drink of the day and it almost seemed to fill that void just a little bit. It quenched a thirst that had been there all day. It was better than medication. I felt better in an instant. However, it was a temporary fix. A person can drink a thousand bottles, and sleep with a thousand women, trying to fill that chasm with every possible distraction known to man, and the void will remain. The more you drink, the more you realize just how empty you really feel. This is why drunks need company. You go out, you find someone else that's sharing your loneliness, and you get shit faced together. A certain bond exists when people drink together. If you don't believe me, go home, grab a bottle of booze, and try to get yourself twisted all by your lonesome. See how much fun you have sitting there by yourself. See how long before you're reaching for your phone, trying to get someone to come over to either drink with you or bang you till you pass out. Drinking alone is miserable. If people didn't have bars to drown in, the suicide rate in this world would be a whole lot higher, that's for sure. And that's why drunks drink. We drink to forget yesterday and yesteryear, and live through another day. You get home after a night of drinking and if you're lucky, you actually have the time or frame of mind to remove your own clothing before you fall face first onto any piece of furniture that will support your weight. Once you hit that bed or couch and your eyes fall shut, mission accomplished.

One day, I was talking about the drinking and carrying on that was going to take place that night and Chris just listened to me without interruption. After our conversation was over, we said our good night, and he gave me his customary hug and kiss on the cheek. He is one of the few people that is allowed to touch me. I am not of fan of physical affection. He told me to be careful and to try to take it easy. I didn't know what he meant so I asked what exactly he had meant by take it easy.

He said, "Look, I know you guys are going to go out and drink tonight, and I just want you to be careful."

I said, "I'm always careful Chris."

He replied, "I know, but you aren't the problem. It's the other assholes that are going out tonight that will be the problem."

He was absolutely right. I had gotten into more than a few scraps in clubs and bars, absolutely none of it had been my fault. He also said something that stuck with me for a long time. He told me that nothing good happens after midnight. He said fun things happen after midnight, and bad things definitely happen after midnight, but none of it is ever good. It was sound advice. Chris was also the first person to tell me, without delivering a sermon, that if I was challenged or confused about what I was doing with my life, to pray about it. Really, it was that simple, just pray about it. At this point I had lost all touch with my God and I was kind of winging it day by day and hating every single minute of being me.

One night, I sat in my house boozing alone, which I have already told you is the worst way to drink. I was honestly looking for a way out. Sometimes I would get so low that six feet under didn't seem too far down at all. I was thinking of pills maybe? No, I didn't know how much I would have to take and I might just wake up embarrassed. Perhaps I could introduce a bullet to the brain? Negative, that's too graphic and my head just might be empty already. Besides drinking myself to death, I really didn't fancy any of the traditional methods of checking out. I thought that maybe drinking myself into a permanent coma could be a viable alternative to making some kind of modern art décor with my brain splatter all over the wall. I drank a bottle of rum and a bottle of vodka in that sitting.

This wasn't uncommon for me, for the simple reason that I drank whatever was available after I finished my rum. I was in my typical, if not daily routine of finding a way to finally check out of this life. How much does a guy have to drink to earn himself a toe tag these days? I almost started to sober up and it upset me further. I was in a drunken craze, cursing God and proclaiming that he really didn't exist. I was begging that he take me, asking that he show some mercy and finally put an end to my misery. I put my fist through the television. I demolished a Grandfather clock my friend had given me right down to splinters. Given that I had destroyed most of my furniture on previous nights of rage, there really wasn't much else to break. It's all why I tend to not own much as I've gotten older. It can get expensive to constantly destroy and replace your furniture.

The night wasn't going well for me at all as I became increasingly frustrated. I then started to hit myself. I began ramming my head into the wall, going right through the sheet rock wall. When that didn't seem productive or quick enough, I

91

started to punch myself in the head and temples trying to put myself out. I vividly remember my own fists crashing into my head, the impact making crunching sounds in my skull as I tried to knock myself unconscious.

It just wasn't working. This was a new level of rage for me and it was all coming out. I was bleeding from several cuts on my head, crying uncontrollably, and I just threw myself onto the couch in frustrated exhaustion. I cried. The guttural sounds emitting from my chest, I continued to scream until my throat was raw. I was shaking and thinking of a different way to hurt myself. Then Chris just popped in my head. It was almost like I was seeing him right in front of me. The words just came out of his mouth.

He said, "Pray about it."

In my emotional desperation, I did exactly that. I prayed for what seemed to be at least an hour. I was crying. I was screaming and whispering at the same time. I was convulsing from sobbing so hard. During this particular emotional breakdown, I was hyperventilating and could not breathe to the point where I was dizzy.

"Pray about it. Don't stop. I know it hurts." I said to myself.

Slowly, I tried to gather my emotions. I could hear the whole world right outside my window going about its' usual business. Everyone was oblivious to the life and death struggle that was going on within my four walls. I went into a trance like state that felt like I was being carried away, floating to a place that was neither here nor there. I didn't hear. I didn't see. I didn't feel anything. I suppose this may the place within every one of us that the Yoga Guru's try to make us find.

"Pray about it. Even if it feels pointless and fruitless, what do you have to lose?" I kept saying that to myself and I really don't know how long I was in that state.

When I finally came out of it, I was amazed to be laying on my futon, with my knees tucked into my chest. I had trails of dried tears on my face, and my head hurt. I sat up slowly and perused the room, half expecting some Buddha like figure patiently sitting at my table. I was alone. I wasn't scared. I wasn't shaking anymore. I was…calm? No, I was serene. That was the word. The rage was gone. I wasn't even drunk.

Who knows how much time had gone by but it was still night, and I was confused about what had just taken place. I slowly realized that I had cocooned myself into whatever mental state I needed to be in to protect myself from further damage. Wherever I went, whether it was deep inside my own sub-conscious state, or if Baby Jesus himself had come down and wiped my slate clean for the night, I was at peace.

I started to clean up the mess I had made, hoping that it was the last time that I had gone totally berserk in my wrecking ball state. I have been known to put my fists through doors and windows and mirrors from time to time. It's a habit that I actively try to tackle and diffuse whenever it shows its ugly face. But because Chris had taken his time to teach me just a little bit, it forever changed the way I view and handle my anger.

I wouldn't draw the line there, however, in detailing all the things that he taught me. He wasn't an overly opinionated man and it never felt like you were being sermonized when he spoke to you. He was just passing on things to me that he had learned years ago. He was simply doing the chore of the older generations, in schooling the young, who refused to be schooled and insist on being baptized in their own mistakes and failures. He was and still is a great man, with a sense of paternal love that was second to none. I loved him for being the great example and nurturer that he is, and I love him for the man that he wanted me to be in the eyes of God and family. He is another person that I only rarely get to see, but when I do have the fortune of his audience, I would always engage him in conversations of our families and our recent mishaps. Then I just listen. On a lucky day, I may have one of my darling offspring at my side, and I would let them absorb if not indulge in whatever it is Chris chooses to share. In truth, he would be speaking to them as well and if they are even a little bit smart, they will take something with them that will perhaps be useful when they themselves are parents and guardians of their own rebellious flock.

RumDog's Guide to....Parenting?

Having children is without a doubt the biggest reason I survived my inner turmoil and made the decision to roll out of bed every single day. Everyone thinks their kids are great and the best things that ever happened, right? Well, my kids are definitely way better than most kids. They are good-looking, smart, respectful, athletic little creatures, each armed with a keen sense of humor that rivals the other. While they are both hilarious children, they differ greatly in their manner.

My daughter is a teenager now, and is honest to a fault. She also dislikes most people and has no problem whatsoever voicing and showing her displeasure at your presence. My boy is almost 13 years old now. He doesn't have a care in the world, and will try to con his way out of everything, no matter how badly red handed he was busted. He is content to play video games, eat eggs at every meal, play with his penis, and avoid showering at all costs. He, on the other hand, is a natural charmer. He loves and is loved by everyone. I'll give you a perfect example of just how different they are.

Many moons ago, I was sitting on a recliner and watching both of them playing with the computer. They were both pretty small at this point, so they were sharing a computer chair as they both stared at the happenings on the computer screen. I guess it was my sons turn to play because I noticed that my daughter took her eyes off the screen, and started to eyeball her brother. He was sitting with half of his butt hanging off the chair and I watched as she appraised just how vulnerable her little brother was. It was like I was reading her mind. I watched as she looked at him, looked at the floor, and then her eyes surveyed him to see just where she should give him a little nudge. I'm watching this whole thing unfold, and I was thinking to myself that there was no way that she was going to knock him off the chair for no reason whatsoever. I was wrong. A second later, the boy was sprawled out on the floor with a bump on his head, screaming his lungs off. He had no clue what had hit him or even why. My daughter was sitting there giggling like an evil villain. I could not believe what I had just witnessed.

I ran over to my son and scooped him up and yelled at my daughter, "Why did you that?"

Her answer was almost as surprising as her action. She looked at me with a very serious face and said, "You know, I really don't know. He was sitting there on the edge of the chair and I thought to myself how funny it would be if he fell off. So, I pushed him. That was wrong, wasn't it?"

I was thrown for a moment because she was so nonchalant about it, but I tried to recover and be the tough parent.

I said, "Yes, of course it was wrong."

And before and I could say anything else, she said, "Yeah, I know. I guess I'm in trouble so I'll just go to my room."

She walked right past me and said, "Sorry!" as she patted her brother on the head and walked into her bedroom.

That was it. It totally diffuses you as a parent when a child fully admits his or her wrongdoing and then administers the disciplinary action.

My son, on the other hand, is a totally different child. He will try and fib his way out of any jam, and will stay committed to the fabrication no matter what. On one fine afternoon, they were playing outside, when I heard a wail from outside in the front. Then I heard sobbing as the front door opened, and my daughter came into the house crying hysterically. She was holding her face, and when I removed her hand, she had a small ugly welt on her cheek. When I asked her what had happened, she told me that he had struck her in the face with a stick for no reason whatsoever. I was definitely skeptical about this story but I called out for him to come into the house immediately. He walked in and he started stuttering and stammering immediately. I asked him if he had hit his sister in the face and he outright denied it. She called him a big fat liar and started crying some more, and I had to hold her back from kicking his ass, and at the same time solve the case.

I asked him again "Did you hit your sister with a stick?" Again, the boy denied any involvement in any sort of assault.

The explanation he offered was a fantastic story, but I had to hand it to him, he wasn't going to crack. After I swore him in, he testified to the fact that there had been a boy outside, a boy he had never seen before, that had been doing tricks on his bicycle. At one point the boy came up onto our gravel driveway, did one final trick launching his bicycle up into the air. He then landed with so much velocity that it kicked up a big piece of gravel, catapulting said gravel into the admiring but his unsuspecting sister's cheek. I asked him if that was that story he was sticking to.

He looked me right in the eyes and replied, "I swear, that's what happened."

I nodded and then I went in for the kill. I asked him "Can you please tell me why it is that you are still holding a big stick in your right hand?"

In his panic and rushed concoction of the bicycle boy patsy, he had forgotten rule number one, ditch the weapon! His eyes popped out of his head and he looked at the stick like it had magically appeared there, then he dropped it like it was hot. He got his ass handed to him shortly thereafter, and when he was in his room whimpering like he had been framed, I chuckled to myself, still thinking of that ridiculous story. One thing is for sure though. If I ever rob a bank or stick up that check-cashing joint, (one of my fantasized capers for years) I certainly know that my son will be my wheel man. If we were to get pinched, there's no way the kid is going to crack under questioning. My daughter is a great kid too, but she would dime me out in seconds.

That is the beautiful thing about them. They are completely different children, but they are equally funny and beautiful in their own way. When there's a party, the boy is in the middle of the dance floor, doing the worm and attracting all the attention. My daughter prefers to hide in a corner with her friends and dance in a tight little group, dancing only with and for them. She will read all day until her eyes fall out, and he will only play video games until his eyes bleed. Don't buy the hype that you should parent all children the same way. Raising a boy and a girl are two very different things. I learned as I went along, and I have definitely made mistakes but nobody is perfect. What can I say?

My first mistake was very early into parenting. I rarely did anything in the day-time, so while my wife at the time finished college, I was usually home with my daughter every day. By the time she was two months old, we had our schedule down tight. We had time allotted for breakfast, bathing, watch ESPN from eleven until Noon, then nap until two. Then we would have a nice lunch, throw on a few colorful cartoons to distract her while I cleaned the house and got dinner together. One day I decided to order some Chinese food, in some garlic sauce and while she ate her mashed vegetables, I was dining on some delicious chicken and broccoli.

She kept eyeing up my plate and I knew that she was very curious about what I was eating because it smelled so damn good. After a few minutes, she wanted nothing to do with her bland veggies.

Her little nasal passages were working fine at this point, because she could definitely smell my lunch and I could tell that she was ready to try something new. So I gave her an itty bitty, tiny little bit of broccoli. I mean, what could go wrong right? The piece I gave her wasn't even the size of my fingernail and when she tasted it, her eyes lit up. She freaking loved it man. She started smacking her lips, and in my head, this was a perfectly acceptable meal for a two month old. I gave her another little bite of food, this time with a little bit of chicken in it, and apparently a tiny piece of pepper had snuck in there with it. Fun lunchtime was over. The pepper agitated her little mouth, she started crying, and that's when I remembered that the garlic sauce had a little bit of spice to it. My poor daughter started to cry and I started to panic. I started flushing her mouth out with water, but she started to cough and gag so I figured that maybe water boarding an infant would be frowned upon in society. Then I had the genius idea of giving her milk because the dairy would help soothe the burning. It usually worked for me, so might as well give it a shot. It seemed like it worked for a few minutes, because she stopped crying and began to drink her milk quite peacefully. I wiped my brow in relief and thought that maybe I shouldn't give her anymore take-out food, no matter how much she wanted it.

She started to fuss around a bit, so I took the bottle from her mouth thinking that perhaps she needed to be burped. I don't know if it is normal or even possible for infants to display facial expressions, but when I looked at my daughter, she locked eyes with me and all I could read from her face was "Holy Shit." Her little face contorted, and then something amazing happened. If you have children, maybe you have seen this before, but if you haven't you just don't know what you are missing. She farted so hard that it lifted her about six inches off her baby seat. I couldn't believe my ears. Right when I was about to laugh and maybe even call somebody to share of the news of my baby's accomplishment, there was a smell that burned my eyes. That smell was followed with an obscene amount of diarrhea, an amount that I would attribute to that of a sick panda.

I jumped off my chair and tried to get her to the bathtub but it was too late. When I got her into the bathroom, we were both covered in baby poop. I couldn't believe that I had my beautiful baby for about sixty days and I had already broken it. She was still fussing a bit while I ran warm water all over her, and it seemed like she had gotten it all out. I felt terrible and I felt like the worst parent ever, even though I had the best intentions in trying to share my food with her and bring her a new joy at young and tender age.

I'm an idiot, and my poor darling child had volcanic magma exploding from her for about two days after. When my wife mentioned that she thought our little girl was getting sick, because of her frequent loose bowel movements, I assured her that it was no big deal and that she was just flushing out the garlic sauce. That got me into a lot of trouble, and for a long time I was still reminded occasionally of just how brain dead I was for giving her spicy food. But the kid has loved Chinese food ever since.

By the time she was about three years old she had developed quite the palate for Asian cuisine, and because Friday night was always Chinese food night, she would go nuts. I would come home and I'd be there barely five minutes when I asked her what day it was.

When she didn't know the answer, I would say, "It's Friday, you know what that means?"

Her eyes would light up and she would scream "Chi-nee foooooooo."

In return, I would yell "Chi-nee foooooooo." That's when the Chinese food dance would commence. This was definitely politically incorrect, but we're allowed to be openly racists in our own home, so then I would pull my eyes back tight and do the Chi-nee food chant and dance. She would start to dance and follow me all over the house singing her chi-nee food praise.

This went on for some time until the shit hit the fan on what I thought was going to be another nondescript Friday. Everything was going according to schedule. We ordered food and before long, the bell rang. I buzzed the delivery guy in and as I was giving him the money for the food, my daughter yanked open the door and jumped into the hallway. She landed in a wide footed stance like a super hero about to do battle. It was then that I noticed to my horror, that her hands were on each side of her face with her eyes pulled back tight.

She yelled at the top of her lungs, "Chiiiii-neee foooooooooo." I didn't know what to do or where to look, I was so ashamed of my offspring. The delivery guy was looking at her and I noticed him grimace as my daughter repeated her mantra. I yelled at her to get inside but she was determined to get her message across.

I quickly apologized to him and tried to get my darling little racist back inside the doorway but she proved to be surprising elusive for a child. She kept squirming around and out of my grasp. When I finally got her back inside, I turned around again and tried to finish the transaction while apologizing profusely for my daughter's outburst. Just when I thought that I could simply over-tip and talk my way out of it, she burst out into the hallway again. I grabbed the door just in time to pin the door halfway open, so now she barely had the right top half of her body sticking out. With her free arm she pulled her little eye back tight and once again yelled, "Chi-neeeee Foooooooo" before I could push her back inside to end the debacle. I was mortified, partly because I knew I would have spit or some other bodily fluid in my delivery if I was ever dumb enough to order from that restaurant again, but also because he knew the child had learned it from her good old dad.

I gave the delivery guy an incredibly generous tip that night and my apologies numbered in the double digits, but I knew that he still wanted to punch me in the face. I had to find a new restaurant to order from, and my daughter had destroyed any chances of having another Chi-nee food parade. It goes to show you how something could seem so innocent and jocular, yet be highly offensive to someone else. I learned that maybe it wasn't a good idea to make racially motivated jokes in front of your children. I make racist jokes all the time and right to people's faces, but it's different to say it to an adult than it is to say it to your child. I guess that's how people learn to parent, through trial and error, and maybe I should avoid turning my child into an insensitive bigot. I think it's better to let them grow up and learn to hate every race individually, including my own, just like I did.

I tried very hard to let my kids make their own decisions, and I avoid downloading all my screwed up tendencies onto them, in hopes of letting them become their own type of normal. Kids are going to do things that are going to throw you for a loop, and while you may not be ready for it initially, you learn to sift through whatever mess they have gotten into, and decipher for yourself what's a big deal and what can go into the recycling bin.

When my son decided to spread the rumor at school that we let him smoke in the house without consequence, it really pissed me off. Yet, as angry as I was, I simply spoke to him about it. If that would have happened earlier, the first thing I would have done was smack him upside his head. We tend to do what we were taught and I was the recipient of many smacks, so I thought it was the right thing to do. I have tried carefully to not repeat the things that I learned. Early in his life, I was on top of him. I was starting to treat him the same way that I was treated as a child. I would yell at him and whack him at the slightest infraction. Yet, for some reason, I was totally hands off with the girl.

I noticed that he would flinch sometimes when I was yelling at him, fully expecting to be hit at any moment, and that's when I realized that my own son was scared of me. I didn't like it. I didn't want my son to walk on eggshells the same way I did when I was a boy. I totally backed off from him, at least physically, until I felt that he was comfortable enough to disappoint me without fearing an assault. It's not a total declaration of immunity. There are still some offenses that can rile me up enough to throw a haymaker or two his way, but for the most part, he is going to have to work really hard to get hit.

I am fortunate enough to realize that I was doing it wrong. I had to back off my own son because I was parenting him physically, not paternally, in the way he deserved to be parented. He's a great kid, with the very same pre-teen tendencies every single one of us had, and I am lucky to have him as a son.

The funny thing is that when I'm around, I can feel that his "man of the house" position is infringed upon. He lives with his mother and sister, so he usually feels like the Rooster in the hen house. He's already almost my height and he should be taller than I very soon, but I still outweigh him by at least a hundred and thirty pounds. Still, I try not to be the boss when I'm around. I will also act like he's doing me a favor by cleaning up the petrified dog shit that's been sitting in his bedroom floor for weeks. I like to keep his little ego intact, so that he is never threatened or uncomforted by my presence. I think it was with my son that I truly learned to parent.

With my daughter, it was different. She showed me how to love. This little precious baby came into my life and I loved her unconditionally in an instant. She has grown into a funky, moody teenager but we have the best communication a parent could ever ask for. It was easy for us. It's a father and his little girl. With him, however, it's just a bit more challenging. He's awkward towards me, and while he is certainly more handsome and funnier than I could ever be, I still feel him being somewhat threatened by me. He still hasn't learned how to "talk" to me. I'm almost sure that he will learn in time that he can talk to me about anything and everything, the way his sister does, but he's just not there yet. When we would do a boy's thing and go out to dinner, just him and I, the conversation felt forced and I could feel that he was just counting the moments until he can go back to his safe haven that is his bedroom, and play video games all night. I never busted his chops about it, but simply accepted what he gave me. I hope that when he is older, he will understand me and will understand the sacrifices I had to make to ensure his well-being. Most importantly, what I truly hope for is that he grows up different, and safe. I need him to be better and stronger than I ever was. I hope he stays confident and armed with a mentality nothing like mine.

Bert and Ernie

This is a two-part story and the second part of the story didn't happen till about two or three months after the original event. My friend Peter and I were absolutely Bay Ridge rats. I was doing well, emotionally and psychologically for the first time in a long time. I felt that I had finally put my troubled past behind me and was capable of living a normal, fun-filled life. All we did night after night was find a different place to drink in Brooklyn. We were in our early twenties at the time and everyone knew us for two reasons. We had a pretty big and popular crew that we had linked up with so everyone was happy to see us. The staff liked us especially because we showed up, turned the place up and spent a lot of money. We were also just two of only a few Latino's that were hanging out in Bay Ridge at the time.

All the bars were stock full of Italian and Irish kids who for some reason, preferred to beat the shit out of each other while Peter and I danced with the women. It got us a lot of dirty looks but we didn't care. We were pretty popular and we were good guys so nobody really went out of their way to fuck with us. After hooking up with a great dude we called Franky Vain and his huge gaggle, we had all the muscle we would ever need. We'd all hit each other up, (via pager or beeper because that's how old I am) before we went out to make sure everyone was going out, or to find out who needed a ride.

There was a group of girls that we ran into all the time. They were a different clique of people but we always ran into them at one club or another, and more often than not, some of them came home with us. One night, Peter had picked me up and we decided to meet Franky Vain and his crew out at a bar called T-birds, which was usually our spot for tequila Tuesdays. How can I describe Franky Vain? He was a really handsome Italian kid from Bensonhurst, which at the time was a predominantly Italian neighborhood. Franky Vain wasn't his real name but since he was a pretty little bastard, the DJ would play the song Mr. Vain every time he walked into the joint. The name kind of stuck. On the night of the first part of the Bert and Ernie incident, I met up with Franky and his fourteen cousins, and as usual, there was a line of women waiting to speak to Mr. Vain or to at least have the honor of dancing next to him while he made out with some other girl.

It was infuriating to see all the girls that I wanted to hook up with, subject themselves to being treated like a bar wench just to have the opportunity to make out with Franky. Still, it was quite an impressive and amazing thing to witness. I walked in and went through the customary long line of handshakes and hugs like we hadn't seen each other in ages. I finally got to Franky, having to skip the line of admirers, gave him the usual one-handed handshake and bro hug, and went on about my business.

These days I tend not to wear stripes, ever, especially if I'm going out. My body, back and shoulders are obscenely wide so stripes tend to go on forever, and it resembles the equator that runs through the lower and upper hemisphere of our globe. However, years ago I was thin enough to get away with it so I wore a striped shirt. Right away, the guys start to bust my balls about the shirt and they started calling me Ernie.

Then someone got clever and said, "Hey, it's Bert and Ernie." Peter was not amused by being called Bert all night, so it just took off from there.

We got our balls busted all night and every time they asked me if I wanted a drink or a shot, they addressed me as Ernie. It has since become my alias every time I meet a girl that I really don't want to talk to, but this was my first time being called Ernie. I actually began to respond to it. At one point I was dancing, putting on a little show, when all the guys started chanting "Go Ernie!" I was laughing hysterically of course and gave everyone the finger, when a young chick suddenly jumped into the circle with me and started dancing and grinding on me. I vaguely recognized her because she was friends with a gorgeous girl named Caroline that Peter had tried to hook up with but failed. I had seen her before but never danced with her.

I had spoken with Caroline, even danced with her and she seemed like a cool girl. That was how I had recognized the girl I was dancing with. She was rubbing all over me, doing splits on the floor while I was amazed that this girl was dancing with me and putting on a show. The guys went nuts and the chants of "Go Ernie" got even louder, with strangers chanting it as well, having no clue who Ernie was or that it wasn't my name. The girl was grinding on me, telling me how hot I was, and that she loved the way I danced.

After a few minutes of her humping my leg on the dance floor, she looked me straight in the eyes and said, "Let's go to the bar and get a drink Ernie."

I was a little banged up by the time this happened so I really didn't realize it until later that she too was addressing me as Ernie.

She told me that her name was Iris and before long, we were making out like teenagers at the bar. I suggested that we go to the car. We went to the car for a little while and messed around in the backseat but she was a bit uncomfortable and suggested that we get a hotel room. I told her that I had my own apartment so if she wanted to come back with me, we could just hop into a cab and go there. She agreed and after I went back in and gave Peter his car keys, we jumped in a cab and went back to my apartment. Before long we were in bed and that's when I realized that she really thought my name was Ernie. We were going at it, and she was screaming "Ernie" at the top of her lungs for the whole thing. I wasn't about to correct her.

The name Ernie had gotten me this far and I was not about to abandon it, especially in the throes of passion. It was a great night and on a few occasions, I had to stifle my laughs in the pillow because she was extremely loud and wouldn't stop yelling the alias. This went on for hours, but eventually the sun started coming up and I politely hinted her exit by calling a taxi and giving her money to pay for it. She insisted that we keep in touch, so I gave her my pager number, which offended her in some way. She said that she wanted my home phone number and that she didn't want to feel stupid paging me and waiting for me to call her back. So I did something that I would usually do when I was very drunk, I gave her Pete's home number. I don't know why I always did that, but I did it often. He still lived at home with his mother and it would honestly bring me utter joy to do anything to cause him headaches at home.

I used to go as far as setting my alarm clock to five am every second day of February. I would go to bed the night before, giggling like a school girl bursting with anticipation. The alarm would go off at five am sharp and immediately I was on the phone calling his house.

Pete would eventually pick up the phone and croak an almost inaudible "Hello" into the telephone.

I would ask, "Hey, what did your mother say?"

He would be totally out of it and half asleep so of course he'd have no clue what I was talking about. He'd ask "What about my mother? What are you talking about?"

Then I would ask, "What did your mother say, early spring or six more weeks of winter?"

He would lose his shit instantly, cursing into the phone, cursing my poor innocent mother out as well, and hang up in my ear. I would laugh all morning long until I finally fell asleep again. So giving yet another strange girl Peter's number was just par for the course. Nothing was different this night, so after I gave her the number, I walked her out of my house and kissed her at the door like a true gentleman. She stopped kissing me and asked, "Are you going to call me Ernie?" I just erupted in laughter as she looked at me like I was crazy. I promised to call her and I waved good-bye as she stepped into the cab. I knew that was never ever going to happen. She was a one-night stand, plain and simple. It wasn't my fault that she was going home with guys that she didn't even know. I went to sleep and when I woke in the afternoon, my answering machine was full of messages from all my friends asking if Ernie the stud had gotten laid.

I usually shut my ringer off, especially in the morning, so when I played back all the messages, there was a good dozen messages for Ernie. I had myself quite a good laugh. As I was walking out that afternoon, my next door neighbor Eddie asked me if one of my friends had used my apartment the night before because whoever the hell Ernie was, he was banging some girl in my apartment all night long. I explained to him what had happened and we laughed for at least five minutes. It was a funny event, and we laughed so much about it but like anything else, before long, we all forgot about the Ernie incident. As far as I was concerned, this was a hilarious one-night show.

PART TWO:

A few months later, Peter and I were out on a Saturday night. We made a few calls to find out where everyone else was, and before long we were all hanging out in Bay Ridge getting drunk again. It had been a non-eventful night, but we did stay out until four am, closing whatever bar we were at. As usual, after a night of drinking and partying, we all went to the Vegas Diner, an iconic eatery in Dyker Park section of Brooklyn. There was fifteen of us so the staff had to move a few tables and chairs in order to accommodate our party. I decided to go to the bathroom before we sat. As I was walking to the bathroom, who do I see sitting at one of the tables? It was Iris, and she was sitting next to her gorgeous friend Caroline. I noticed her give Caroline a little nudge with her elbow and nod her head in my direction, no doubt saying, "There's that asshole that never called me."

I knew that she had seen me but I just turned away, perfectly content to ignore her if she was willing to do the same. After I was done, I went to the huge table that the staff had built in the middle of the diner. I found myself a seat and really didn't give Iris any thought as I went on with my business of ordering breakfast.

We were all talking and being obnoxiously loud as usual, drunk off our asses and stealing food off each other's plates. We were having a fine old time, when all of a sudden I see the beautiful Caroline, with her long slender legs and perfect ass, walking straight towards me. Her face looked like she was pissed off and she was staring daggers at me. She walked right up to me, and stood defiantly an inch from my chair with her arms crossed.

I looked up and said, "Uh, Hi Caroline."

The whole table full of people stopped chewing, talking, or doing whatever it was that they were doing. Everyone froze in anticipation of what was about to happen.

Then Caroline asked me "Ernie, can I talk to you for a second?"

The whole table exploded in laughter. I had forgotten the entire Ernie thing, but as soon as she said it, I too exploded in hysterics. This made Caroline even angrier.

She asked, "What the fuck is so funny Ernie?" and again I was laughing so hard that I could hardly breathe. This was a different crew of guys than the guys that had been out that night at the original Ernie incident. Nobody knew what the girl was talking about, but it didn't take away from the hilarity of a hot girl cursing me out and using the wrong name the whole time.

They started chiming in, "Yea, what the fuck is so funny Ernie?"

I couldn't even get a word out. The harder I laughed, the more pissed off Caroline got, and since she was a stunning girl that everyone wanted to hook up with, she wasn't accustomed to people laughing at her, especially in a crowd. She lost her shit in just seconds, her face turning red with anger.

She started screaming at me, "You're a fucking asshole Ernie! I thought you were a nice cool guy, but you're a real fucking jerk. You used my friend Ernie and you owe her an apology."

At that point, everyone at the table was laughing so hard that people were falling off their chairs. The Vegas diner is a fairly big diner and it was packed that night.

Even people that didn't know us were yelling "Ernie you're a fucking asshole, apologize to the pretty girl," Which made it even funnier.

The entire diner was cracking jokes and cursing at the fictitious Ernie. I could not breathe, much less speak, or explain to Caroline that my name wasn't Ernie. Finally, Iris came over and started to pull Caroline away, telling her to just forget about it, but before she walked away, she decided to lob a few insults at me.

She had pulled her friend away, but then Iris came back and yelled "Go to hell Ernie, you're a piece of shit. Fuck you, and fuck your nasty bitch mother who keeps hanging up on me every time I call."

Everybody went ape-shit. Iris finally walked away and they couldn't believe that this girl had actually gone ahead and insulted my mother who had nothing to do with this. I was laughing the hardest of course, because right on cue, Peter chimes in that he couldn't believe I was going to let that girl get away with talking about my mother. I was still unable to get a sentence in because I was still laughing so hard.

When I could finally speak, I said, "She wasn't talking about my mother, you asshole! She was talking about your mother. I gave her the phone number to your house."

Apparently, that poor girl had kept calling Peter's house and his mother had cursed her out after her many requests to speak to Ernie. That was the knockout punch for all of us. Once again, everyone exploded in laughter, and some people actually had to run to the bathroom before they pissed themselves. Pete absorbed what I had just said and all of sudden his face turned to anger when he realized that she had called his wonderful mom a nasty bitch. He got up to go after Iris, acting like he really wanted to go fight her in the parking lot, as a few guys held him down telling him that she wasn't worth it. Then he cursed me out whole heartedly for giving Iris his phone number and causing his mother undue stress. The entire diner was laughing at us, and it was really one of the funniest surprises that I have gotten in my life. As the waitress came over to give us the check, she was laughing as well. She said that she had seen a lot of crazy things as a waitress, but she had never laughed so hard in all her life. This was just one night with us, out of thousands, which ended with insane things happening. And Peter was usually involved.

Peter the Skel

The funny thing about Peter is that he was not always my friend. Many moons ago, Pete and I were enemies in our childhood years. It was something dumb really, he had done something silly involving a girl and some other classmate that liked my girlfriend, and it almost cost him his head. That's how long we go back. The story of how we met is really quite amusing.

I had a girlfriend in elementary school, well at least something as close to a girlfriend as a kid could have, and she had many suitors to say the least. This girl was willing to go to second base in the fifth grade so she was quite the commodity. I was a lucky enough chap to land her as my main squeeze, even though she was no less a foot taller than me. One day after class, Peter and a few of our classmates decided that the girl, Christina, was probably better off with another one of the kids in our class named Nefi. I don't know what kind of name that is but if my memory serves me correctly, he was of South American decent.

As it went, Peter and his friends decided to run interference and accost me as Nefi passed my girlfriend a love letter. I tried to fight them off but there were four of them and they each were taller than me and outweighed me easily, Peter being the biggest of them. They shoved me against the wall, and told me that if I was smart, I would break up with Christina, because Nefi liked her and they were his friends. I simply smiled at them, and decided that I would take care of this matter quietly. As I walked out with Christina, I took the love letter out of her hand, read it briefly, and threw it in the garbage. I looked back at Nefi who had a shit-eating grin on his face, and told him I would see him tonight with my brother. Unbeknownst to young Nefi, I knew where he lived, and it was barely one city block away from me. I had seen him playing outside a few times during the summer but I hadn't met him until the school year started. Straightening him out would be very easy.

As I was walking away, I heard Peter say, "Yeah, go get your brother!" and they all laughed.

You see, they didn't realize that Gilbert was fully grown and had a mustache by the time he was in the sixth grade, and that he had been left back in grade a few times, so it was safe to say that he was bigger than most of the kids in our school.

The thing about big goon sized kids in school is that they tend to hang out with other big goon sized kids. After school that day, I told Gilbert what had happened and he was pissed that someone had decided to pick on me for no reason at all, especially over a girl. We paid Nefi a visit that evening, and he was completely apologetic. We let him off the hook that day, because he had shown guts in coming to apologize to me, even when he politely declined when I challenged him to a clean, one on one fight. He promised that he would cause us no further trouble, and it seemed sincere to me.

Gilbert was never a bully, but still he asked me, "You want me to smack him?" Then it was my turn to decline.

I decided that Nefi was guilty of being dumb, but overall he didn't seem like a bad kid. We let him slide, and the next day at school, it would be Peter and the rest of his friends turn to answer to us.

I never saw it happen. Gilbert had asked around school, trying to find this Peter character and everyone rolled on him. Gilbert and his friends found Peter and his cohorts, and then cornered them in the schoolyard. There was nothing more than apologies and flowers thrown his way, and five minutes later, Peter and his friends were in front of me saying how sorry they were and pledged their undying loyalty to me as long as I would call Gilbert and his crew off. They offered their lunch on pizza day, comic books, or whatever else I wanted in exchange for their safety. I told them it wouldn't be necessary, all I really wanted was not to be messed with, which was a pretty simple request. That is how I came to know Peter. They readily obliged, and it all blew over. Well, kind of.

One day, I had spotted Peter riding a bicycle in my neighborhood, and I decided that he wasn't going to be allowed to ride freely in my space. We sent one of our crazier friends to go kick his ass. It was supposed to be just a warning but the kid got a little carried away and knocked Peter off his bike, and started to beat him with a baseball bat. The assault caused him to have a near fatal asthma attack right on the spot. From what I understand, he was carted away in an ambulance.

I didn't see Peter again until High School, and by then, it was water under the bridge. He had actually turned out ok it seemed, and when I had re-introduced myself to him, the first thing he did was look around and behind him for Gilbert.

His memory certainly hadn't failed him, and for some reason, we became instant friends. I started to spend a lot of time with Peter, and before long I was over his house, doing dinner, and plotting picking up girls at sweet sixteen's. He was always on my case, to do better in school, to maybe try attending more often, and he was always pestering me about my drinking. I was already drinking heavily by freshmen year and when he came along during sophomore year, I was truly a mess. I would stay out for days at a time, and would sometimes show up to school the next day wearing the exact same clothes as the day before, or have a black eye, or have scratches and cuts on my face from whatever fracas I had gotten myself into. I was very much a different guy than him, yet he accepted me as a friend and treated me as family whenever I came to his house.

Peter was the first person that ever trusted me to use my brain for something good. In an unfortunate circumstance, a racially motivated killing in the late eighties was very big news at the time. A few black kids had come to Bensonhurst, Brooklyn, where my High School was located, to buy a car and visit a girl in the neighborhood, and one of them had been gunned down for no apparent reason. The story was never a big deal for any of us, just business as usual, but on the first day of school, there were news trucks and cameras everywhere, sticking microphones in our faces asking how it felt to go to school in such a racially charged area. We had no clue what racially charged even meant, because it was really a diverse school and most of our friends were of all different races.

The cameras didn't go away. The story grew legs, and before long, they were civil rights marches and riots going on just blocks away from our high school. A civil rights activist had gotten stabbed by one of the guys from the neighborhood during one the riots and before long, the reverend Jesse Jackson had to get involved. We had gotten word that Jesse Jackson was going to appear at our school to give a speech regarding peace and racial unity, and that as a special gift, Reverend Jackson was going to sit down with the school President and have lunch, perhaps to discuss the current foreign policy, or the price of chocolate milk in the lunchroom.

That's when Peter requested my services. He said, "Rummy, I need to be President."

At first, I had no clue what the hell he was talking about. He went on to explain that he had been in the Student Organization office and that he had gotten wind about Jesse Jackson's plan to visit the school and have lunch with the school President. I still had no clue what he was getting at. I knew about the visit because I had my own little birds chirping in my ear, but I didn't know what that had to do with me.

He then looked at me with the most serious expression he had in his artillery and said, "You need to make me President."

I started to laugh a little while I explained to Peter that he wasn't a terribly popular kid, and that he knew maybe fifteen people in the school. He said that he knew this all too well. Then he said something that made sense.

He said, "You know everyone Rummy, just make them vote for me. I need to have lunch with Jesse Jackson."

I looked at him, wondering if he was serious, and judging by his stone faced expression, I deduced that he was indeed.

I said, "Ok". Just like that, I was his campaign manager. School elections were being held in a week so we had maybe three or four school days to get his campaign off the ground. It didn't leave a lot of time for pressing palms or kissing babies, but I figured I could get a few posters up in a short period of time. I never got around to the advertising but it didn't mean that I wasn't busy on the campaign trail, getting in touch with every person that I knew, and then talking to whoever it was they knew.

I even got Gilbert involved. I reminded him that Peter was one of the kids we were going to kill in the fifth grade but good thing we didn't because he turned out to be a pretty cool kid. He got all his cronies involved. We were also friends with the bad ass kids and criminals of the school and their vote counted every bit as much.

I'm not going to claim that I ran a clean campaign because if I did, those would be just empty words. I never put up as much as a poster, a banner, or anything that had Peter's name on it. But I made many promises of free candy and chocolate milk to the chubbier kids. To the kids that were small and somewhat nerdy, I had Gilbert promise them protection from the goons that would abuse them every day on the campus. However, there was not one banner announcing Peter's candidacy. He was totally invisible and a dark horse to say the least. The day before the election, Peter came to me in a panic, saying that nobody even knew he was running. I looked at him, and I told him that he had nothing to worry about. I had it handled and even though I could tell that he was extremely skeptic, he accepted my answer. He shook my hand and stated that he trusted me, but I knew that he had totally given up on the chance of ever having lunch with the good reverend. The next day, Election Day, was a thing of art.

For the record, our school had roughly three thousand students enrolled at the time, but on the average only about five hundred kids or so participated in the elections. The fact is that most kids didn't care one bit who their President was because it affected them very little, if at all. Most of the "Voters" were kids from the Drama Club, Math Club, the student athletes, and kids that were involved with the Student Organization. Other than those groups most high school students troll around in anonymity for four years, until they decide to grow side burns and become cool in college. There were almost two thousand five hundred voters that day, and over two thousand kids voted for Peter. As his "Campaign Manager" I was afforded the luxury of skipping the morning classes while the election took place, and I had the dregs of humanity lined up ready to cast their vote before school had started. You had to show your school schedule, also known as your "Program Card" as proof that you went to school there. Many of the voters saw their program card for the very first time that morning. They had shown up to school, just to vote, and then left immediately afterward to go play handball or maybe even go back home to go to sleep.

All the bad boys had girlfriends, so they lined up to vote. I was friends and had played with most of the kids on the baseball team, so they lined up. All the kids we knew from the old neighborhood came to the same school as us, so they lined up to vote. Then we lined up all the geeks, and I pointed them all out to Gilbert and his goons, making a big show of letting them know that all these kids were not to be touched from now on, as they were now part of the cause. I don't know if you know this, but if you line up five geeks, within minutes you're going to have ten geeks behind them inquiring what possible geek-dom was at the beginning of the line. Word got around that if you voted for Peter, you were no longer cannon fodder on the bus ride home, and the geeks showed out in ridiculous numbers.

Then we got the Special Education vote. Yes, you read that correctly. Somehow,

Gilbert had corralled that evasive caucus, and while they were really nice kids, they could hardly speak. We taught them two words, "Vote" and "Peter". And they lined up. It was a long day for the Student Organization and the school Principal as they were truly unprepared for the record turnout that day. It was a landslide to say the least. They stopped counting after Peter had tallied a little more than two thousand votes. He was mathematically impossible to beat. One of the girls that also ran for President broke down in tears thinking she was a shoe in for posting a hundred flyers with her name in pretty colors all over the school. She couldn't comprehend how this person no one knew, or had ever met, had gotten so many votes. Peter could not believe the amount of votes that were piled up and counted in his favor, nor did anyone else. A short time later, after the Peter's Presidency was confirmed, he did get to sit down and meet Jesse Jackson, also fulfilling whatever need he had to split a turkey sandwich with him.

I never took any credit, nor did I ever grandstand about my accomplishment that day, it just made me happy that Peter had wanted to do something, and I had made it possible. What it made me realize, was that perhaps I did have some value, some worth. Perhaps there was more to me than I had ever perceived. While it meant absolutely nothing to me, and though I had no confidence in myself, Peter had entrusted me with a task that was important to him. And I had gotten it done. For many years later on in life, it became something I was rather good at, fixing things. Especially for Peter, who just like many politicians, was definitely a degenerate. That made him endearing to me almost instantly. It seems like eons ago that we were running the streets of Brooklyn, creating havoc in the lives of single women. Sometimes he would get himself in trouble with women, or with their boyfriends, and I had to go places, stick my neck out to get him out of trouble without being harmed.

One night, while we were out drinking, one of my girls' called me to see if I wanted to hang out. I told her that I was hanging out with a friend, but if she could dig up a friend for my friend, we could pass by her house after or get some drinks. She informed me that she was hanging out with her sister, and that maybe we could link up at some bar. We were already drinking, so it seemed like a fine plan to me, but Peter was a little skeptic because none of us had any clue what the sister looked like. My girl, Nancy, was a beautiful girl. She was tall, had a rocking body, and had gorgeous green eyes. She was really a lot of fun to hang with. I actually tried to avoid spending a lot of time with her because she had children, and on our first night together, she tried to make plans with Gilbert's wife to get all the kids together for Halloween. Nancy had spent the night, and by the time I woke up the next morning, she was in the kitchen having coffee with my family, and planning our lives together.

This was a red flag and I decided that I would distance myself a bit, but I still kept her on retainer. We had kept in touch, and dated from time to time but for the most part, I needed to keep it casual with her. By design, I had never met her friends or family, and I wanted to keep it that way. Tonight would be the first time I would meet her sister, and Peter was none too happy about it. We jumped in a cab, and I told him to relax and see what happens. He insisted that I allow him to punch me right in my face if she was ugly at all. This was a common request from him when he was drinking, and perhaps it was because he was still scarred from the beating he had received in grade school. For some reason I agreed to let him hit me and we went on our merry way.

By the time we had arrived we were almost sober, but not quite. We walked into a restaurant with a bar that was within a block of Nancy's apartment. They were sitting at a table and apparently, they had been drinking as well. Nancy greeted me with a wet sloppy kiss that suggested she had other things in mind. When she introduced her sister, we couldn't believe our eyes. She was absolutely gorgeous. She had short black hair, a beautiful face, and the body of a porn star. I looked at Peter and he had a huge smile on his face. Within seconds, he went to work on her. Before long we had confirmed that she worked in a strip club, but she and her sister insisted that she was only a bartender and didn't shed any clothes, which we knew was a lie. We were so fascinated with her sister that Nancy began to get a little jealous. She was giving me dirty looks every time I looked at her sister, who was canoodling and whispering in Pete's ear. I decided that we should probably leave and go back to Nancy's apartment, before she picked a fight with me or was turned off by the fact that I wanted to take her sister back home with me and maybe tie her up in my basement for a few weeks.

We paid the tab and on our way back to Nancy's, I could definitely tell that she was feeling regretful about bringing her sister along. I insisted that I only had eyes for her and that I would prove that when we got inside. When we got back to her apartment, she thanked the babysitter and we decided to start in on a bottle or rum. Then her kids woke up and it definitely killed our hook-up vibe instantly. Her kids were crazy to put it bluntly. They were maybe seven or eight years old. The boy was trying to set the couch on fire, and her daughter decided to drop her stockings to her knees, pick up her dress, and show us where she had a crack while she was giggling hysterically. I hadn't noticed that the girl was half naked because I was too busy fearing for my own life, trying to dissuade the boy from burning me alive.

The night was definitely falling apart. Thank God at that moment Nancy, who was off making us drinks, came in from the kitchen, yelled at the kids, and dragged them off to bed. It took her roughly a half hour to put those psychopaths to bed, and we had made good use of the time to interrogate her sister. We ascertained that she was indeed a stripper, and she was kind enough to give us the address and her work schedule. She made us promise that we would not tell Nancy, but that if we wanted to pay for a private show, she was willing to for a price. This night was definitely getting interesting, and I could tell that Peter was in his glory. Stuff like this is what he lived for. When Nancy came back, we abruptly changed the topic, sat around and talked for a bit, before I suggested to her that we should probably take our conversation to the bedroom. But now she was hesitant. It took a little convincing but we finally went into the bedroom and started to get it on. She kept asking me if Pete was a nice guy. She wanted to know if he was going to be good to her sister, and I kept insisting that he was aces. I said he was good guy, and they were adults. I knew him my whole life and I'd trust him with my sister. Lies, yes, but it was necessary.

We finally started to get busy, and we were barely five minutes in when strange sounds began to come from the living room.

Every few minutes, I heard "WHACK" and then whispering.

A minute later, again we heard, "WHACK" then murmuring.

She asked me, "What the hell is that?" and I pretended not to hear anything at all. Again, there was a "WHACK" followed by Peter's voice saying, "Yeah? You like that?"

She asked me "Babe, don't you hear that?"

This time I couldn't pretend that I didn't hear anything. I thought to myself that Peter was probably in the living room spanking her sister, but I had my own thing going on so it really wasn't my business.

We heard the sound again but this time it was really loud and you heard her sister say, "Ouch, please stop, it hurts."

Nancy pushed me away and jumped off the bed, barely stopping to put on a robe as she stormed into the living room. I wrapped the sheets around my waist and decided to see for myself what was going on. I expected to see them naked on the couch, rolling around, but what I walked in truly surprised me. Peter and her sister were fully dressed. She was, however, straddling Peter's lap. He had her lipstick smeared all over his mouth and face which was evidence that some kissing had been going on but he also had a Visa card in his hand, which was baffling to me. Then I looked at Nancy's sister and I could not believe my eyes. She had red, credit card shaped welts on her face.

Apparently, Peter had been smacking her around with his Gold Card and asking her if that's what she wanted. She wasn't even offended or mad. They had simply been negotiating and Pete had gotten a little carried away. Nancy however, lost her damn mind. She started screaming at Peter to get the fuck out of the house. She was yelling at the top of her lungs for all of us to get out.

Pete said, "What are you mad at me for? She said she doesn't do anything for free and I didn't have enough cash."

I have never seen a woman so enraged. Not only did she not know that her sister was a stripper, but she also didn't know that she dabbled in prostitution. I was truly amused by the whole scene. I was still half naked, watching Pete as he argued with Nancy, who defending her sister that was sitting on the couch with rectangular bruises on her face. I started to laugh, and that's when Nancy turned on me as if I had something to do with it. She pushed me and told me to get dressed, and to get the hell out of her house as well.

I asked "What did I do?" but she wasn't in the mood to answer questions.

We got kicked out of the house, and two minutes later, we were walking down the stairs. We could still hear the two sisters arguing inside of the apartment. I was pissed at Peter, pissed that my night had been cut short, and pissed that I hadn't gotten laid. Now I had to find a way home now from the Brooklyn/Queens border in the middle of the night. Pete tried to speak to me, but I put up my index finger in front of his face and advised him not to speak to me.

He tried to explain himself again, but again I warned him "Not now Pete. I really want to choke you. Give me a minute."

So we stood there until some guy walked by and I asked him if he knew any cab companies in the area and he gave me a number I could call. We waited for a good while in silence and when the cab finally arrived, it was a long gray limousine. We hopped in and I instructed the driver to take us to a bar in Bay Ridge. It was just too early to go home and I wasn't done drinking for the night. A few minutes into the ride I could feel Peter staring at me and I looked in his direction.

He said, "I could definitely get used to this," referring to the Limo.

I said, "Yeah, it's nice."

He asked if he could now explain himself and I told him that he could. He told me that the minute that Nancy and I had gone into the bedroom, they had started to mess around on the couch. He said that she went with it until she was sure that he was completely hot and bothered, and that's when she said that she didn't sleep with men for free. She was expensive and that she wasn't sure that Peter could afford her. He asked her what she meant and that's when she told him that he was going to have to pay for it. After he informed her that he didn't have much cash, she said that there were other ways that he could pay for it. He asked her what were the other ways that he could pay for it, and she asked him if he had a credit card with a big spending limit on it, and somewhere around then is when the negotiations broke down.

At first, he was rubbing her seductively with his credit card, all over her body, and things were progressing nicely. I don't know if he tried to swipe it somewhere. Maybe it was declined, whatever happened, it led to him smacking her with it and asking her if she liked and wanted it. That's when Nancy burst out of the bedroom. It seemed like a perfectly good explanation to me, and we left it at that. I told him that since he had ruined my night he should have to pay for the cab ride. He reminded me that he didn't have any cash.

I guess the limo driver overheard him say that because he quickly said. "It's ok, we take credit cards."

The Hoff

One night, perhaps the funniest thing that ever happened to us occurred in a bar in Park Slope, Brooklyn called 200 5th. It's actually the address of the bar, and it's a great place to meet people, pick up women or just to watch a game. Nowadays, it has over one hundred flat screen televisions, where they show anything from sports to the President's State of the Union address, depending on the night. Football Sundays are absolutely mobbed. The booze flows, the wings keep coming, and it had become home for a lot of us misfits. Many of my friends were people that I have met at 200 5th. Some were patrons, some were employees but we somehow bonded and formed a merry band of misfits, and we spent a lot of time together. But it wasn't always a sports bar.

Years ago, it was just a bar and restaurant but on Friday and Saturday nights it would become a club. If you were there early enough, there was no cover charge and we would be there drinking and dancing all night long. It was a great place to meet women and we were regulars so we were always taken care of by the bartenders, while they hit everyone else over the head for drinks. One night we were at the bar and it was looking like it was going to be a slow, boring evening.

Now when I say, "We" I mean to say it was me, Cee, and Hasselhoff. We just called him "The Hoff" for short. He got that name for two reasons. The first reason was because of his constant, thick seventies porn mustache, Secondly, because for years he drove around a total piece of shit hatchback that we nicknamed" KITT".

This car was tiny and totally beat up, with holes in the floor of the car so wide that you could see the road underneath. When it rained or snowed, you had to cover the holes or you would start to get dirty water all over you from the road. Since he was the only one that had a car at that point, we would all pile into his little piece of shit and go out to dance and booze the night away. It was truly a spectacle but it was better than taking the bus or the train. Watching all of us pile out of that car had to be a funny sight to behold. We are all dressed up, wearing shiny shoes and ties, climbing out of that decrepit hatchback dragging its muffler about two feet behind it. A little embarrassment was much cheaper than taking a cab. Mind you, the Hoff is about 15 years older than me. He looks great, he's youthful, in great shape, but no one has told him that he's a terrible dancer in his more than half a century of existence. He dances like he's a puppet, and the puppeteer is having an epileptic episode. Watching him dance was always a treat. He'd get his liquor in him and he was like a wind-up toy.

On that slow but awesome evening at 200 5th, we are standing around the bar doing a few shots when a crew of off-duty teachers started making their way to the dance floor. The Hoff is one of the cheapest people I have ever met in my life. He's incredibly giving and good hearted without a doubt, but he has never enjoyed spending money. Before long, the Hoff shook off the rust and started to wiggle his way out to the dance floor to our delight. He started dancing with a beautiful Asian woman who began to give him a run for his money.

They were rocking on the dance floor and I gave Cee a little elbow jab and said, "Look at this guy."

Cee smirked and said, "Yeah I know, those two are making love."

He wasn't kidding. The Hoff and Ms. Saigon were wrapped around each other tightly, grinding and humping away to a different beat than any song that was playing that night. And to boot, his leg was up in the air wrapped around her upper thigh. That's how we knew that the night was going to get interesting. When the Hoff's sneaker boot ceases to have contact with the earth, shit is about to go down.

Cee and I were watching this debacle and noticing that little by little, the place was starting to get pretty crowded. We were eye-balling all the talent coming in when all of a sudden the girl gave the Hoff a shove and told him "Get away from me!"

He claims that she didn't shove him but we saw it happen. He raised his arms and was thoroughly confused by her action. I could barely make it out but he said, "What's the problem?"

She told him again, in no uncertain terms to get the hell away from her and she walked away. Her friends all walk out right behind her like a pack of teachers usually do in bars.

Cee looked at me and said, "What the hell was that about?"

I was thinking that maybe he grabbed her ass or something. The Hoff is known to get a little "handsy" when he drinks. He was still standing there on the dance floor, all by his lonesome, still amazed at what just transpired. He turned and started to

121

shake his head.

He made his way back over to us and said, "Hey, did you guys see that? That chick is crazy." At this point, is when we realized that the Hoff was sporting a massive erection.

"Jesus Christ, dude get away from me!" I said.

Cee was just standing there, totally in shock, with his usual two drinks in his hand. He was just speechless. The only thing he could do was shake his head. Also, the place had gotten completely crowded so there was nowhere to go.

To the left and right of us was completely jammed up with people and I was trapped like a cornered animal while the Hoff was pointing Excalibur at us through his fancy pants. There was no retreat, and I certainly wasn't going to try to brush past him. Being Latino, I would be impregnated instantly. So I was forced to continue yelling and trying to back him away from us.

Once again I said, "Dude, would you please get away from me?" but he just stood there looking at us like we were crazy. The only other option was to turn my back on him and pretend he wasn't with us but I wasn't one-hundred percent in love with that option neither. Finally, I have to do a little see and say and I pointed directly at his crotch.

I yelled, "Animal, look down!" and when he did, he seemed genuinely surprised at his condition. The only thing he said was, "Oh".

Cee was leaning on the bar, laughing so hard that he was practically in tears. I was almost ready to laugh but not until The Hoff got the hell away from me.

I said, "No wonder why she pushed you away, she probably thought she was getting mugged. You're lucky she didn't give you her purse before she ran away."

I started to laugh a little but Cee was doubled over, laughing so hard. I don't remember where the Hoff went after that, maybe he went to the bathroom to rub one out, but all I know is he went in some direction and didn't return for some time. We probably laughed for about 2 hours.

The Hoff was always good for that. He's just a good guy, even if he is also one the cheapest human beings ever born. He'll give you a ride, help you move, or put you up for the week when your lady kicks you out of the house. I have honestly lost count of just how many times some girl has kicked me out and he's come to pick me up without questions. For a few years, it became routine to pile up a few garbage bags full of clothes into his little hatchback, and making the Hoff's apartment my headquarters until I got my own place or went to stay at my sister's house in Jersey. I think he's got something like a credit score of 800 but there's just no way he's ever going to spring for a new car. Don't get me wrong, I wouldn't change him for the world. His tendency to be frugal is just part of his charm and it gave us plenty of grenades to lob his way.

The Hoff is also famous for always claiming to have had "Just three beers."

When that bar tab came at the end of the night, he'd usually be up in arms protesting the amount of the tab. He always asked, "What the hell did you guys order? I just had three beers."

We would start to laugh. Cee and myself anyway, because the Hoff would disregard the seven shots of Jagermeister he downed with us. The truth is that he probably had about five or six beers but bartenders usually take care of us. So there might have been just three beers on the tab, but he drank a lot more than that.

I'd say, "Hoff, you are totally wasted right now. Are you trying to say that you are this drunk on three beers?"

That's when he'd say that maybe he had one shot. Again, we laughed. For a period of time, he started to claim that the only reason he was so drunk was because someone was spiking his drink with some mystery drug. He'd be on the floor, vomiting his liver out, while complaining of someone "slipping him a Mickey". One afternoon he got totally legless off of Mimosa. I drove the Hoff home, because he was completely wasted and insisted that someone had drugged him. I rang the bell and handed him over to his son, Little Hoff, who is pretty much a cardboard cutout of his father, and although he's not quite as cheap as his dad, I can certainly see him having the tendency to grow T-Rex arms when the bill comes. This stuff is in his DNA and there's really not much you can do to combat nature. The Hoff and I were living in the same apartment building at the time so it was very convenient when it was time to go out to a club, or even just to split a cab home. He was literally one flight away from me at all times.

We had returned from the bar sometime around five pm. Seven hours later, around midnight, my phone started to ring. It was Little Hoff. The Hoff was still deposited on the bathroom floor.

I asked him "Is he breathing?" He took way too long to respond, so I started to get a little nervous. I was starting to think that maybe we had killed the guy with champagne and orange juice. Finally, little Hoff answered that maybe, just maybe, he had heard the Hoff snore.

I said, "Ok, good, don't worry about it." He asked me if he should pick him up off the floor. I answered "No, fuck him, serves him right for talking shit about drinking mimosa. Let him wake up in the morning on the filthy bathroom floor with a face full of piss."

Little Hoff seemed to get a decent amount of joy and amusement from that and wished me a good night. I did the same and laughed myself to sleep. The Hoff managed to survive, but he was severely hung over the next morning. And he never said another word about mimosas again.

The Reveal

I can't deny that I've had a lot of fun and had a ton of laughs. I've been lucky enough to have come in contact with some great people, but the way I was forced to grow up has stricken me with a very quick temper and a tendency to be extremely violent, amongst various other side effects. Regardless of however the past has affected me and no matter how traumatic it was to my childhood; I still have to find a way to live somehow. I'm sure people have spoken and repeated the story of when my hidden nature was unmasked. For me it was not flattering, but it was nothing but the truth. I could not deny it. It was my fault, and my fault only for allowing someone to unsheathe the secretive personality quirks that I deal with. I usually do a better job of hiding who I am. A better way to put it is I usually do a better job of hiding who I can be. I've always warned people that have tried to get to know me that they are better off looking at and enjoying the show. Do not dare peek backstage because I guarantee you will not be happy with what you see. Yet, sometimes it simply could not be helped, and I paid the price for my indiscretion.

The day had begun like any other, innocuous by all means. When I was in possession of self-control, I had allowed myself a social life. I allow myself to enjoy a sense of normalcy, a social life with a small but varied circle of friends. We would meet from time to time, in my favorite watering hole of course, where there was a barstool with my name on it. The bartenders knew me, and the owner, Mark, was a large man who had mood swings that varied between cantankerous and extremely charming, and all within minutes. He was cut from the cloth of the neighborhood, and growing up he had to be a tough guy, being the only Jewish kid in a neighborhood of Latino, Black and Irish toughs. Even the Italians owned a big piece of the neighborhood a little bit down the road, but back then, everyone knew everyone. There were no outsiders that owned the stores and tenements. No big chains, no fancy coffee shops, just neighborhood people.

I liked that about Mark. He was successful, no doubt, but it had not changed him one bit. He liked me too I think, and maybe that's why he never complained even when he knew the bartenders were taking care of me. He was "Brooklyn" so he and

I clicked immediately. Once in a while, he'd sit with me to shoot the shit, and insist that the barkeep brought me yet another shot on the house. After a while, it was really the only place I felt comfortable. I had agreed to meet up with the Hoff, Cee and another neighborhood guy named DJ. He was a bit more refined than the rest of us, so he would show up to the bar wearing a perfectly tailored suit and fancy shoes, much to our delight. He was a handsome guy, well over 6 feet tall with perfect white teeth, so he did very well with the ladies wherever he went. As opposed to me, who only dated with infrequency, or whenever Nina went on sabbatical. Nina is the closest thing that I can call a girlfriend. When she's not around, I'm left to my devices and getting into trouble with my friends. DJ and I had made up a rule, though unspoken, that whatever one of us said, the other had to play along. He would ask me how my Herpes was and I in turn would give him an update on my condition. Whenever he would walk in with a new woman, I would approach him and make a small scene, inquiring as to why he would choose this place of all places, to flaunt his new "heterosexual" lifestyle. He would retort by telling me to move on, and to start seeing other people. So, if everyone thought I was gay and was stricken with a sexually transmitted disease it was fine, as long as we adhered to the rules.

Back then I actually kept a social calendar and carried a cell phone. I had a very bad habit of leaving my phone on the bar whenever I got shit-faced, which was quite often. One day, after I had gotten a very big head start on happy hour, Dj walked in and saw that I was completely hammered and not paying attention. He stole my phone, and changed the picture on the home screen to a picture of his wrinkled testicles. I was very surprised when I went to check my phone for missed calls or messages and encountered his brown balls instead of the usual picture of my kids. At first, I thought I had picked up the wrong phone because the crafty bastard had also changed the input language to Spanish. Now I speak, read and write Spanish fluently, but I was so drunk it might as well have been German. I surveyed the room, asking who had a phone with a pair of low hanging nuts on the screen, without realizing that it was actually mine. It was borderline genius on his part, and Dj earned my adoration immediately.

Years later, on the day of my unmasking, we were up to our old shenanigans. The entire bar was lined with people so we opted to sit in a big booth because it was really the only place to sit and grab a bite to eat while we caught up. Our waitress came over, a girl named Zimmy, who at the time held the title for the best ass in the tri-state area. I didn't know her well but Dj had known her from the neighborhood for a long time. She was cordial but not super friendly, as she took our orders then disappeared into the kitchen.

After Zimmy reappeared to bring us our drinks, and after we all remarked of her physical stature, we went back to our usual ball busting and shit talking. Suddenly a group of good looking girls walked in, one better looking than the next. They were searching for seats to no avail, and were just about to give up when DJ introduced himself, and asked them to join us at our booth. They appraised us rather quickly, and decided that we weren't exactly eye candy but we weren't hideous either. They joined us and the introductions went around the table. Funny enough, we all hit it off pretty well, and had a very good conversation going which was odd for me. I don't like strangers. I don't like many people, much less sitting with them as I tried to get my head upside down just the way I like it. I drink to drown myself, not to be social. They told us that they were actually here to meet up with a group of guys who so far hadn't shown up. If we didn't mind them killing time and hanging with us, it was fine by them. We hung out with these girls for a few hours, and phone numbers were exchanged by a few of them with a few of us, myself not included. I was knee deep in rum at that point and was more interested in going waist deep if possible.

After a good long while, some bar stools opened up after happy hour let out but the girls opted to stay with us at our table a bit longer. I wasn't quite sure what was bothering me, but I had always been able to see things coming. I didn't know exactly what it was but I had always had a sixth sense of what was approaching and this night would be no different. It was a weeknight, so most of the after work crowd began to disperse, leaving a lot of room to move around. DJ had left after working his magic, which left just the Hoff, Cee, and myself at the table with the girls. A group of guys walked in and one of the girls got up and went over to them, giving them each a hug hello. They weren't exactly a rough looking bunch, but from the daggers that were being stared into us, we knew that they weren't exactly thrilled to walk in and find the girls sitting with us. One guy in particular, a black guy with long braids, looked especially unhappy.

The rest of the girls bid their farewells to us and thanked us all for a wonderful time, then went to join their group which sat down on the newly open bar stools right across from us. I don't know if they sat there purposely, but it certainly didn't matter to them that we were within earshot. The comments started right away, some under their breath and some were said especially for us to hear. One of them in particular, the one with the braids kept mentioning what a bunch of bitches we were, and how he felt like putting "a few holes in some people tonight."

That really bothered me. I've never been much of a talker when it comes to any sort of confrontation. As a matter of fact, I usually don't say a word. There are times when it is certainly better to talk things out if possible, but things almost always go the way they are supposed to go whenever there's talk of shooting someone. Someone gets shot, or somebody runs. That's usually how it works. Of course if both parties have a gun, then everyone but the intended targets end up getting loaded with lead. Still, doesn't leave much room for chit chat. The minute I heard the guy with the braids say he felt like hurting me and my friends, that little switch inside me just turned on. I've always had it, but I hide it. I've kept it a secret for most of my life. I've done a pretty good job, especially in the last few years of keeping people at bay, and not allowing anyone a glimpse of the violent nature, but it tends to seep out everyone once in a while. Without much thought or trepidation, I react. It wasn't really about me. I could live with someone hurting me. I took on so much hurt as a kid, there wasn't much anyone could do to scare me. The thought of my friends being hurt, however, was all the motivation I would ever need to react.

Once I am in that mode, everything moves in slow motion. Even though I was the only one aware of what the guy at the bar had said, I felt like everyone was watching me and my reaction. Everyone else was oblivious to the threat that lay right ahead of us, and went on with their conversations as I kept an eye and an ear concentrated on the loud mouth. I thought for a moment that maybe I was giving this guy too much attention. It was business as usual at the bar, people talking and cracking jokes, my friends included. Maybe he was just blowing hot air, when he had mentioned putting holes in some people, and maybe tonight wouldn't end in a disaster. It was wishful thinking.

Cee had noticed the change in my demeanor, and asked me what was wrong. I remember telling him that the guy at the bar had mentioned shooting us to his friend, and Cee's eyes widened as he looked at the guy. I told Cee and The Hoff, who was clueless about the situation that I wasn't going to let anything happen to either one of them.

I think my exact words were "If these mother fuckers got guns, I got guns too, and we could all settle up right now."

I was louder than I wanted to be. One of the girls overheard me, and walked back over to the edge of the table and told The Hoff that maybe I should calm down because they could hear me quite clearly. My eyes never left the guy at the bar.

One of his friends walked over to him, and whispered something in his ear. He looked back over his shoulder, at us, and then back at his friend. His words were clear.

He said, "Hold up right here, I'm gonna go get the chopper from the car for these fools."

I'm not ashamed about what happened afterward.

A chopper is the word that is used on the street for a gun, a machine gun to be exact. This guy had just said to his friend that he was going to go to his car to get a machine gun, to use on me and my friends. I told you about that switch. I never see it coming, nor do I recall with complete clarity what happens when it does. I stood straight up at the booth, and pulled out my 9 Millimeter.

I pulled it out from behind my back, and slammed it on the table, then gave it a hard spin. I told them all, "Go get your fucking chopper. I got sixteen shots for all you mother fuckers!"

Needless to say, the conversations and everything in the bar came to a grinding halt. Everything except for my gun, which continued to spin and spin until it finally stopped with the barrel pointed in Cee's direction.

I yelled again, "What the fuck are you waiting for? Go get the fucking chopper. Don't just talk me to death. Go get it!"

I was seething. The Hoff was standing with his mouth agape as the tough guys suddenly began to leave. One by one, they left their stools, nodded in our direction for some reason, and left without saying a word. Perhaps they understood the situation was about to get very ugly and decided that they wanted no part of it or me. A few words were murmured under their breath, but not one person addressed me or looked at me directly. Especially not the tough guy who allegedly had an automatic weapon in his car. The girls followed them right out of the bar, and never looked back in our direction. There was utter silence at our table as well. The Hoff decided that maybe it was a good time for us to pay our tab and got us all out of there.

I don't remember much of the ride home, but I don't imagine there was much chatter. Cee had been quite shaken by the way things went down, and had decided to go his own way and take a cab. I was buried deep in one of my zones, trying to decompress. I didn't snap out of it until I heard the Hoff shut the engine of his car off. I looked at him and noticed that he was looking at me rather strangely. I could tell that I was being judged.

I asked him, "What?"

He looked at me like I was crazy, and repeated what I said. "What? Are you seriously asking me what? What are you fucking crazy?"

How do I answer that? I know that I can be volatile. I know that people might believe that I over-react, but I think I simply react. While the nights happening seemed more like a dream than a memory to me, I was pretty sure that I hadn't actually hurt anyone. The asshole with the long braids had certainly asked for it, hadn't he? Maybe he hadn't expected to come across someone like me, but that was no fault of mine. I was perfectly happy to keep myself immersed in rum, pleasantly distracted by my own inebriation all by my lonesome. It was he that decided to antagonize me by threatening me and my friends. I wasn't quite feeling the appreciation I believed I was due for chasing off the bad guys, and I let the Hoff know as much.

I opened the car door and let myself out. I was still angry. I was only getting hotter as I felt the pressure building within, and I was going to pop at any moment. I was trying not to explode in front of the Hoff who was walking a few feet behind me. I was already annoyed with myself for showing that particular side of me at the bar, and I'm sure there would be a ton of questions about the gun. My friends had no clue about what I did to earn money. I rarely had people in my life long enough to get into detail about career choices.

The only person who really knew me was Nina, who I had met while I had been on a "Job" one day. I had gotten her out of a very serious situation, and we had been connected since. It was no fault of her own, but her father's debt, which had put her in a quite a precarious position. I had been called in to fix the situation, and had been blind-sided by Nina's awesome and overpowering aura. She was innocent, but she was in danger nonetheless. I called in a few markers and had tried unsuccessfully to cash in on some debts to negotiate on her father's behalf. At the end of the ordeal, she walked out with me as I whisked her away to safety. I'm not going to lie. Blood was spilled that day. Mine as well as the blood of a few others. I never bothered to check on anyone's vitals after it all went down but I can't be sure that life wasn't lost. Perhaps it was Nightingale Syndrome, or maybe it was fate that had kept Nina in my life afterward. Whatever the circumstances were, we had been brought together, although unintentionally, by the sins of her father. We had never looked back ever since.

My friends, however, had no clue about my past or my childhood for that matter. They had no clue what I did for a living, so maybe a little bit of gunplay would be a big deal to them. These things just happened sometimes, but they were strangers to that world. Cee had refused to ride home in the car with me that night and the Hoff kept going on and on about how totally out of control I was for my behavior. I tried to walk away from him before I erupted but I never really stood a chance. My anger had been uncorked, and now it would erupt with destructive force until my steam would slowly fade. As I walked away with haste, my hands began to itch with that old desire I used to have to dismantle everything around me. I used my left hand first. I cocked a fist back and punched a side view mirror clear off the car, sending it flying down the street. It did little to satisfy me. I passed the next car on my left and repeated the action, punching it as hard as I could. The second mirror didn't go flying, but it shattered and hung from the side of the car. That made me angrier. I switched hands, punched at the mirror until it snapped off, and fell to the street. I went to a third car and repeated the process.

I had walked about fifty feet up the street and had destroyed the sides of every car I passed. The Hoff was frantic. He kept yelling and asking me to calm down but I was a lost cause. I turned the corner and the half minute it took me to reach the next vehicle felt was a tortuous eternity. It came to my attention that both of my hands had been cut, and I had shards of broken mirror glass embedded in my knuckles. I don't know why, but this made me burst out in laughter. I felt invincible. I was bleeding profusely, but I felt no pain. Inexplicably, I thought of the dog that had tried to get me when I was a tiny little hostage in Alphabet City, and I dared it to come get me right then while I was fearless and brimming with impunity. I screamed from the top of my lungs for it to come, so that I could sink my teeth into its mane and rip its life right out. It started to rain.

The Hoff was speechless. He followed me at a careful distance as I continued to walk down the street, dismantling everything in my path. I was aware of his presence but there was nothing I could do now. It had to come out. When I got closer to my house, I spun around and The Hoff froze in his tracks. I could see the apprehension all over his face. He had no clue what was coming next.

I pointed a bloody finger in his direction and said, "What I did tonight at the bar was for you guys. I did it for you. They were going to hurt you. They were talking about hurting all of us, and I cannot let that happen."

The Hoff nodded and said, "Ok man, just calm down, ok?"

I hadn't realized it until then that I had been speaking through clenched teeth, but I was so angry and was shaking so much with the need to explode out of my own skin. I closed my eyes and tried to imagine the rain as a soothing wash to remove the angst from me. I held my hands in front of me and let the rain wash away the blood and glass that was stuck to my skin. I was lost in my own little world.

The Hoff broke the silence when he said, "You need to go inside before the police come. I'm sure someone called them by now."

That didn't scare me much. I had been handcuffed before. Nina had heard the commotion outside and came out to see me standing there in the rain, but by then the anger I had been teeming with had begun to melt into sadness. I knew that The Hoff had never seen that side of me, and that he would probably distance himself from me after doing so. I wanted to explain to him that I had lost too much already.

I wanted to say that I could not possible bear another loss in my life, and those men at the bar were threatening to do just that. I simply could not live with that, but I could see in his face that all he wanted at that point was to get away from me. He had seen just a little piece of everything that I carried, but it was more than enough.

Nina called to me before I could open my mouth to say anything at all. She said, "Come on, get inside and out of the rain."

Her voice could always soothe me. I looked at her and then looked back at The Hoff who was still standing a safe distance from me. It broke my heart to see that expression on his face. I turned away before he could see that my mood could swing from anger to uncontrolled emotion in an instant. As I walked towards Nina, I tried to put my hands in my pockets but was hit with sudden jolts of pain as the shards of glass embedded in my hands reminded me that I was not invincible at all. When I got to Nina, she grabbed both my hands and shook her head in disbelief.

She asked, "What did you do? Why would you do this to yourself?" I could not explain.

It was a long night. When she finally accepted that there was no way I was going to go to a hospital, we decided that the only thing to do was to grab tweezers and remove every piece of glass from my hands. I was a good patient. I winced every once in a while, and took in large amounts of alcohol to numb the excruciating pain I was in. I had also broken a few knuckles during my fit but I was none the worse for wear. These were things that I had great experience with.

I reached out to The Hoff and Cee several times in the weeks to follow but I was unsuccessful in my attempts to speak with them. I knew it was coming, but I was trying to keep some sort of stability in my life. I had known those guys for a long time, but again, people never really stay with me. I decided to move from the apartment building I had been living in, and I left a note on The Hoff's door wishing him well. He had been a great friend to me, but my unpredictability proved to be yet another chasm between me and those that I care about. After all these years, I still hadn't figured out how to keep the ones I loved.

Exorcising Nina

The thing about Nina, the thing that nobody would ever understand is that she somehow manages to love me no matter how unlovable I really am. Nina is in possession of the softest and gentlest spirit I have ever come across. It is true that you can fall in love with someone's spirit, someone's being, and I fell in love with Nina's soul long before I decided to loiter and trespass upon her garden. I am ugly, especially when my blood is up, but she loves me no less for it. It's a guarded love, a private love, if not a secret. She hates when I use that word. She absolutely abhors my use of the term, "Your dirty little secret." I admit it, I say it on purpose to hurt her. I also say it so that she can share in the hurt and misery that I feel whenever she leaves my bed, and goes back to her loving, doting Indian family.

A relationship with me is forbidden in her culture. She has to marry someone who is Indian, just like her, and anything else would be unacceptable. It's hard to believe that in modern day time, restrictions and arranged marriages are still alive and well. Sometimes I appreciate that even though her entire family would disown her, she still comes to me. I am a magnet to her, this I know, but just like a magnet she also has a side that repels me when I try to get closer to her, to involve myself in her life.

Unfortunately, this is exactly how it's been since the beginning of our relationship. It's funny how my life goes from being completely empty, devoid of love or human contact for days at a time. Sometimes, I am sitting at home and I realize that I haven't spoken to another human being, not one word, for days. I lose track of the days and it amuses me somewhat. Sometimes I will gauge just how many days it has been since I've spoken a word just to see if I can beat my own personal record of four and a half days without speaking. It's not like I go out of my way, it's just the way my life is fashioned. I don't have a lot of people to speak to. I used to have a lot of friends, but one by one they have dropped off my radar. I don't blame them. I am quite the handful, but I do wish sometimes that my really good friends, like Cee and The Hoff would drop by sometime just to see how I'm doing. I fantasize about it on lonelier days, and imagine I'd put on a pot of coffee or make a nice hard drink for us to talk over. Those guys are long gone now and Nina, she is my one constant. And oh, how we talk.

She has a habit of stopping by unannounced, with her stock of wine in tow, and by the amount of liquid courage she's holding, I can tell whether this will be a short visit or if she will be staying for a few days. I am always happy to see her. I pretend to be more annoyed than ecstatic to see her, but she sees right through me. She's always had the ability to do that.

When I wake up before her, there's nothing better than to open my eyes with our legs entangled and her long black silky hair in my face, and draped over my arm. I'm always surprised to see her, always delighted to feel her, and completely excited to wake her in any manner that I please. She emits soft murmurs as I kiss her neck and shoulders, and I'll always know right away if she wants to be had, or if she would rather lay there and be held, be entirely loved as she negotiates with the rising sun for more bedtime. If she lets my hands wander, she wants more and I gladly oblige. If she takes hold of my hand, and holds it to her chest, letting me feel her beating heart and deep sleepy breaths, I begrudgingly let her have her way. I must admit, that though I had other intentions, it still thrills me to have her in my arms, basking in the loving protection that my muscled, tattooed arms provide her.

When we wake together, we never leave the bed separately, but instead join each other as we brush our teeth, wash our faces, and take in the morning aroma of brewing coffee. She says beautiful things. Or maybe she says everyday things, and it becomes beautiful because it comes to me in her soft soothing voice. She is the only woman, the only voice that makes me forget about all that I came from. She believes in me and inspires me to heal. I can tell her all my funny stories, and some of the stories that make her eyes water in sympathy for me. I share all of it without fear of her judgment. She always reminds me that whatever happened, it was a long time ago. It is ancient history. She tells me things like, "Let it go" and learn to love and live freely, and it works for a few days at times, but before long, I'm returned to the guarded, wounded psyche that encumbers me.

As I mentioned earlier, while she is amazingly beautiful, it's her incredibly loving and nurturing spirit that surrounds me and somehow overpowers all the years of ugly strife that still lives in me. Many nights, when I'm at my drunkest and most belligerent, she still comes to me and allows me to unload whatever it is I am carrying. I have literally knelt at her feet, crying and sobbing uncontrollably, while she held me up, rubbed my back, and encouraged me to let it all out. It's a scene that has played out over and over, yet she never tires of being my pillar. She never says, "Not tonight" nor is she ever too busy to listen. I imagine that she has things on her own mind, things that hinder our relationship and love as well, yet she is completely receptive to all that unravels me over and over again. I know, despite limitations, Nina truly loves me.

I still remember the very first second that second that I had laid eyes on her. It was that moment that they talk about in movies and romance novels. A moment is all you need as your eyes communicate wordlessly. She broke the connection of our eye contact first, but I already knew at that point that I had to have her. I knew that Nina was going to be something meaningful and maybe even cataclysmic in my life. So goes love. I have always known these things. Nobody grows on me. Love is very much like heroin. It's addicting. And withdrawal from love is equally crippling to the human heart. I wasn't sure if I would ever actually see her again, but I knew if I did, it was because of fate. She quickly became a friend and then my best friend. I would care for her when she became very ill shortly after we met, and we decided that maybe we could take care of each other. She listened while I ranted, and I rubbed her feet the minute she came home and took her shoes off. I fed her, bathed with her, and drove her wherever she needed to go. Her presence brought me the elusive peace of mind and heart that I had long struggled to find. The rest of us was shot out of a cannon, as we quickly achieved an amazing connection, a hungry attraction, and a need to share a bed nightly.

I once took the liberty of putting together a little cubby for her to keep her things in. Some pajamas, hair products, or whatever storage space she could possibly need on her longer stays. To be honest, it seemed like a good idea at the time, but when I saw her face contort in that unpleasant manner, I knew that I had crossed the boundaries of who I was to her. She did thank me, but in the same way you thank someone on Christmas for an ugly sweater. It hurt, and I made mental note to make sure to pick a fight later so that I could make her feel as shitty as I did at that moment. That's how my mind works. My passive aggressive tit-for-tat manner. I won't voice my displeasure outright. Instead, I swallow it and let it fester within me for hours or days at a time, until I muster enough angst to explode like a volcano destroying everything within my reach. I'm not one of those people that play the victim card and can't see why I'm without a mate. I know exactly why I'm alone.

I ask her many questions, because I want to know the truth at all times and because I am a glutton for punishment. I even ask the questions that I know the answers to, just to reassure myself that I am fully correct in knowing that she will never truly be mine. She sees it coming of course, and she tries to head me off at the pass. Sometimes it works, and I am talked down. Sometimes, however, I am a proverbial runaway train and I have to give her some credit, because she stands directly in my path anyway and takes the brunt of it. She can only do this for so long, only for a few days, then she retreats to whatever hideout she finds until she is ready to deal with me again. It's not always like that. Many times, she will come and I will be in complete bliss for days at a time. We talk, we laugh, and I will usually break out my latest recipe to impress her palate. We eat way too much usually, and lay down together on my couch, which is much too small for two people. Yet, we squeeze in, her back to my chest with my hands around her waist and our feet always together. On these days, when I have a face full of hair and her light little snore is barely audible is when I feel like I've found my home. I can only sleep for a few minutes when we lie like that, because she is always cold and I run hot. I wake up and I watch her sleep for as long as she continues to purr peacefully in my arms. This can go on for hours at a time and when she starts to stir, so do I. I begin by kissing her neck and shoulders, and I can tell when she begins to cross the barrier from being unconscious to being seduced. Her sleepy eyes begin to flutter as she wakes, as she lets out a small gasp of pleasure. Her moans are soft and ever so feminine. Slowly but surely, her hands begin to wander as well. That's when I know that she is revived and ready to be taken. That's exactly what I do. Our lovemaking is enigmatic.

Nina and I dwell somewhere between unbridled passion, and constant fear of losing one another. I know that I have to be careful, and I also know exactly how this ends, with me alone licking my wounds. It ends with her someday walking down the aisle with a man simply because he has matching skin. In my head, I've replayed the future scene over and over. I imagine that I go to the ceremony, hiding and suffering in my secret pew, and watch her as she promises her heart, body and undying commitment to someone she hardly knows. In some of my fantasies, she sees me watching and starts to cry right before she runs off in blinding tears. In others, she sees me, smiles at me, and mouths "Thank You" to me as she appreciates me lending her support even if it kills me. Sometimes, she doesn't even notice me and I am the one that runs off with tears streaming down my face. Never, not once in all of my hypothetical scenarios, does she come to me.

That's what drives our sex, I believe. Some of it is appreciation for each other and some of it is resentment for keeping me in a box for so long. It's powerful, and when we do lay down together, it's an amalgamation of pure love, passion, lust, anger, hurt, which mixed together makes for quite a physical synthesis. Our spirits converge into a sweaty, moan laden wrestling match, which takes us to heights where nothing else exists except us. The world, her family, even time ceases to matter. We are in our place. She knows me well. When I move she counters, where I revel, she lingers, until we are both entirely physically and emotional spent. It's more a pugilistic bout than sex, but the deep suffocating kisses in between the constant grinding and raising of fresh bruises re-establishes our union. That is my variant of passion. She will usually climax two or three times during our sessions, and when she is ready to finish, she knows exactly what to do. I can never finish in a traditional manner. The only way for me to achieve final gratification is to watch her pleasure herself, as she watches me do the same. I clearly have some issues, which prevent me from allowing someone else to physically bring me to orgasm, but she never complains.

Sometimes, her expression will convey disappointment when we are rocking the entire room and she believes for a brief moment that I may burst, but then of course I don't. She never complains, but assumes whatever position I desire for her. Sometimes she stands against the wall, and sometimes she kneels over me within reach, and masturbates for me to enjoy in full view. I am always pleased by that and before long I am in spasms as well. On the luckier nights, we convulse together.

We both sleep a lot easier afterwards. You would think the opposite, but I am the one that feels safe when she is in my bed. I'm not a small man, and I have developed muscles and many skills that would guarantee my own safety in sticky situations, but skilled or not, the things I fear would overcome me in seconds if I were ever to allow myself an unguarded slumber. The different boogeymen and soul-takers that I encountered long ago would never be forgotten or disregarded as harmless. Nina knows my secrets. She knows what I'm capable of and does not hold it against me. She is the only woman in this world that I trust. I say this because the only other person I trusted on this globe with my secrets was a saint of a man named Anthony. He was surely a man of God. He was no priest, but he was the closest thing to the ritual of confession that I have ever had in my life. I surely loved him, and still do, as a Brother. He too, has gone his own way. Nina, however, had a different love for me. A woman's love is completely different from a man's. We can love our own parents, our own brother's in a way that is bound by blood. A woman's love envelops you in a very exceptional way. It is safety, accommodating, fulfilling, and territorial. When a woman stops loving you, when she shuts the door on you, it's the coldest and loneliest a man will ever feel. Nina's love, though strange and too complex for me to understand, still encased me in security. I knew somehow that her love only belonged to me and while I had no clue where she went on the days and nights that we were not together, her ever embracing love would remain mine.

I could never leave things be. We had had many fights over the years. She would promise me things, then take it back as an impossibility. The things I hated most, is when she would cave and tell me that someday, she would bring me around to her family and circle. I hated this because I knew that I would believe her. I would eat it up, hook, line and sinker, knowing full well that she was never going to do such a thing. I wanted to believe, however, that she loved me enough to stand up to her family, to her friends, to her culture, and that she wanted for us to be together just as much as I did. When she would recant her prior promises, she would ask for time. She would ask for the space and ability to work me into her life slowly. I would be irate, cursing her and her culture, saying whatever vile insult could come to mind, while she sat there and took it, every single time. She knew she was breaking my heart, destroying what little spirit I had left, but she remained at my side. She would pretend to leave, grab her belongings, and make for a hasty exit. When I followed her footsteps, minutes later I would find her still sitting at my front door, crying softly and that would tear me to pieces. It would somehow validate our love, because she was just as hurt and upset as I was. I always invited her back in and we always finished whatever talk we had to finish. Sometimes, it would end with a goodbye. She would stay away for months at a time until I would reach out to her, but Nina always came back.

We would talk, and catch up on the last few months of our respective lives, knowing full well where we were heading, but still unwilling to face it head on. I would playfully invite her to come by to do something totally foolish.

To my amazement, she would show and I would think to myself that she was just as much as a glutton for punishment as I was. The connection was instant and electric and we always seemed to make our way back to my house, to our bed, and hammered out whatever differences we had by giving each other a new batch of soreness to carry throughout the week. I loved to be that bruised afterward, to walk around completely sore is an awareness that kept our encounters fresh. People that exercise seem to get a high from feeling that ache after a good workout, and this was no different. I would wake in the morning and instead of seeing muscles, I noted every single welt, and bite mark that she had left on me. I would turn and see the new scratches she had left on my back, to see if any of the new marks traced the ones that she had left at another time.

While it sounds that our attraction was purely physical, it certainly had an emotional edge to it that we were both afraid to unleash. When we spoke of love and togetherness, it always ended ugly and empty, just like me. It was easier to show our love, yet do our best to never speak of it and let the angst seep out of us like mini explosions during our meaningful but carnal sex.

This is how we are. There is always going to be that one person in your life, and in your bed that you should stay away from, that person with which you feel a kinetic energy, regardless of circumstance. Yet, it's the same person that leads you to countless dead ends and seemingly endless disappointments. No matter how many times you manage to get your finger caught in the door they undoubtedly slam shut in front of you, it is never enough to drive you away for good. You think and actually recite that this will be your last time and that you have finally learned that lesson, but in truth, it is just an emotional timeout you call to take the time you need to recover before you are ready to take on that challenge again. I know that I can never deny Nina. I know that I will always be her muse, if she'll have me. I belong to her, even if she won't have me.

Things changed for the worse of course, when I tried to outsmart her and began going through her things. It had been three hard years of being a secret love which everyday felt more and more like a paramour. I had always suspected that there had been other men. It was the only logical conclusion to explain her disappearances and clandestine behavior. We never shared a birthday, or holidays, as I was never allowed or welcomed to partake in the festivities with her people. I would reward her by forbidding her presence at any of my happy occasions as we continued our toxic vengeful behavior. Then I found a picture of another man, an Indian man, in her bag. The long fuse that had been lit for all this time finally sparked a long simmering fire.

For Nina, having been caught with such damning evidence, there was no denying that this unknown man was someone of significance. Try as she did to soften the blow, she finally confessed that this was a man she had met recently, while away in Washington D.C. This was the first that I had heard of this trip. She told me that she liked him enough to believe that her father would approve of such a man for her. He was in fact, someone that she would consider for marriage.

I wish I could say that I handled it well, but anyone that knows me at all, could imagine the explosion of rage and betrayal that coursed through my veins at that very moment. I had struggled, cried, begged, forgiven, and cried again for Nina to take me home to her family. I had beseeched her to find the courage and love somewhere within her to announce her love for me, as if somehow that would validate the last three years of my miserable and unreciprocated commitment to making a life together. On my fiery days, I would threaten to ring her father's doorbell and introduce myself as the man his daughter called home every night that she wasn't with her family. On her more defiant days, she would tell me point blank that the notion of bringing me home to her parents was "Non-negotiable". But most nights, with our hearts and naked legs intertwined, we would settle down with her promise of a future reckoning, if we were to just let things be for now. That last night, however, would be our worst.

Nina never worried about me hurting her. She knew of my actions, and she knew of what I was capable of, but she never worried for herself. She would nurse my various wounds and injuries while shaking her head at me and telling me that I was going to have to stop being an ogre someday. She had always believed that no matter how angry I was, that I would never lay my hands on her. I am in possession of two very different, but extremely effectual pairs of hands. One set is used for touch. These are used for coaxing, to massage, to knead, to trace every bead of sweat, and to express my limitless appreciation for every single amusement park like curve of Nina's exquisite and receptive body. My other set of hands, she had never seen. She would never want to meet the latter pair. They are ugly, and harmful. They are strong and driven by an objective to gain compliance. Yet, they have also been known to break free in an uncontrolled flurry of rage of destruction, if only for a short while, before they are brought under control.

After her confession, I went to her. I don't recall the words I used, but there were words I hadn't used before. Words that certainly weren't suitable for the ears of women or children. I moved swiftly without realizing that I was actually moving towards her, as all the years of unrewarded patience and heart breaking disappointment exploded if not erupted out of every single pore. I was a ball of hatred hurling towards her and she knew that there was no place for her to retreat. She was stammering an apology, but the words froze in her throat as I reached for her. Nina, and these other hands of mine, were meeting for the very first time. I grabbed her shirt collar, and pulled her up so that we could be face to face. I needed her to see my eyes. I needed her to see the cold, savage intent that lay there waiting for her as penance for her indiscretion. I relayed the message. That I am sure of because her eyes were giant orbs of fear, incapable of any another expression or tear. I didn't want to merely hurt her. I needed to eradicate her existence. In my mind's eye, I saw my powerful hands wrapped around her throat ever so tightly, leaving her mouth ajar, moaning a wordless spittle as she made a last desperate gasp for air that would never come.

I let her go. I released my grip on her collar and backed away from her. She watched me move until my back was against the wall and I could move no further. She had seen what I wanted her to see. For the first time, she was no longer safe from the damage that I am capable of. She had seen it before, but she had never known the precarious position of being the intended target of my rage. She was shaking, but this was not to deter her from making a hasty exit. She began to say that I was right, and that she was going to tell her parents all about us. She was nervously stammering, and asking for just a few more days to introduce me to her family. These were all lies, of course, but for the first time we both knew it. I nodded and said that I would look forward to the day, even though I knew full well that I would never lay my eyes upon Nina again. She gathered her things, gave me a curt hug and dry kiss upon my lips, and escaped my apartment in one piece.

She called me days later, from the safety of her own home. She told me that she could not find it in her heart to tell her parents and that she needed to end this thing of ours for good. It was no surprise to me. We flirted with the idea of remaining friends, staying in contact, somehow, but again, we knew we would be telling lies. Nina left for California shortly afterward. It was a trip that she had dreamed about making many times, and I suspect that perhaps it was her love for me that kept her here for a short while. When she left, in our last conversation, she told me that she did not want to know me, or hear from me ever again. Whatever this was, this short period of our lives, would never be forgotten, yet never needed to be re-lived. She told me she loved me, and that she always would, and I expressed the same. She wished me well, and while I strongly suspected that she meant every word, she never looked back. The next and final thing I heard was the haunting dial tone. The menacing pitch that echoes into your ear after someone hangs up the phone forever.

The Bell Tolls

No matter how hard I tried to shake the harsh lessons Indio had burned and beaten into me, I always reverted back to violence, even if I had managed to avoid it for a lengthy period of time. I do believe in nature versus nurture and somewhere within me lies a much kinder and gentler soul. Naturally, I believe myself to be a good, God-fearing man that ultimately would prefer to never hurt another human being. I am certainly capable of acts of violence when I am pushed, but the latter was something I was taught. On the other hand, Indio was simply incapable of doing good for anyone other than himself. There was nothing he wouldn't do to get his way. As we got older, it became more difficult for Indio to manipulate and take advantage of us like he had done when we were kids. Vilma had also grown up so he would be careful not to hit us when she was watching. We caught on to that little fact pretty quick and decided to stay glued to her side whenever Indio was around. My sister was an adult now with a full time boyfriend, yet we were all over both of them, not giving them any privacy or a moment of peace. But that was our life, and sometimes we took a beating when nobody was keeping an eye on us. He would come and go, disappear for months at a time, especially after the very long cold winter we had endured in the condemned house. I was never proud of myself for stealing from him, but the way I see it, I earned every single penny in bruises and welts. I earned it every single day when his accounting of the drug money didn't add up. Still, I simply did what I had to do to survive.

When we were living in the Midwood section of Brooklyn, he had shown himself again for a few weeks. Within that short period of time, he had gotten into two fist fights. First he fought with Gilbert, who handily kicked his ass to my delight. Then about a week later, I had walked in with my girlfriend at the time, and he decided that he wanted to start with me.

I introduced my girlfriend to him, being polite as ever, and he just bluntly remarked, "Oh, I thought you were a faggot."

I called him a faggot in return and he smacked me in the face. I remember the rage inside me that day. I can still feel the burning sting on my face from the smack I had just gotten and from the embarrassment that it happened in front of my girlfriend. I had about eighteen years of abuse locked up inside and it was dying to come out. I punched him as hard I could in his face and he recoiled back a few steps. He was in shock that I hit him back. Then he came at me and for a few moments, I was taking a beating just like I had when I was a kid. I was still rather small and thin but there was still a rage inside me that fueled a comeback in me. My girlfriend was screaming her head off and that's when I rocked him. All my boxing lessons I had taking alongside Gilbert came back to me and I hit him with an uppercut that startled him and knocked him into a corner. I started swinging at him with all that I had but my girlfriend kept trying to drag me back. I was punching him on his head, his shoulders, his arms, wherever I could hit while he was trying to cover up. I was crying hysterically and trying to unload every single amount of resentment I had for him at one time.

Then Indio got dirty. He grabbed a broomstick and hit me on the head with it a few times before I was able to grab it as we started to wrestle for it. It was a good thing because I was starting to get a little fuzzy after the last blow. The funniest thing happened right then, the phone rang. I pushed him away, but he managed to keep his grip on the broomstick. He back peddled about ten feet down the hallway, but still kept the broomstick in threatening stance, ready to crack me over the head with it again. My girlfriend got between us again, and started to drag me out of the apartment. We were still yelling and screaming at each other, as the phone rang. Then he just kind of called a timeout and picked up the phone, calm as could be.

He said, "Hello" like nothing was going on, and apparently, it was someone he was expecting to hear from.

I was still cursing and screaming and he had the audacity to hush with one finger in the air, signaling that he needed a moment of quiet. I couldn't believe it. My girl was crying hysterically as well and begged me to stop and to please come with her. After a few moments of calming myself down, I went with her. We went to Ocean Parkway, which is a long stretch of benches and trees. It's usually teeming with bikers, skaters, or joggers getting their exercise in. When we sat down on the benches, I just unloaded all the shame and anger that I had held in for the past 18 years. I told her everything that he had done to Gilbert and me, and how he had maligned the family for all these years.

She cried with me that day and held me as I sobbed heavily on her shoulders. We stayed out as long as we could. I took her home that night and we hung out at her house as late as possible before I went back home. I fully expected a war when I got back home but when I did get back, all was quiet, like nothing had happened. Indio was nowhere to be found, so I went into the Gilbert's room to tell him what had happened. He was happy that I had finally stuck up for myself and he asked to feel the lumps all over my head. We laughed and stayed up talking for some time that night, and we were both wondering how it would be and what would happen once Indio came back but he never did.

Apparently, the phone call he had received was an important one. Some big drug deal he had been waiting on came through and he was on his way again. But the spell had been broken. Gilbert had kicked his ass, and even though I had ended up on the losing end of my fight with him, I had finally fought back. We had announced that enough was enough. My next conversation with Indio was a few years later. I had moved out of my mom's house and I was dating a girl named Jeannie, who I was walking with down the street while we were headed to my apartment. It is kind of funny the way it happened, because while I was walking down the street, I heard a car horn. Jeannie and I kept walking and then I heard my name being called out. I looked to see who it was and it was Indio who was in the car and had honked the horn at me. I must have tensed up because Jeannie, who I was walking with hand and hand, asked me if I was ok. I assured her that I was fine, and I went over to the car, but I told her to stay by the sidewalk, not knowing what to expect from my brother.

I said, "What's up? Long time no see."

He said that he had been traveling and that he had met a woman in Ecuador that he was in love with. He asked me who the girl was and I told him that she was my girlfriend, and he said, "Really? I thought you were gay."

Two things were different that day. He had used the word gay instead of the derogatory term "Faggot," which believe it or not meant I had earned some sort of respect from him. When he said it, he was smiling.

I half smiled back at him, and replied "You remember what happened last time you called me that?" and I held my stare right into his eyes.

I wasn't looking for a fight by any means, but in a subtle manner, I had just let him know that if he was looking to fuck with me that day, he was in for a surprise. He just laughed and asked me where I was going. I told him that I had moved back into the neighborhood recently, but I was hesitant to tell him exactly where. All I needed was Indio popping up unannounced, ruining the sanctity that I found while living on my own.

We made some brief small talk about the family and when the pleasantries were finished, he asked me if he could borrow twenty bucks. I had to laugh out loud when he said it because it had caught me off guard and I asked him if he was serious. He was serious, he explained. Before he could give me a long drawn out story about why he didn't have any money, I reached into my pocket, being careful not to show him just how much money I was carrying and I peeled off a twenty-dollar bill. I gave it to him without question, fully knowing that I was giving him the money, not lending it to him.

He said, "Thanks little bro, I'll see you around." We shook hands, said our goodbyes and those were the last words that he and I ever exchanged.

The very next time that I saw Indio was a few years later. He was lying dead on a cold metal slab at the Queens medical examiner's office. His mouth was slightly agape and he looked older and somewhat bloated because he had been lying dead in a hotel room by the airport for some time before housekeeping had discovered his body. My sister couldn't handle seeing Indio that way, so Gilbert and I went with my sister's husband to identify the body. We went with a detective who was asking all kinds of questions, as if we had the answers he was looking for. Apparently, Indio was going big time into the drug business.

He had bought a pharmacy in Ecuador and was using the store as an establishment to smuggle drugs out of the country and into the United States. He had gotten a little greedy, however, and on this trip, he had swallowed fifty bags of heroin. He had checked into the hotel airport immediately upon landing so that he could pass it and sell it to whoever he was supplying to, but he never made it. One of the bags broke in his stomach and it killed him instantly. Just like that, Indio was gone.

I was playing basketball that day in the park, and my pager kept going off over and over again. When I finally took a look at the screen, it was my sister's home phone number and I knew it had to be bad. I politely excused myself by telling my friend Sal that I had to go and he definitely saw something on my face because he asked me if everything was ok. I explained to him that my sister hardly ever paged me, and that I had gotten many texts from her with the numbers 911 following her phone number. I told Sal that it was definitely bad news and that somebody was probably dead. I was banking that it was either my mom or Indio. Had to be, I thought to myself. Gilbert never came to mind. When I finally got to a phone booth and called my sister, she told me that Indio was dead and that he had been found dead in a hotel room. I went home, showered, called my girlfriend at the time, who told me she'd leave work and meet me at my sister's house immediately.

I didn't cry at all, at least not yet. When I arrived at my sister's house, it was the typical somber scene that you would expect. Everyone was crying and hugging each other but I really couldn't find a very good reason to mourn his passing. I wouldn't say that I was happy or relieved that he was dead, but I couldn't find it inside me to feel any kind of emotion about it. That night I went home with my girlfriend and she asked me if I was ok, I had to be honest. I told her that I was fine. I didn't feel everyone else's sorrow, not even a little bit. I explained to Denise everything he had put us through and that I had never had a real relationship with Indio. The only memories I had of him were bad memories and I wasn't going to lose any sleep over his passing.

I don't think she quite understood my experiences with him, because she looked at me like I was crazy. But there was no way that she could begin to fathom what my life had been like growing up. She tried to be very supportive and did the best she could which I greatly appreciated. She was definitely there for me and I think I would have had a harder of a time if not for her. When we went to identify the body, the detective assigned to the case was asking all kinds of questions and was trying to appear very sympathetic, asking us if wanted to help find justice for Indio's death. He didn't really believe that Indio was a victim, but he was trying to pull all his tricks out of his hat, trying to get us to reveal to him the dealer the Indio was supplying. We all told him that we didn't know anything and we really didn't. Indio was his own entity since he was young. He came and went as he pleased and never asked for permission, even when he was taking that which belonged to you.

We all explained to the detective that we would be of no help and that this was pretty much an open and closed case.

We made the funeral arrangements and it turned out to be a pretty decent turnout. We even had to designate a small section of the funeral parlor to house the various young women who arrived, in tears, claiming to be Indio's girlfriend. It was kind of amusing after the third or fourth girl and we just pointed them in the direction of the other girlfriends who were probably forming a support group by then. On the last day, perhaps the last hour of the viewing, before he was taken away to be cremated, was when I knelt at his coffin, and said a prayer for his soul. I knelt there for a few minutes. Knowing the he would be gone forever once they closed that casket was what pushed me over the emotional ledge so to speak. I began to shake and finally cry at the thought of him being burned to ashes never to be seen again. But I was angrier than hurt. I was angry that another one of my siblings had been taken from me. I was angry that I had never really had the chance to know him as an adult or as a true brother. I was also incredibly angry for the years of abuse that he had unleashed on us. And I was angry that he would never have the chance to atone for his trespasses.

He would never have the chance to apologize to us, to tell us that through it all, he had loved us in some way or another. This was it. The book was closed and there would be no chapters added later. That's when I cried. I let some of my emotion out but my sister grabbed my shoulder as I started to erupt, and she saw me about to lose my composure. My hands tensed up so hard that that my fingers went right through the leather cushion that you use to rest your elbows on as you kneel in prayer.

Vilma has seen me unravel. She placed her hand on my shoulder and told me, "No, Don't do this here. Please calm down. Don't let mommy see you like this, she's had enough this week."

I swallowed it. I kept whatever was fighting to get out, and pushed it back down to wherever it dwelled within me and that's where it has stayed until now. He's dead twenty years now, but the scars he inflicted upon me are here to stay.

The Good Wolf

I still had my Gilbert. As bad as it got, he was always in my corner. My children, lucky enough for me, are truly wonderful children. I am positive that they love each other to no end, but I can never quite explain to them the love that Gilbert and I had for each other. Our bond was incumbent on life and death at times and when you suffer with someone on those terms, something else is created. Something is created that is even more powerful than love, something that makes you fight, not for yourself, but for the person next to you.

When Gilbert was stabbed and almost died in his late teens, I nearly had a nervous breakdown. I can say with certainty that what transpired that day was an eerie act of fate. I had been walking up the street earlier in the day and I saw my friend Calvin being chased around a car by a kid holding a knife. I had never seen this kid before so I thought that this might be serious. I snuck up on the kid and while he was busy chasing Calvin, I knocked the kid on his ass and took the knife out of his hands. The kid started screaming because I had twisted his arm so bad, and was on the cusp of breaking his wrist before he finally let go of it. Calvin came running from the around the car and started yelling at me to let him go, which I had no intention of doing. Calvin explained that he really wasn't chasing him with the knife to stab him, they were kidding around, and the kid was just being stupid. I let the kid get up, but for some reason I hesitated to give him back the knife. I told them they were both assholes, and what they were doing in jest was a good way to get somebody killed. They apologized for being so dumb and said all the right things kids will say to get something they want.

In this case, the kid wanted his knife so I gave it back to him. I swear that it felt wrong, like some bad energy was being passed but I simply couldn't get a read on it. I gave him back his knife and I told Calvin, who happened to be a very good friend of Gilbert's, to be careful and smarten up. I walked away and went to hang out with my usual crew on the corner of Thirty-eight Street. Not ten minutes later, I was smoking a cigarette with Joe, who still remains one of the few people that I can still call a friend. We were just shooting the breeze with another friend Willy, contemplating what kind of forty-ounce beers we were going to get into that night.

Gilbert happened to walk by and saw me smoking a cigarette, which pissed him off for some reason. He asked me what the hell I was doing smoking and I told him I smoked all the time, which I did. I wasn't about to deny it and as I was about to take another drag on the cigarette, he slapped me right on my face, sending the cigarette flying onto the floor. For a second I thought about hitting him back. I did sometimes but on this night, I decided against it. I simply didn't feel like getting into it with him and certainly getting my ass kicked that night. I called him a fucking asshole and told him that he was going to get his or some empty threat along those lines. He told me he was just trying to protect me and stop me from getting cancer and I told him to go fuck himself. And that's how it ended.

He walked away to go hang with his girlfriend and I got myself another cigarette, and a beer. Not even an hour later, some kid from the neighborhood came running up to me in hysterics, telling me that Gilbert had gotten into a fight and had gotten stabbed. I shook the kid pretty well and warned him that he better not be kidding. He was in tears at that point and it was a safe bet that this was not some sort of sick joke. About 20 kids and myself ran to Gilbert's girlfriend's house and I started to ring the bell, getting close to hysterics myself. After nobody answered, I started to break the door down, imagining my brother's lifeless body lying on the other side of the door. One of the neighbors started yelling out of her window that Gilbert was no longer there.

I started to run. As I was running, I started to think of the last conversation I had with Gilbert. After all the strife that we had endured together, it would have broken me to have our last conversation go as it did, with him slapping my face and me warning him that he was going to get his in return. I did catch up with Gilbert that night and after I got the full story, it gave me a chill that weakened my knees. Gilbert ended up in surgery, and the knife that was used to pierce his ribcage and puncture his lung was the very same knife that I had taken from the kid barely an hour before. That same kid that was chasing Calvin with the knife had said something distasteful to Gilbert's girl and before long they were fighting. The kid started to lose the fight quickly of course, so he pulled the knife and stabbed my brother.

Hearing this was like being in a twilight zone movie. I actually got light headed and had to sit down. My damn fingerprints were probably still on the knife and it was just used to nearly kill my older brother. I really don't know what you would call that. It's really some sick happenstance that you would only see in the movies, but yet I can truly attest that it happened exactly that way. Had Gilbert died that day, I never would have recovered. Not mentally, emotionally, nor spiritually in any shape or form. It would have killed me too knowing that I had that knife in my hands and I had given it right back to the kid that would go on to stab Gilbert. God can be quite the prankster sometimes and I had learned a painful yet valuable lesson. I vowed to never take Gilbert for granted ever again.

I remember when he won the boxing Golden Gloves, it was probably the best moment that we ever shared together. He won the golden gloves in 1988, I was 15 years old, and it felt like Gilbert had won the heavyweight championship of the world. As a prize, the Daily News, which was a sponsor of the fights, gave every champion of each respective weight class a solid gold set of boxing gloves that hung on a necklace. Many times I have watched that fight on video. Until this day, even though the quality of the tape has seen better days, you can still hear me cheering for Gilbert while I was screaming my head off in the audience. The day of the knife changed the course of history, I believe.

After Gilbert got stabbed, he was never quite the same. His lung had been badly damaged and he had lost the desire to train. As a result, he started to gain a lot of weight and he just accepted that he was going to be an average Joe destined to toil away at some meaningless job instead of being a professional boxer. It was heart-breaking for all of us, but I can imagine that it was probably a lot harder for him. When Gilbert was lying in the hospital with all those tubes running through him and with all the machines attached to him, it was the first time in my entire life that I felt Gilbert just might be mortal. He had saved me so many times and always bested whoever wanted to challenge him, but he seemed incredibly fragile lying there in that hospital bed. I would go see him and I wouldn't stay long, always making some excuse about having something to do or having to see a girl. It hurt me to see him in that condition. He was my own private version of Superman and I loved him fiercely for it. Seeing him so human and mortal was too much for to see.

Gilbert could make you absolutely crazy though. He duped me once in such a manner that it caused a huge riff between us. I was living on my own for quite some time and partying like a rock star every single weekend. Gilbert was still living at home with my mother, who was seeing a man, and was trying to gently prod her darling son out of the house finally. I was living in a one-bedroom apartment and paying about a thousand dollars a month, which was a little steep at the time but between two jobs, I was having no trouble at all making the rent. My mom had found an apartment close to the old neighborhood we used to live in and right next door there to her was another apartment for rent that Gilbert had his eye on. He decided to get me involved and I really should always go with my gut but Gilbert, ever the salesman, talked me into leaving my apartment, and moving into the new apartment with him. The numbers were definitely ideal. I was paying a thousand a month for my place and the rent for the new apartment was much less. It was twice as big as the apartment I was living in and the rent was eight hundred dollars a month. My half of the rent was four hundred in total, with the utilities included so it was a no-brainer financially. Still, something didn't seem right and I went into it with the expectation that something was going to go wrong.

The apartment had three bedrooms, and I had suggested to Gilbert that maybe we could turn the extra bedroom into an office or perhaps even a music studio to play around with some DJ equipment I owned. I was always experimenting with music. He just shook his head and blew off the idea, then abruptly changed the subject. A week before we were to move in, we went in to clean the place and make some last minute touches. I went into the extra bedroom and I noticed that it had been painted pink.

I looked at Gilbert and I said, "This room wasn't painted before Gil, why is it pink?"

He tried to convince me that it was always pink and that I simply had failed to notice it when I had come to view the apartment. I assured him that I was not crazy and I that was one hundred percent sure that the room was white just like the rest of the house. Again, he blew me off and changed the subject. I knew something was wrong but still I couldn't put my finger on it.

When moving day came, everything went without a hitch. We paid the first month of rent and the security deposit and Gilbert and I were officially roommates. I suggested that we throw a huge house warming party in a week or two and he looked at me like I had two heads. Gilbert didn't want to have anything to do with a party. He suggested that maybe we invite my sister and my mom, but that we should keep it small. I thought he was going nuts.

I said, "Dude, we are in our twenties, and we have this huge bachelor pad to ourselves and you want to invite mom and Vilma? What the hell is wrong with you?"

Once again, Gilbert was stoic, and that's when I knew that whatever was going to happen was going to drop at any moment now. I asked him repeatedly what the hell was wrong and why he was being so weird, but he insisted that everything was fine.

About a week later, I was in my bedroom sleeping off a raucous night of boozing in Bay Ridge, when all of a sudden, I felt like I was being watched. I opened my eyes, and in my bedroom is a little girl who looked to be 3 or 4 years old. I thought I was either dreaming or maybe I had really gotten fucked up the night before. I closed my eyes tight and shook my head, and when I opened my eyes, the little girl was still there. I was thinking maybe this little girl was going to kill me like in a horror movie and maybe I should try to escape. When I moved to stand up, the little girl ran out of the room. I laid there for a minute, thinking maybe I dreamed the whole thing, then I heard cartoons being played in the living room. I walked out of my bedroom and I started to slowly and carefully sneak out of my bedroom, still deathly afraid of the strange little girl that was just in my bedroom plotting my demise like in a horror film.

I ran into Gilbert in the hallway, and I asked him, "Did you just see a little girl running around the house or am I losing my mind?"

He said, "Yeah, that's Cheena."

I asked, "Who?"

Again he said, "Cheena."

I asked, "Who the hell is Cheena?"

Then he said, "That's my girlfriend's daughter."

My next question of course was, "You have a girlfriend?"

He proceeded to explain that he had a girlfriend and she had nowhere to go right now. She and her daughter would be staying with us for a while. I completely lost my shit before he had a chance to finish and I cursed him out at the top of my lungs. He had planned this all along. He came to me under the guise of getting our own bachelor pad, but the truth was that he wanted to provide a place to live with his girlfriend and her daughter but he couldn't afford the rent on his own. I guess he knew I would never go for it if I knew that those were the circumstances, so he came up with this whole plan to dupe me into paying half of the rent. We weren't in the apartment a full week before he dropped this huge bomb on my lap. I told him I was moving out immediately, but he begged me to stay.

Truthfully, I had blown all my cash on new furniture and a nice little trip that I could suddenly afford with the new decrease in rent. So at the moment, I was stuck there with their new happy little family, but I was pissed that he had totally lied to me and never once thought about what I wanted for myself. It was a really selfish thing to do to me, and it came out of left field, especially from someone who I had always viewed as a straight shooter. I finished cursing him out that day and I started to sulk back into my bedroom when I suddenly turned around, having to get one last thing off my chest.

"That fucking room wasn't pink when we saw the apartment! You painted it after I left so that you could make it into a bedroom for that little girl. Didn't You?"

He nodded sheepishly and admitted. "Yeah, I painted it last week".

I yelled, "I fucking knew it. I knew I wasn't losing my damn mind. You're an asshole!" I walked into my room and slammed the door.

I was livid. I got on the horn right away and tried calling a few of my friends hoping one of them was looking for a roommate. There were no takers. I ended up staying until I got married a few years later. Nevertheless, while I was still living there, I was going to make Gilbert pay dearly for screwing me over. After a while, we could actually talk about it and laugh about it, but I still resented him for it. Just to mess with him I would come home drunk as hell, late at night with a girl or sometimes two and we would party like animals in my bedroom till four or five am. Then we'd sleep in late, and in the afternoon, I would parade the girls through the house. The girls would still in their high heels from the night before, and I walk them out with a huge grin on my face. Gilbert and his girlfriend would be sitting on the couch having coffee when I would walk out of my room like a crazed rock star leaving a hotel with his groupies. His girlfriend hated my guts for it and Gilbert would then come to my room and yell at me for causing him strife. And I would smile. The poor guy was being yelled at every day, but I couldn't care less.

Sometimes I would tell the girls Gilbert's name and told them to make sure they said goodbye to my brother when we left. That made his lady even crazier and again he would come knocking on door in a fury. I would have myself a good laugh over that and tell him to please close my door on the way out. The funniest thing is that I ended up loving Cheena so freaking much that I could not have imagined living there without her always hanging around us. I would play with her all the time and every Christmas I made sure that I got her the loudest, most obnoxious toy that I could possibly find. Since she woke up every day at six am, you could hear her toys making all kinds of noise all through the house as soon as the sun came up. Oh, I cannot describe the joy that it brought me.

It's hard to believe that these things happened twenty years ago. Cheena is in her twenties now and it's hard to believe that she is an adult considering that if felt like yesterday that I was picking her up at school and walking with her as she held my hand. She is every bit my niece as Gilbert is my brother. I still remember her standing in my bedroom that day and that's the memory that I will always keep with me. She was a tiny thing with a little speech issue and the cutest thing I had ever seen. Cheena and her younger sister Kelsie are my brother's daughters. Sometimes I look at their pictures and wish for that time back, but it's just not part of the deal, is it? I am happy, however, that my kids have cousins and pseudo cousins everywhere they go. It's not like us. When we were growing up, we had no real cousins, aunts, or uncles to speak of.

I was the happiest that I have ever been in my life, for only a short time unfortunately, after I had moved out and gotten married. I was happy because I had finally achieved something that I had wanted my entire life and I no longer had to look to other people's family to fulfill it. I had married a girl that was one of my best friends through High School and we had a great apartment. I was working two jobs and she was finishing up college within the year. Soon she would be working as well and we were talking about buying a house. Can you imagine that? A kid like me that had grown up bouncing from place to place, being homeless and living in condemned shacks, talking about buying an actual home. I had everything that I wanted. We had gotten married in November of 1997 and we hosted that very first Thanksgiving at our place. It is truly one of my happiest memories. My wife and I cooked and my brother came over with his family. My sister came by with her family. People from the neighborhood kept stopping by to have a bite or have a drink and it all felt so right. The house was full of kids, playing and yelling. The usual Thanksgiving domino game was about to start as my mom sat at the table deciding who was going to partner up with whom. We were finally a family. More importantly, this was my family, and I had brought us all together. It was the only time of my life that I felt like a complete human being. It was also the closest thing to perfection and happiness that I ever experienced.

Right around the time that I had gotten married, Gilbert had been diagnosed with cancer. It truly took the wind out of our sails. I had been getting ready for my whole world to fall apart yet again, but on this very first Thanksgiving as a married man with my family, I felt like I was going to be ok. Perhaps all my sufferings were a thing of the past and I could finally strive to be someone "normal" if such a thing existed. I was surrounded by family and with trusted friends, beginning a new life. I was officially home. My wife did a really great job of hosting and cooking and I felt like it was only to get better from here.

I had no clue that my happiness would be so short lived, but I was blissfully unaware of the nightmare the next few years had in store for me. Gilbert's cancer was an ordeal for the entire family. Between the operations and surgeries, we were all running around and pitching in as best we could. Those were very hard years for me. My marriage was unstable, but it hadn't fallen apart yet. When I got news that my wife was pregnant, it built me up again. I was struggling to hold on to my sobriety, but I didn't let anyone know that I was such bad shape. In hindsight, I probably should have spoken to someone about it, but a man's pride is a formidable foe, especially when it's his own. I had been sober since 1995 and right when I felt like my wheels were coming off, I found out that I was going to be a father. It was the just buoy that I had needed. It would keep me afloat for the time being and at the same time, anchor me to something solid that I could look forward to. For some time, my wife and I had endured a separation or two and even though we had a few weeks at a time that were decent, I was having a lot of trouble turning back the clock and letting go of the anger that I felt towards her. She had made a few mistakes along the way, like anyone else, but none of them unforgivable. She had lost her mother right before we had gotten married and it might have been a good idea to postpone the wedding for some time so that she could have the proper time to grieve. Maybe it would have helped in the long run, but we didn't change our plans.

The way I saw it, the time was never going to be right. She was living in Tampa, Florida and she needed to get back to NY and finish her schooling. Everything was booked and paid for so it was just a matter of walking down the aisle. So we did. We had the love for each other for certain, but we didn't have the patience. My beautiful baby daughter was born in April of 1999, and it reunited everyone. Everyone was thrilled to see this little piece of heaven in our bassinet and again it seemed like everything was going to work out. I was still struggling not to drink, as my wife and I went through yet another period of separation, but I was hanging on and dealing with working two jobs and helping Gilbert get back and forth. Even though I had advised him against it, he decided to let the Doctor's amputate his cancerous leg from the knee down. I was completely against it of course, because it was just further proof that Gilbert was just as human as the rest of us. He had always been a superhero in my eyes, but the reality of his humanity was too much for me to witness. I told him that whatever this world has in store for us, it would better to face it on his own two feet.

I was being selfish undoubtedly, because I didn't want to see him that way. He knew that his odds of survival were better if he had his leg amputated, but the thought of him being crippled that way was very difficult for me to handle. He went through with it and that was only the first of many surgeries he would have in order to prolong his life. After his surgery, we were all at the hospital and he was lying in the bed in unimaginable pain. I walked in and seeing an empty space where his leg used to be made me dizzy as the room started to spin. I didn't fall, but I had to lean my back onto the wall so that I wouldn't go over. I think this was probably my first experience with having an anxiety attack and before I knew it, I had to sit down on the floor of the hospital room in order not to fall on my face. I was trying to regain my composure because I didn't want Gilbert to see me that way, especially now that he had bigger things to worry about. A nurse snapped me out of it, although I don't know how long she'd been standing in front of me trying to tell me to stand up. Eventually, I did, and I went home feeling like a piece of me had been cut off as well. Gilbert's cancer was an ordeal for everyone and anyone who has ever had someone in their family battle that unforgivable animal called cancer, will tell you just how much effort and support is required of everyone involved.

On the long days of chemotherapy, we took turns picking up Cheena from school. Some days I had to drive Gilbert back and forth from the hospital. Well, he would drive himself there knowing that the next round of chemotherapy would wipe him out and leave him much too weakened to drive his own car. Sometimes, after the chemotherapy, he was incapacitated for a few days and I would have to go to work for him. He had a job driving a truck delivering pager parts and cases for two Jewish brothers that owned the business and we worked out a deal. On the days that Gilbert could not get behind the wheel, I would drive them around to all their stores all over New York.

Those guys loved my brother and they constantly went out of their way to make it work for him. They didn't want him to lose his job, but they needed a steady reliable driver in order to run their business so I agreed to drive when Gilbert could not. I would be half asleep behind the wheel at times, having just finished a twenty-four hour shift at eight am. I then had to drive for ten to twelve hours until they had finished whatever business they had for the day. I would get home after working thirty-six hours straight and still I could not sleep. I would stay on the computer for hours, until the sunrise sometimes, because I couldn't find it in me to sleep and relax. Gilbert was constantly on my mind and I could not figure out what to do in order to save him. I knew that there was nothing that I could do. I would pray and beg God to spare him somehow, but truthfully, I knew it was completely out of my hands. Maybe that's what kept me up at night.

Gilbert went through another surgery and at one point, it seemed that they had gotten all the cancer out. He had undergone a few PET scans and they could not find any cancerous cells in Gilbert's body. It was nice to see Gilbert with a smile on his face after suffering so much in such little time. He had pieces of his lung removed and been through countless rounds of chemotherapy in the past year, to go along with the amputation of his leg. We had a few months of relative quiet in the family, but between my wife and me brawling over the silliest things and Gilbert being in and out of the hospital, this thing called life was really taking a toll on me. I really have no right to complain, considering that Gilbert was the one who truly suffered for so many years. He suffered the pain, suffered the countless surgeries, and suffered the knowledge that his time with his family and children was extremely limited. A few months later one of Gilbert's PET scans came back positive and just like that, we were back in the struggle. They had found cancerous cells in his spinal fluid and he had to go through another round of tests, just like he had done before. A few months later, they found cancerous spots in his lungs again and he went through another round of chemotherapy, to shrink the spots they had found, followed by another surgery to remove pieces of his lung.

I had lost track of just how many surgeries he had endured at that point, but it was clear to me that my brother was being cut away piece by piece, and if something didn't give, there wasn't going to be anything left of him. We were adults now and I probably outweighed him by thirty pounds, without discounting the fact that he now had a prosthetic leg that he was slowly learning to walk in, but no matter the circumstances, he was my big brother. We still argued and disagreed about everything in general, that hadn't changed and I knew for the first time in my life, I could finally kick Gilbert's ass if we got into a fight. Well, that was a maybe. Sure, it had taken cancer, an amputation and years of toxic chemicals being pumped into his body to put us on at an even match, but the truth is that at this stage of our lives, there was no way we would be taking that avenue ever again. He would always be my big brother. I could have been one hundred pounds heavier than Gilbert and it would matter not, for he still held a very powerful and authoritative position in my life and that could never change. He had been in my corner for my entire life. The time had passed for our fist fighting and any kind of physical confrontation.

We were men now and we kept our disagreements to verbal confrontations every once in a while. I'm more than a little ashamed to admit that I truly did not understand what he was going through and I vehemently disagreed with some of the decisions he was making. I was opinionated and combative when I really should have been quiet, and listened to whatever Gilbert wanted to say and do. You see what I really didn't understand is that while we are all on a clock that will expire someday, people that are seriously ill have a clock that runs a lot faster than normal. Gilbert was facing life and death every single day, trying desperately to extend his life to raise his two daughters, and I actually had the audacity to tell him that he was doing it all wrong. But in fact, I wasn't really fighting with Gilbert. I was fighting with the reality that I was going to lose him sooner than later and those were circumstances that I simply could not accept. I knew that I was not strong enough to lose Gilbert and I was terrified of the downward spiral that I would enter if that ever happened. I was getting used to being an everyday citizen, but my unraveling loomed over me like a death sentence. I knew just how close I was to having a drink and I knew that once I put the bottle to my lips, it would just bring me that much closer to going off the deep end again. I would talk to him sometimes when I would drop him off at home, or when I would bring him the truck that he was going to drive the next day and he would always talk me down. Some nights I saw it in his face that he did not have the energy to talk to me, much less drive me back to my house with the truck. I would take a nice long walk home on those nights. I was never in a rush to go home those days, because there was no comfort waiting for me at all. So I would walk and sit on Ocean Parkway, the same stretch of road that I had sat down many years before and unburdened my tortured past on my girlfriend. I would sit there and just think, sometimes for ten minutes and sometimes for hours. I would lie to my wife and tell her that I was at the gym, or was playing basketball, or whatever story I could come up with in order to avoid being home.

I felt like I had no one to talk to, because Peter had changed. He had gotten involved pretty heavily with gambling and cocaine and those things were just not for me. He had also gotten serious with a girl so I rarely saw him anymore. I was becoming incredibly insulated, which was definitely a sign that I was becoming unraveled at the seams. I can be loud person, without a doubt, boisterous and somewhat obnoxious in some ways. When I'm quiet, however, is when I'm at my worst, internally speaking. I tend to be melancholy, withdrawn and removed from conversations when I drift off into my own psyche and it never leads anywhere good. When I reach those lows, that's when I find the bottom of every bottle. But

161

for the time being, I was barely hanging on and praying for the road ahead of me and my family.

There's one memory of Gilbert's battle with cancer that brings me joy and every time I think about it. It makes me laugh to myself, but then the momentary laughter is followed by the sting of sadness. One afternoon, Gilbert had to go to chemotherapy and right afterward he had an appointment with a prosthetic company in Long Island that was going to give Gilbert a prototype prosthetic limb. They were testing the product and decided that he would be a good candidate to test out the limb on. It was actually very cool looking with a Nike swoosh on it in the thigh area. After his fitting, we drove back to Brooklyn and once again, I find myself taking Ocean Parkway home. I was driving Gilbert's car because he was worn out from his session and I estimate that I was driving somewhere around forty miles an hour. I leaned back to make myself comfortable after the long drive and the steering wheel came right off its mantle and into my lap. Here we were, traveling at a high speed, in the middle lane of traffic and the steering wheel was sitting between my legs.

My first reaction was to scream. Gilbert's reaction was to scream as well, but at me.

I was yelling at the top of lungs, "Oh my God, Oh my God."

Gilbert was screaming at me "Put it Back, Put it back."

In my panic, it never dawned on me to perhaps hit the brakes and try to put the steering wheel back on. Instead, I was trying to stick it back on while the car was in motion. Somehow, the car didn't veer left or right so thank the good lord that the car had a proper wheel alignment. It simply continued to travel straight and perfectly within the traffic lane, as I wrestled back and forth with reattaching the wheel. After what seemed like an eternity, it clicked back into whatever groove it was sitting in before I had leaned back. It was more like twenty or thirty-seconds, but can you imagine traveling at forty miles an hour on the highway, without a steering wheel and having no control of the vehicle.

We came to a traffic light and I looked at him with my eyes surely bugging straight out of my head.

I looked at him and said, "What the hell is wrong with this steering wheel?"

He looked back at me like I was crazy and his expression told me that he felt like I had done something wrong. He then said something that until this day, I can still hear his voice and I don't believe he actually said it.

Gilbert said, "You're not supposed to lean back, asshole." He was actually blaming me for the steering wheel coming off.

As I learned later, Gilbert had unscrewed all the bolts holding the steering wheel to the steering column on purpose as an anti-theft deterrent. At night, he would get home, pull the steering wheel off, and take it inside with him. The next morning, the crazy bastard would grab the steering wheel and reattach it without ever putting on the bolts again. I'm sure this method was full proof and made it very hard to steal his car, but it's not something you want to find out while you are in motion on the highway. After a few blocks of driving and arguing, we started to laugh about us screaming at each other at the top of our lungs when I had initially pulled the steering wheel off. We laughed and laughed for the rest of the trip, debating who had yelled the loudest and who had panicked the most. When we finally got back to my house, we were still having a hard time catching our breath from all the laughing. It was the most I had seen him laugh in a very long time. Actually, it had been some time since I had seen him laugh at all. But for that day, maybe even for one moment out of the past few years, we were ourselves again, laughing and joking about each other like we always did when we were kids.

Eventually I had to leave him and go upstairs to my own family, but it was nice to have that moment with him. It was nice to laugh with my brother. He went in and out of the hospital for the rest of the year, until they decided that they could not help him anymore. He never said anything about being diagnosed as terminal but I could tell that something had changed somewhere along the way. His breathing continued to worsen, and his ability to get around was becoming extremely limited. It was only when he started to use an oxygen tank that I knew our days together were truly and undeniably numbered. We tried to go to his house for every holiday because asking him to leave his house in his condition was too much to ask.

On Father's day of the year 2001, the whole family went to Gilbert's house to celebrate together and he was unable to leave the bed. I sat in bed with him for hours. We watched TV together and I was doing most of the talking because he was wearing a breathing apparatus and the tubes were in his nose, making it a chore for him to speak clearly. His skin had changed to an unnatural yellow tint and I could see every bit of pain and suffering that he was going through. I loved my brother more than I have loved anyone else, but on that day, Father's Day, I prayed that God would go ahead and end his suffering. I prayed and begged our God to take him, to end his painful journey. It was no different from when we were children, and I did bad things so that Indio would stop hurting Gilbert. I could no longer watch as my brother died little by little, piece by piece, every single day. I went home that night, waited until everyone was asleep and prayed not for a miracle, but for mercy. I could take pain, but I could not take his.

Two days later, I received an urgent call. I raced to St Vincent's Hospital in the middle of the day because Gilbert had been rushed to the emergency room due to his inability to breathe. I arrived at the hospital and everyone was standing around his bed as he lay there with as more machines attached to him than I could possibly count. He was actually talking to his wife and his daughters. He actually looked a lot better than he did two days earlier on Father's Day. He looked content and happy which was a bit confusing to me to say the least. The doctors needed to perform some emergency surgery to clear some sort of mucus plug that was hindering his breathing, but they also warned him that he might not survive the procedure. His lungs were weak, his heart was laboring, and they told him that if they did the procedure, in likelihood he would go into cardiac arrest. That's when I understood why he seemed to be at peace. He was tired of the battle. His struggle and any amount of fight he had left for his life was now exhausted. Gilbert and I spoke quite candidly.

I asked him if he was sure that he wanted to go through with the procedure and he told me that he was absolutely sure. I nodded and for some reason that I cannot really explain, I knelt at his bedside and I took his hand in mine. Kelsey, his beautiful little daughter came over to the bed and shared her candy with him. It was either the innocence of her eyes, or the gesture of sharing at this moment, that gave me the slight nudge I needed to go over that emotional shelf that I had been teetering on. I began to cry. I held his hand as tightly as I could and I buried my face in his lap. I recovered my composure for a short period of time so that I say things I needed to say.

I said to him, "I love you so much Gil. I could never ask for a better brother. I didn't deserve you Gilbert. I have never done anything to earn a brother like you. I'm not sure how or even when, but we will be with each other again. I promise you this will not be the end for us. Whether it be on this side or the other, I will indeed be face to face with you again."

Gilbert looked at me and said, "I know that already. This isn't the end little brother."

I know it now and I knew it that day. I will see him again. He had both my hands in his big paw of a hand and while I wept into his lap, he told me that he loved me when I felt his other hand softly stroke my hair as he assured me that it was going to be fine. Wouldn't you know it, that even now, in what we both knew were his final moments, it was he that consoled me.

I sobbed like I had never cried before.

When I could finally speak, I still held his hand tightly and barely had the strength to pick up my head and look him in his eyes, but when I did, I said, "I'm going to see you later Gilbert, ok? I have to see you again. You understand that right?" He nodded.

He looked at me with completely certainty and said, "I'm going to see you later."

I nodded my agreement, and I left it at that. We were in accord, for better words could not possibly be spoken. We all walked out to give him a few private moments with his wife before the Doctors came in. Minutes later, after four years of battle, My Gilbert was finally at peace. My Brother, my hero was gone, and I have never truly recovered. That day, that very minute, was the day that I broke apart into many pieces and I've spent the last fifteen years of my life trying unsuccessfully to put myself back together.

I had sat there with Gilbert and told him everything that I needed to say to him. We didn't have a lot of time that day but everything pertinent was passed between us. I had the honor and privilege of holding his hands, looking at him straight into his eyes when it came the time to divide our journey. I promised him that I would see him again and I intend to keep that promise. Sometimes, as I'm driving, I think I see him driving in the opposite direction and it makes me do a double take. It takes me a moment to realize that he's not here anymore, at least not in body and it takes me on the usual roller-coaster of emotion. I have that one moment of recognition of his familiar face and it's followed by the somber thought of his departure after such a short time on this earth and in my life. I know that I will see him again and that is why we never once said Good-bye. And contrary to whatever I thought at the time, he did go out on his own two feet. He was merely tired, and ready to embark on wherever the next phase of his journey would take him. He was calm, serene, and not one bit afraid of dying. It was us, me especially, who was afraid to continue life without Gilbert in it.

Father's Day

The funny thing about me is that even though I'm somewhat dysfunctional in my own private life, I still managed to be "Johnny on the Spot" for most of my friends. I think that I have always been someone that you can count on, especially when your neck is on the line. When people needed something done, whatever it was, I just got it done. Sometimes it was using my head and sometimes I had to result to my physical nature. After going through what I had gone through as a child, I had begun to hate violence. I had become almost completely nonviolent during my earlier teenage years and I couldn't figure out why I didn't want to touch or hurt anyone. Now, of course, I realize that I was severely traumatized by what I had gone through as a child and maybe I had just had enough of it. I guess I would think of all the pain I had experienced and I couldn't see myself inflicting that same pain on someone else.

After I turned 18, something changed within me yet again and I almost began to welcome violence. I had absorbed so much abuse that it never worried me or made me nervous. I would walk into any volatile situation without a care in the world, ready and sometimes hoping to get my own head cracked wide open. I would get a phone call and someone would tell me that their little brother was surrounded by a pack of thugs or they were about to get jumped by a gang. I would tell whoever it was to come pick me up. And when we got there, I'd get out of the car, take off my jacket and shirt off and do my best to get into a fight. Sometimes we did fight, but the odd thing is most of the time we didn't.

I don't know if maybe people saw the recklessness in my eyes and wanted nothing to do with it, or maybe they didn't want to be embarrassed by me. I was still kind of small and thin but I had no fear. And that's where it came from I think for me. I had been hurt so many times that there was no way anyone else could do anything worse to me.

I would walk up to guys, six foot three inches tall, and twice my weight at the time, and say, "Hey, are we going to do this or are we here to talk?"

I was always a fan of the fair fight. I would always say win or lose we shoot a fair one. We're men, not pussies. Nobody jumps in, that's where the truth lies. All of sudden, there was the possibility of getting your ass kicked in front of everyone and too many people worry about their reputation to allow that to happen. They talk tough and want to fight when they have a gang behind them, but when it's just you without any help, they are a little more reluctant to step into the ring. And guess what? I got my ass kicked a few times. So what? I had plenty of experience with that. I'd put my neck on the line for my friends so that nobody else had to get hurt.

I have to admit; I was never a great fighter the way Gilbert was. He had skills that I could never match. My thing was that I never did mind getting hurt. I didn't really wake up or get angry till I started to bleed. Sometimes Gilbert would have to hold me down and he would have to say that he quit, because I wouldn't stop coming. He'd beat the shit out of me after we fought for some reason, but I would not quit fighting.

We actually had a fist fight inside of my friend's car. My friend Willy and his brothers were all in the car and we were squeezed into the backseat. These guys were like brothers to me and we spent a lot of time together in my teens. I made a joke about Gilbert and we started cackling like hyenas in the back. Gilbert got pissed off and smacked me right in the face in front of everyone. Everything was silent for a few moments until I hauled off and punched Gilbert in his face as hard I could. We started to brawl and he started to get the best of me, so I covered up while he peppered me with punches. Finally, he stopped swinging at me and just when he thought it was over, I punched him in his face again. Again, he started to beat on me as I was trying to cover up but he was tagging me all over the place. He might have stopped to catch his breath and there I went, POP, right in his mouth. This went on for a while and everyone in the car was screaming and yelling, trying to stop the fight. Every time they thought it was over and believed me to be beat into submission, I'd surprise them with a little jab into Gilbert's face or ear. Finally, Willy and his brothers had to hold me down and sit on me for the rest of the car ride.

When I look back, I think that maybe I was so miserable inside that I was asking someone to take me out. I guess that made me pretty handy to have around when someone was in trouble. I never fancied myself a tough guy, but my willingness to put my own safety on the line made me an asset. Truthfully, I never did mind a bit of pain. I had taken so much by the time I was barely a teenager that there was nothing anyone could threaten me with. I knew that I could take it. What I couldn't take was friends of mine or someone that I loved being hurt. I cannot watch or hear someone that I care about being hurt in some way, because it makes me furious and sad at the same time. So I guess I just would always rather that it be me.

But many times people would come to me in other situations that had nothing to do with fighting and there were times that I actually had to use my brain. I had always been good at getting the old gray matter working. I think I realized that for the first time in that sophomore year of High School, when I had gotten my friend Peter elected President, even though nobody in the school actually knew who he was. I had actually become quite good at fixing things when they were broken. Most importantly, when shit went wrong, really wrong, I was usually the one that got a call. If things were bad, I fixed them. It's vague, I know, but it's also quite simple. I fixed broken situations. Sometimes it was a financial thing. Sometimes it was a domestic violence thing, but whatever it was, I handled it. I readily walked myself into sticky situations, without regard or worry for myself and never once did I fail to deliver or receive any repercussions. It just fit for me since I had very little regard for myself. I was good at keeping calm and collected in potentially dangerous situations. And most importantly I was good at keeping my mouth shut about it. People in desperate situations also tend to pay well. For years, because of my demeanor, I had made quite a bit of money by keeping my head in the worst of times. As I've mentioned before, my chaotic childhood has left with me some pretty interesting side affects. Some of them bad, but my ability to adapt and access on the fly has proven to be priceless. My reputation grew and before I knew or intended, it became a business. This is what I had become.

Sometimes you get called upon to get someone out of somewhere while there are surrounded by an angry mob. Sometimes someone had overdosed. Or sometimes you get called by someone in need while you are having breakfast with your kids on Father's Day morning, like I was. That's when you realize just how fast your happy go lucky little life can spin completely out of control.

I was a different man by then. I had settled down, gotten married, and had my children. I had decided that I was going to try my hand at being a tax paying citizen.

I'm not ashamed to say that I had a lot to fear those days, because it was actually a healthy fear for my own well-being. My biggest fear then and still is, is to do something that would bring shame or embarrassment to my children. If something happened to me, I was deathly afraid that my children would be subjected to the same poor and hopeless childhood that I had experienced. Just with that, I felt like I had too much to lose. I also had a somewhat normal life by then. I had gotten much closer than I ever was to my family and I had managed to surround myself with very good people. I was having marital woes already but my wife and I still managed to keep the nucleus of our little family together. We would still meet every Sunday morning and attend church as a family.

On a particular Sunday, it was Father's Day and I was not in the best of moods. Being a dad, you would think that I would look forward to Father's day every single year. It's the one day of the year that we as men finally get a pat on the back, albeit a small one, but a pat on the back nonetheless. Growing up fatherless, it never had been particularly meaningful to me by any means, so all the commercials and sales that were announced in the honor of all dads everywhere went right over my head. It was only after I became a father myself that it dawned on me just how important that day is, never mind the fact that we never get gold or expensive gifts like mom's get on Mother's Day. We're happy with a bag of new socks or maybe some under shirts from your children and a hand written card. The sentiment is still there though the expense is not. That is fine with me. During one of my early days as a father I had something happen that was, for all intents and purposes, out of the ordinary. After I had my children, I was convinced that I had finally achieved a respectable level of "normalcy" and would never have to put myself at risk ever again, but life doesn't always go as you plan.

This Father's Day would be like no other. After church, we decided to go get a nice breakfast together as a family and while I was sitting and enjoying my western omelet, I got a phone call from one of my past cohorts. My friend Peter, who I had known for many years, was on the other side of the call and he was screaming at the top of his lungs. I could barely understand him but from what I could make out, his brother had gotten himself into some serious trouble. He was absolutely frantic. I could hear screaming and unknown objects being smashed to pieces all around him.

He begged me to come to his brother's house and even though I had never been to his brother's apartment, I knew that he lived in the same building as Pete.

Still, I wasn't in that business anymore. He would have to call someone else to go clean up whatever mess they had going on in that apartment. If that wasn't enough, then I'd be forced to remind him that it was in fact Father's Day. I hadn't seen Peter in years and even though we had been extremely close at some point in our lives, life had gotten in the way and we had gone on separate paths. It had probably been seven years since I had seen Peter and I really couldn't recall how we had left off, but I'm sure that it had something to do with his wife hating me as well as his increasingly bad and dangerous habits. I had saved his neck and life on more than a handful of times, yet when it came time to stand by me as a friend, he chose to appease his wife and abandoned the brotherhood we had cemented in blood.

So goes life. Shit happens, right? There was no chance in hell that I was going to leave my family on this special day, to go fix a situation that Pete's brother had most likely played a big part in until it had spun out of control. This is almost always the case. People play. All is fine and dandy as long as the game you are playing stays within whatever safe boundaries you have established for yourself. Then it gets out of your control and you try to contain it, only to make it worse. That's when people reach out for help, and they try to explain that everything was fine, until it wasn't and somehow they just don't know how things had gotten out of hand. That was usually when my phone would begin to ring. After my phone rang that day and I explained to Pete that it was out of my hands, he said something to me that most people will only say out of sheer desperation. He promised me anything I wanted. He said money was no object and that he would be eternally grateful, thankful and in debt to me if I were to make this one exception. I figure that this had to be pretty bad if this guy was promising his life. To be honest, it would be nice to make a little bit of invisible cash and feel alive again after being on permanent daddy duty for the past few years. Maybe I was speaking a bit facetiously earlier when I stated that there was absolutely no way that I was going to clean up that mess. Perhaps I just needed the right motivation. It also added a little extra satisfaction to know that after all these years, Pete had come back to me on his hands and knees begging for my help.

Before I knew it, I was asking my wife for the green light to go take care of "something" and I promised to be back within the hour. An hour is all you usually need to clean up any kind of mess and that's usually double the time allotted to anyone in a pinch. Anything more than that, more often than not, you were hopelessly fucked. Wouldn't you know it, I went. I figured that I'd be back with my babies before nap time was over.

I wasn't always on the right side of the law. I'd been known to carry a small arsenal at times, but those days were long behind me. I still had a few weapons lying around so I stopped at my house for a mini Glock 9MM that I could carry without much of a noticeable bulge. It fit nicely into my waistband, which was a plus, but I never liked the way it felt in my hand. It was somewhat small and just didn't feel right in my grip. My aim was surgical with a bigger firearm, but the mini Glock had many advantages. It was virtually undetectable which was great and I would feel a lot better going into a possibly volatile situation with a little steel.

When in doubt, come heavy, that's what I always say. It is certainly better to have it and not need it, than to need it and not have it. I was satisfied with my current level of protection and was pretty sure that it really wasn't going to be necessary anyway so I went on my way. Time is money and I was there very quickly. I arrived at Pete's building in five minutes, and after scanning all the names on the side of the doorbells, I ascertained which one belonged to his brother. I rang the bell and I was quickly buzzed in without anyone inquiring just who it was that was ringing. Mistake number one was made just as I arrived. For all they knew, someone could have heard the ruckus and called 911. They could have just let a whole squad of cops in without them having to ring twice. I took the stairs even though the apartment was all the way up on the sixth floor. I have nothing against elevators, but they tend to have cameras mounted somewhere. In these unknown situations, it's most certainly advantageous for self-preservation not to have footage and a nice eight by ten photo for the boys in blue to go by if for some God forsaken reason, things were to go wrong. As I got to the sixth floor, I was a bit out of breath, so I took a few extra moments to compose myself before I went in.

It's much harder to gain control of a situation when you yourself appear to be flustered and sweaty. When I was ready and felt sufficiently in character, I knocked on the door. I gave three forceful knocks as is my custom. Not forceful enough to rattle the door, but enough to announce my arrival. You knock too hard and you attract attention. You knock too soft and you come off like a rabbit, meek and helpless. And you also lose precious time if you have to knock again. I could hear harried whispers on the other side of the door and then I heard Pete's strained voice as he asked who it was that was knocking.

I quickly answered, "It's me" again as is my custom and a very good idea not to use names.

I heard rattling on the other side of the door and then the door opened, but only as far as the safety chain on the other side of it would allow. Pete's harrowed face popped into view, and when he saw it was me, I could see the look of relief on his face. He closed the door and undid the safety chain. He opened the door, and rushed me in, pulling me by the shirt before he rushed to close the door again. I asked him politely to keep his hands to himself. I wasn't in the habit of being man-handled by anyone other than my woman and him pulling on my shirt was going to get on my nerves in a hurry. He apologized absentmindedly and we both knew that he had bigger things on his mind than offending me.

There was a smell in the air that was very familiar. I had been hit with mace once or twice before in my life and when you get hit with it, it's an aroma that you will never forget. I'm not exactly immune to it, but it doesn't have the same effect on me that it has on most people. It irritates me quite a bit, but not as much as the rest of the population I suppose. The apartment was rank with a cloud of mace. I started to think that maybe I had wasted my time if I had come here for someone who had been playing around with mace and had permanently screwed up somebody's eyes. That's a dilemma for a hospital or an emergency room, not for me. Peter had one minute to persuade me to stay. He reached out to touch my shoulder, maybe to guide me into the kitchen and when I looked at his hand he pulled it back quickly remembering our short exchange just moments ago.

He stopped short of the door, as if he didn't dare to go any further and then he said, "She's in there."

I looked at him and was debating whether to ask him what he was talking about, or to wait for him to elaborate on just what was behind the door. My first thought was

173

whoever "She" was, might be dead. Then I heard a noise from the kitchen and I looked at Pete. Whoever it was, she was moving around, unless Pete's brother was in there making more of a mess of it in there.

Pete shrugged his shoulders, and said, "I don't know her name, but she's in there. She's been in there all morning and refuses to come out."

This was going to be easier than I thought. She was still alive so that was one less headache to deal with. I really couldn't believe that he had called me here for an out of control chick, probably high as a kite, who was apparently armed with mace and had barricaded herself in the kitchen. This was a proverbial lay-up. I asked Pete where his brother was, and he said he had to lock him into his own bedroom just so the girl would stop spraying mace all over the house. That was a bit of a head scratcher but I guessed that I would ask later if the need came. but usually I'm not too inquisitive about the details. You just get lied to.

I asked, "Just you two and the girl in the house? Nobody else?"

"That's it, just us", Peter replied.

I instructed Pete to go into the bedroom with his brother, it would certainly be better if it was just me. I knocked on the doorway three times before I walked in. The noise and scurrying came to an abrupt stop as I announced myself and told whoever she was that I was coming in, alone. I really didn't know what to expect once I had crossed the threshold into the kitchen, but whatever happened, I knew that I would definitely have an intense and possibly drug induced maniacal set of eyeballs fixed on me the minute I entered through the doorway. There was no response and as I had done many times before, I walked into the unknown.

How do I say this? She was fucking beautiful. She was of Latino decent, of that I was sure. She was tall, had long beautiful hair, and even longer legs. She also had a body that women normally pay for and can only achieve after they endure one painful surgery after another. However, she was completely natural. I've never seen a better body and I knew this because she was completely naked. Her completely bloodshot eyes were fixed on me just as I expected, and that was where her beauty ended. One of her eyes was an odd color that I had never seen before. It had been a different color before, most likely the same as her other eye which was a hazel green. The defective eye was now a milky gray. It was odd seeing a woman so beautiful which one little flaw that completely un-nerved you. I tried to imagine what exactly had happened to her eye.

Ah yes, there was one other little detail. In her right hand, she was holding a meat cleaver roughly the length of my arm from the elbow down. That was certainly one little detail that I would have appreciated from Pete. Just a little "Hey by the way, there's an ax wielding maniac on the other side of that door" would have been nice. The look on her face was unmistakably rabid, as she had every intention of putting that knife to work.

I started to doubt myself and my abilities, even though I had walked into far worse situations and I had diffused more volatile events than this. Yet something, perhaps something as usually unnoticeable as the density of the air, was off that day. Was it the smell? Whatever it was, I was not one to ignore my senses. In contrast, it made me pay even more attention to the little details that other people might normally miss. Most people might take one look at this woman, at her small stature and completely naked ample attributes and think that this was going to be a piece of cake, but not me. I coaxed the rest of my body through the doorway and took a small step into the room. I was not exactly barging in, so that I had a little bit of room for retreat in case things got ugly in a hurry. Her eyes were glued to me but the expression on her face changed to something that seemed like bewilderment. Also, though it seemed impossible, a degree of recognition. I had never seen this woman before in my life but I'll be damned if I didn't see her cock her head to the side like a confused dog. The sneer on her face appeared to dissolve as well, but I knew that meant absolutely nothing.

Having nothing else to say besides the obvious, I slowly picked up my right hand and waved.

I said, "Hi".

She didn't return the salutation. Instead she continued to stare at me.

When the curiosity became too much for her to bear, she finally asked, "Who the fuck are you?"

I smiled at her, trying to break down her completely reasonable and pragmatic apprehension. I said, "My name is not important. Let's just say I'm a friend."

A small sample of her previous sneer creased her face again, as she said, "You ain't my fucking friend."

Perhaps I had used the wrong terminology. Or maybe even used the word "friend" in an improper context. Either way, she called me on it and I was going to have to circumvent around that word. I didn't apologize, an apology suggests sorrow and weakness, but I excused my use of the word in such a cavalier manner.

I tried to clarify as I said, "I should say I am a friend to this situation."

I added "I have no ties to either party here miss, I was just called in to make a situation go away and that's what I'm here to do."

I was rustier than I thought. I had used the words "go away" and within seconds she digested and processed that I was there to make her go away. I noticed the grip on her machete tighten and her eyes change back from confusion to aggression.

Before she flew off the handle, I said, "I am not here to hurt you."

The muscles in her arm were noticeably taut and I noticed that her stomach muscles were quivering as well. Her body betrayed the fact that she was scared. There is nothing worse than a scared and cornered animal. I had no control of this situation, but I talked to her as calmly as possible. I asked her name but she just continued to stare right through me. I knew that she was on the fence. She was still deciding whether she was going to come at me with the machete, or to maybe give me a few minutes and hear what I had to say, then come at me with the machete. She started to yell that she didn't need any help and that I should leave. She also hinted at the fact that she was going to chop Pete and his brother into pieces the minute I walked out the door.

As her voice rose, she started to shake the machete around in the air as if she was trying to hold it back from its intended purpose. Then she directed her attention to me, and pointed the top of the edged weapon at me as well. She informed me I was going to meet the same fate if I didn't get the fuck out. I've been threatened with bodily harm and decapitation before so it really didn't wrinkle my collar. I simply smiled impassively at her and told her that there was no need to get ugly in this situation. I also offered several alternatives to chopping everyone's head off to see what it was that she really wanted.

She said that she had been raped repeatedly all weekend, and that she had been forced to smoke crack and do heroin the entire time as well. When a woman says she is raped, people tend to believe her. The whole thing about being forced to do drugs against her will was plausible as well, but if that was really the case, why hadn't she once reached for her clothing to cover up the shame of being taken against her will. She was perfectly content to be standing there in front of me, barefoot and knife in hand, with all her clothing folded neatly into a big duffel bag.

I looked at her and thought for a moment, then asked her, "Do you want me to call the police?"

She was shocked by this and I could tell by the expression on her face that she wanted absolutely nothing to do with the cops.

Anyone who just got raped would probably want Johnny Law there as soon as possible. She had shown a little bit of her hand and I saw it. Furthermore, she saw that I saw it, and this got her a little more agitated as she started yelling and threatening to kill everyone in the apartment again. I waited until she was done and again I asked her what exactly it was that she wanted. Did she want to leave? Did she want money? Did she want me to take her somewhere? Whatever she wanted, she could have. All she had to do was tell me her wishes. She was intrigued at the mention of money, so she was certainly paying attention.

Out of the blue it seemed, she blurted that she wanted three hundred dollars and it came out as if she believed this was a sum of money that had very little chance of being given to her. If she had asked for a million dollars, maybe that was something to worry about, but three hundred dollars was quite easy to come up with in any situation. I thought that she had unintentionally low balled herself, hoping to maybe get two hundred dollars at best. I probably would have given her a thousand dollars on the spot just to avoid further mess, police contact, and having to split her head like a canoe with a hollow point round if she came at me with that machete. I also showed my hand as I agreed to the money much too quickly. She saw that too and maybe for a second she thought that she the upper hand because she started to talk about payback for what had happened to her this weekend and three hundred dollars wasn't going to be enough. She started to talk tough again and started to inch towards me as she spoke. She was also pointing the business end of the machete at me again.

I cut her off abruptly and asked her why she carried that machete. This question caught her completely off guard as was my intention. When you ask someone a question, they always seem obliged to answer. I saw the momentary confusion on her face as she stammered a bit, perhaps a little annoyed that she had not fully finished threatening my life with the full gusto that she had wanted.

She asked, "What?" But I knew that she had heard the question just fine. She was just stalling to think of a good menacing response. I obliged her nonetheless.

I asked her again, "Why do you carry that Machete?"

She answered, "I carry this shit right here for when people fuck with me."

For the last time that I was going to tolerate it, she pointed the machete in my direction. I nodded my head in full comprehension of her message and I had one of my own to deliver. I raised the front of my shirt up just a few inches to show her the Glock sitting ever so neatly and patiently in my waistband.

Her eyes were fixed on it as she attempted to look frightened, but I knew she wasn't. She wasn't terrified, or wide-eyed by my gun. She simply had to re-think her strategy was all. She tried her best to pretend the gun had scared her and she went as far as changing her voice to sound like a meek little girl.

She asked me in that faux little voice, "Why do you have a gun?"

I answered as calmly and soothingly as possible, "I carry this shit right here, for when people fuck with me."

We stared at each other for a moment, and then I went on, "You see, if I wanted to hurt you, you'd be hurt by now. I would have walked in, ended this quickly and that would have been that. There would be no talking, no back and forth, no bullshit. But I'm here, you're still here and I'm thinking there may be a better way to end this without anybody getting hurt."

She nodded her head. She asked me who I was again but that question was already asked and answered. She said that if I gave her the money, she would be on her way and nobody needed to get hurt. She didn't want to get hurt. She seemed to understand that she had brought a knife to a gun fight and maybe she would use her head and live to fight another day. She asked if she could reach into her bag and start pulling her clothes out, so that she can get dressed. I had absolutely no problem with that. Surprisingly, her entire demeanor had somehow switched, to complete cooperation. She dumped the entire content of her bag onto the kitchen floor and managed to put on a very sexy black thong.

It's funny how we men are, because even in that moment, I was looking at her and fully appreciating every inch of her. She knelt down and started to put everything back into the bag except for a few articles of clothing, when she stood up suddenly. If I had been distracted by her body, it was short lived because as soon as she stood up my senses were going off all over again. Her face hadn't changed. It was still that fake scared senseless expression, but that mask was hiding something behind it that I could not make out. I'm usually pretty good at seeing these things, but I couldn't figure this one out. Even though I know it's physically impossible to wear two different expressions on your face at the same time, I could somehow make out something behind her mask of fear. She was grinning. No, she was snarling at me behind the mask. I saw teeth and rabid eyes behind the veil she wore to disarm me. It was then my turn to cock my head sideways in confusion.

She saw that I saw yet again and abruptly dropped down to her knees again and started to rummage through her bag. She dumped the contents out all over the floor, as if she was looking for something. I granted her another minute before I opened my mouth.

Then I said, "Babe, now you're just stalling."

Yes, I actually called her babe. And as she stood up, there was something different about her now. She was back to having one face. The shit eating gnarling teeth were suddenly gone and it was the just the fake frightened little girl expression again. But her eyes had changed. I'm sure we have all seen someone with eyes that were completely bloodshot. But I'd never seen anyone's eyes actually change from white to blood red right before me. The process took seconds but it was as if I could make out every single blood vessel as it popped and turned color until all the white was gone. And there was something in her left hand, something small that I could not fully see. There were things all over the floor and as she took her dainty little pedicured foot, and swept the debris out of the way, clearing the path between us, that's when I saw it.

At the window directly behind her was my old friend, the dog that had almost gotten my soul many years before. It was staring at me intently, baring its teeth menacingly. I was no longer confused. Everything probably happened in under a

179

second but for me it felt like the next few minutes transpired in slow motion. I knew who this was. I now knew why she had somehow recognized me when I walked into the kitchen that day and why she had cocked her head just like that goddamn dog. It wasn't here for me. It was here to collect another soul, probably that of Pete's brother who apparently had done enough harm and wrong to attract this unforgiving beast. But how fortuitous was this for it? I was the one that had gotten away decades ago. I had somehow vanished from its sight. I had immersed myself under God's protection and tattooed a crucifix on the four sides of my body in order to defend myself from every angle of attack should the day ever come we met again. It had been decades since our last encounter and if you ask me, that wasn't nearly enough time.

Had she not moved slightly to her right to clear the path between us, I never would have seen it. Now that I did see it and I realized that it knew who I was, I strongly suspected that I probably wouldn't get out of that room alive.

As unbelievable and unlikely as it is, everyone, and perhaps everything has a "tell". A little weakness or a little flinch before the big bang. Skies rumble with thunder before they unleash the heavy water onto the earth. Cars sputter before they break down. Cats hiss before they attack. That little bit of warning is the telltale sign of what is to come. This dog, this hound derived from pure evil, is also governed and enslaved by the same laws we live under on this earth. The creature's weakness was in its eyes. When I had first encountered this creature many moons ago, it had come to the window hungrily seeking to devour whatever had been left for it to feed on. But when we began to rebuke it with the words of God, it had flinched slightly, giving Indio the time and courage to run directly at it and close the window right in front of its snout. I'm sure the window wasn't what prevented it from coming in after us, but the words we used to defend ourselves.

This time would be no different. I knew what this dog wanted as I was in full comprehension of its purpose in this world. I could see the dog clearly now, in full view and it had not aged a day. It still had a full black mane of hair and even though it was sitting impossibly at the window sill a full six flights up, its presence was in the room. Yes, that's what was wrong with the air when I had walked in. It was too still, too heavy. What I had mistaken for her sweat and body odor was actually that of the rank of a dog.

The girl was fuzzy in my peripheral vision but I could still feel her acute presence in the room. She was frozen in place, out of focus, yet I was keenly aware of everything in the room. I could hear a fly flapping its wings near the top of the window where the dog was seated. I could hear the distinctive hum of the florescent lights above our heads. The one thing I could not hear was my own breathing as I became aware that I had been holding my breath. It was a moment, but all the pieces on the board were set. It was the dog's move. The girl was no longer important; for I knew she had absolutely no control as to what she did next. Again, it was but a moment, but I had a flashback of her perfectly manicured feet sweeping in front of her, those pretty little feet. All of a sudden, it all became clear. I looked up at the ceiling, but I was hoping to see and reach well beyond it to the heavens as I beseeched my creator.

"God, No!"

Before I had a chance to finish, there was the "tell" that I had been waiting for. The Dog's furtive eyes suddenly looked in the direction of the girl and without hesitation I reached into my waistband to pull out my Glock. It was always in the eyes. Man or creature, the eyes do not lie. I heard her exhale sharply as she started to run straight at me, and her eyes had nothing but murder and rage behind them. Had I not seen the dog avert his attention to her, she probably would have gotten the jump on me.

The average person can close twenty-one feet on someone before they have a chance to pull out a weapon or defend themselves. We were a mere twelve feet, half of that distance, so I would have been Dead, Dead, Dead. When I saw its eyes move, I knew what was to come. I instinctively started to draw out my weapon before the deadly message to remove my head was delivered to her. She came at me with the machete cocked over her head and from her left hand, a fine red mist was coming straight at me and into my eyes. My left arm went up in defense, hoping to catch her arm on the downswing and hopefully jar it out of her hands. Any miscalculation on my part would mostly mean losing a limb during the attack. I could live without my left hand I supposed, but I wouldn't get too far in life without a head.

Well, maybe I could go to Law School, but who had the time to go back to school after all these years. I stepped forward and to my right as far as I could go before I would be pinned against the wall. Being close to two hundred and thirty pounds at the time, I was quite a wide target. The only thing going for me was that for someone with such broad shoulders and a back that you could take ad space on, I had a pretty small head. My left arm was up defensively, my next and only move was to block her left hand with the mace, but there was no way I could concentrate on both. So I picked my poison and let her mace me while centering my focus on the machete. I caught her hand right in the middle of her swing downwards. If I had been standing in the original spot in the kitchen when she attacked, the machete would have hit me squarely in the center of my forehead. Right between my eyes. But because I had also closed the distance between us, she was forced to short arm her attack taking most of the steam out of it. My left hand caught her right arm and the machete stopped in its tracks, after cutting through the top half inch of the cartilage connecting my left ear to my head. I felt the cold steel immediately, followed by the warm blood flow streaming from the side of my head and down the back of my neck. Immediately I thought, "Damn, that's going to leave a mark" and somehow laughed at myself momentarily for my clever little quip halfway through a fight for my life.

I didn't know the extent of the damage done to my ear and as far I knew, it had been sheered clear off my head for all the blood I felt pouring out of me. Still, I was thinking to myself than if an ear was all I lost then I had made out pretty well so far. I was prepared to lose my left arm so I was still ahead of the game. Besides, an actual ear serves no real purpose other than decoration. They could probably sew it back to my head upside down and it wouldn't make a difference in how well I could hear. I had her right hand firmly gripped in mine so the machete was neutralized after it had found at least a bit of its mark. I still had to remove the mace from the equation. At such a close distance, it can still hit your orb with some force and blind you regardless of your tolerance for the chemical. I spun around trying to grasp both her hands, which was impossible with the Glock in my right hand. Instead, I used the gun as a shield, blocking the stream coming out of the mace container. I used my left leg for leverage, and lifted her off the ground with my knee in between her legs.

We both landed against the wall with a thud and I heard the air escape her lungs momentarily. Her legs were dangling in the air, with my knee in her crotch and my left hand was holding onto her machete hand. I used the rest of my left arm and elbow to pin her mace hand with sheer weight and force. I was still getting hit with the chemical and it was starting to sting my face pretty good, but the Glock had blocked most of it. Then the container started to sputter and let out the harmless gas that acts as the propellant. It other words, it was out of juice. And so was she. We were face to face now, my body pinning her body to the wall and my knee planted firmly in between her legs. Since I outweighed her by at least one hundred pounds, it was safe to say that she had nowhere to go. I saw the surrender in her eyes. Oddly enough, she smiled. A coy, flirty smile that a woman uses on a man right before she teases him one last time and then finally allows him to enter her. Suddenly I felt immense heat coming from her area. She was….aroused? Inexplicably, I also began to feel that all too familiar pang of want deep within as I started to feel a stiffness against her and between us that was unmistakably….erotic? Clearly, there was a few things that I hadn't realized about myself until that very moment. She looked down as she felt me against her and smiled at me one last time before she tried to bite my face. I recoiled just in time as I heard her teeth come together, being sparsely sprayed with a bit of her saliva. That was her last move.

She opened her mouth and all she got out was the word "DO" before I pulled the trigger.

Blow back. That's what you get when you fire a high velocity round into someone's head at close range. It's neater than hitting a watermelon on stage with a sledgehammer, but the difference is the spray comes right back at you in the opposite direction of where the pressure is coming from. I was in front of her and my Glock was to the right of her temple, still, I got a nice amount of blood and fragments of skull deposited on me and into my mouth. Those of you that have gotten their teeth knocked out can agree with me, it's an odd feeling to spit out little shards of bone out of your own mouth. It is even odder when it's little pieces of skull, and you taste the iron rich blood flooding your mouth that isn't your own. I didn't spit it out just yet.

I listened carefully for any commotion, any screaming or yelling or indication that someone had heard what had happened. Other than the scurrying and loud whispers coming from the bedroom where Pete and his brother were cowering, there was nothing else. She had gone limp immediately, so it was my weight against her that was keeping her up against the wall. I let her slide down the wall slowly and as quietly as possible. After I put her down, I went into the bathroom so that I could finally spit out the blood and everything else directly into the toilet, being very careful not to leave any trace of my DNA anywhere in this place. I searched underneath the cabinets and found some bleach that I could pour into the toilet. I flushed several times, and washed off as best I could in the sink, but there was nothing that could be done about my shirt. It was then that I noticed that my ear was still attached to my head, but the top had been cut at the joint, leaving the top of my ear detached from my head. It was bloody and sticking out at an odd angle but none the worse for wear. A few well-placed stitches would probably alleviate that condition.

Next, I thought briefly about what to do about telling Pete and his brother, but there really wasn't much choice now was there. I went to the bedroom door and knocked my normal, forceful three times. After walking into the kitchen and nearly being decapitated, I wasn't up for any more surprises. Pete opened the door and I could tell by the look on his face that he knew things had gone horribly wrong. I was covered in blood and I looked like I had tried to pull a Van Gogh but had stopped halfway through. I stepped into the doorway into the bedroom and closed the door behind me. That's when I noticed Pete had a small five shot thirty-eight revolver in his hand. That annoyed me immensely, knowing that this whole time Pete could have put an end to this nonsense without getting me involved at all.

When did Pete start carrying a gun? Not only did he fail to warn me about the woman wielding an obscenely big cutting device, but he also forced me into this, on Father's Day of all days, because he didn't have the balls to handle this himself. The fact that he had a gun told me that he very well knew that there was no way in hell this situation was going to end with a peaceful resolution. After all these years, he just decided to get my hands dirty, so that he wouldn't have to. That was the thanks I got for risking my life for him countless times before.

I told Pete, "I have good news and I have bad news."

He looked at me and couldn't resist looking back and forth between my face and my ear.

He said, "Ok?"

I said, "The good news is she's gone. She came at me with the machete, as you can see but she didn't get as far as she hoped with it. The bad news is, I shot her. I definitely shot her, but she managed to get away and out of the fire escape by the living room window."

Human nature is so predictable. They both scrambled to the bedroom window hoping to get a glimpse of the girl climbing down the fire escape with a bullet wound. He didn't give a shit that I was hurt. All he cared about was the fact that the girl was finally out of the apartment.

I did Pete first. Not because he was holding a gun, but because he would be the hardest to do if he turned around and looked at my face. At one point of my life, I had loved him very much. He was like a brother to me in so many ways. Over the years we had certainly drifted, through no fault of my own, but it was he that had decided I was no longer a necessary component in his life. Please do not dare to mistake the brevity of my decision for not caring about Pete. It's what I do. I process and make decisions quickly and this would be no different. He had gone from someone that I had laid my life down for, to someone that I used to know. Without a second thought, he decided to put me and my family, my children and their future at risk just so he wouldn't have to stick his neck out for his own brother.

When he turned around to look out of the window, I pointed the Glock at the back of his head and this time I was more mindful about the blowback. No sooner than the trigger was pulled, there was blood and little pieces of brain raining dripping down the window. A second shot would not be necessary as his body slumped down against the wall. He hadn't felt a thing. Pete's brother looked at the glass in horror. I could see his reflection in the very little bit of window that wasn't covered in blood, and his mouth was agape with shock. He was trying to say something but he was obviously too overcome for words. He began to bring up his hands to his face and his mouth was open so wide that he seemed about to scream at the top of his lungs. He never made a sound, not even after I aimed the Glock to the left.

185

Moments later, he joined his brother Pete in eternal slumber.

Two brothers, gone, just like that. Three people, faded to black, just like that. Funny how life can be all fun and games and thirty-seconds later your whole fucking world can be upside down. Pete had gone right down without a sound, but his brother was making gurgling noises and twitched for a full minute before he finally succumbed. I knelt by his body and inexplicably felt the need to console him as he continued to spasm involuntarily. I put one hand on his body and advised him. "Embrace the inevitable brother." Eventually, he did.

My next thought was just as much as a reflex as anything else. I immediately began to sift through my memory banks trying to remember who I could call that would be good for some quick paperwork-free stitch work and could also be counted on to keep his mouth shut. A few names popped into my head as I gathered up all the weapons and took everything I had touched with me. Lastly, I put my bloodied shirt into the woman's bag along with her machete and grabbed one of the shirts from the closet. I was careful to wipe down the door handle after I found a shirt to my liking. I suddenly remembered the dog and spun around to the kitchen window fully expecting it to be there, waiting to pounce on me. I was sure it would sink its fangs into my throat and drag me out of the window and down to wherever it dwelled, but the dog was nowhere to be found.

Ironically, I crossed myself, as I looked up again and asked for a forgiveness that I knew would never come. There was no doubt about it now. I now belonged to the hound. He had not gotten me this time but he had succeeded in laying claim to damned soul that I was now in possession of. I was his, of this I was sure, but he would have to wait to come collect. I had a job to do. Kids to raise. A family to provide for. I refuse to let my children be burdened by the sins of their father. When the whole show is over and it's the final curtain for me, there is no doubt in my mind who it will be that will drag me kicking and screaming into the afterlife. As for my body, I was going to be laid out at the Leone funeral parlor on fourth avenue in Brooklyn, just like my two brothers before me. Until then, I was still in charge and Fido was just going to have to wait his fucking turn.

Repose

This couldn't be real. I understood every single word and syllable that fell out of Rumdog's mouth with ease and completely dispassion. He had just admitted to me that he had coldly committed a triple homicide, one of his victims being his lifelong friend. With the same nonchalant and impassive tone that one would use to tell a stranger on the subway the time. He never once blinked or stammered, but instead looked at me with his usual assessing eye. Ever evaluating the weight of his words and just how much I was willing to accept. I was frightened. Afraid to look him directly, I continued to jot everything he had said down in my composition book, hoping that he would not be looking at me when I finished writing. God knows that I was taking my time and stalling as long as I could while I formatted a plan in my head as to how to get out of here in one piece. I couldn't believe what I had gotten myself into and at the same time, everything he said sounded like something I had read or heard before.

Was Rumdog telling me the truth or was he just pulling my leg and repeating something he himself had heard? This could not be the case. I had believed every gripping word he had said to me and I had gone as far as somehow viewing it in my head as if I was watching a movie. It all seemed so real to me. So familiar?

I had gotten so entrenched in my writing that when I looked up, I noticed for the first time that Rumdog had left the room. This was my chance to get out. I could simply walk out of there, or rather, smartly run out with my laptop and composition books in tow. Is this what he wanted me to do? Was he testing me yet again, seeing if I would bolt and give him the excuse he needed to kill yet another friend? Would I be victim number four? I am assuming that the triple murder he had just confessed to had been the only time he had killed. What if there was more? What if this was simply old hat to him and he had lured me here in order to continue killing.

No, this was my idea. I had insisted on coming here and hearing his tale, wanting to put his story on paper. This whole thing had been of my own volition and there was no way around that. The nosy, probing and desperate for a story writer in me had gotten me into this and now I had to somehow get out of here with my head firmly attached to my shoulders. I started to shove all my belongings in my backpack quickly and was thinking of the quickest and wittiest excuse to leave so abruptly but I knew that he would see right through that. The one thing I needed to avoid was provoking him in any manner whatsoever. If what he said was true and believe you me, I did believe him, he could snatch the life out of someone with relative ease and little remorse. I would have to think of something better. It came to me suddenly, but I was reluctant to leave behind the tools of my trade. I could tell him that I needed something from outside but in order to do that, I would have to walk out of here without my backpack. I would have to leave my books and computer behind and run for my life the minute I got outside the door. What was I thinking? As long as I got out of here alive, it doesn't matter what I left behind. No story was worth my life.

I needed to act now. When I stood up, my knees were weak and my legs were shaking. I had never been so scared in all my life. I attempted a step forward but the fear had completely paralyzed me. My legs felt grounded by gravity, making them feel like each weighed a ton and it took all my energy and nerve to take one simple pace forward. I heard the floorboards creak underneath my weight and I froze again. I tried to listen for movement but the sound of my heartbeat in my own ears was deafening. I had never been a brave man, but to be terrified like this was simply a new level of helplessness. For a moment, I felt someone behind me and I spun around, fully expecting to see Rumdog standing behind me, with the business end of a firearm pointed straight at me. I even imagined his unemotional steely eyes fixed on me as he prepared to dispose of me quickly and without regret, but when I turned, I was alone in the room.

The chair I had been sitting in had its back to the wall, making it impossible for anyone to sneak up behind me, yet I could feel his presence still in the room. Even though my ears were completely occupied with the incessant pounding of my heart, my eyes were still working fine. I scanned the room and every hidden corner until I felt satisfied that the living room was populated by just me. I finally worked up the nerve to take a second step and it was equally betraying. The floor squeaked even louder this time and again I froze, taking shallow breaths so that I wouldn't pass out or breathe loud enough for him to know that I was on the move. Again, I tried to listen for movement, but there was none.

I had always been one to become engrossed in my writing, shutting out the world as I tried to put my thoughts down into words, but how was it that I had gotten so lost in my work, that I had not heard Rumdog walk in and out of this room. My first two steps had been careful and wary, yet it had announced my movements throughout the apartment. After listening closely for a few seconds, I finally mustered the courage to make a break for it. I didn't want to go like this, killed and anonymously dumped somewhere for the rats to feed on. I had a family to provide for and that was the exact thing I needed to motivate my lower extremities into movement. I could see the front door of the apartment and simply put, I ran for my life.

I'd like to tell you that I made it out and got away. I'd like to tell you that I ran out of there like a bat out of hell. That I got home and hugged my kids, promising that I would never leave their side again, but happy endings only happen in Hollywood. I made it as far as the front door and when I reached to unlock the door, I noticed for the first time that it had one of those double-sided locks that Rumdog had mentioned before.

When he was a child and the woman had kept him and his sibling's captive, she had locked all of them in with a double-sided lock. The lock would require a key to get into the apartment, as well as a key to get out. I had never seen one before and when he had told me the story, I had imagined what it might look like. There was a cylinder on this side of the door as well and I was without a key. I hadn't noticed Rumdog lock the door behind me when I had walked into the front door, but who stops to notice these things? Somebody lets you into their home and you don't stop to watch them lock the door, hoping that they won't lock you in. You simply put your things down and look for a good place to sit.

I was in a full panic now and I spun around with my back to the door, again fully expecting him to be right behind me, but I was still alone. To my left was the kitchen window. Briefly, I thought about jumping but I was way too high to pull that off. At my age, both my legs would shatter and as bad as a prospect as that was, it still beat being murdered. I was trapped. I was scared and there was nowhere for me to run to. I contemplated calling the police but he would surely hear that. Even if the police did come, what was I going to say? I still had no clue what Rumdog had in mind for me, and I think they'd need a good reason for them to respond. Besides, I didn't see a phone nearby, or in the apartment for that matter. I glanced against the kitchen walls and back towards the living room, but there wasn't any evidence of a phone line anywhere. What I did see, however, was a set of kitchen knives sitting on the table.

This part of the apartment had tile floors so I would be able to cover the distance without a sound at least. I walked as quietly as possible and removed one of the knives from its wooden sheath. It was the biggest of the set but I still felt vulnerable. No way I was going to go without a fight, so I removed another knife and decided I would go with the two handed approach. It would have to do.

This was it. I crept slowly back towards the living room, because for some reason, I suddenly felt the urge to fight for my life. I not only intended to win this fight, but I also wanted to take my things with me when I left. I put the smaller knife down and started to slowly and quietly pack all my writing materials into my bag, keeping a keen eye on the door the entire time. I zippered the bag using my one free hand, then slung it over my shoulder. I switched the knife from my right, my dominant hand, and slung the other strap over my shoulder. I then picked up the second knife and gripped both of them tightly, as I began to creep my way over to the other side of the apartment. Other than my footsteps, there hadn't been a single sound in the apartment other than those made by yours truly.

Can you imagine what I looked like? Can you imagine the embarrassment I would feel if I opened the bedroom door, and Rumdog had been in there resting? Still, simply being embarrassed was worth the risk. I needed out of the apartment and I didn't appreciate being locked in at all. Even if I was overreacting and he had no plans to kill me, I had to get out of there quickly. I continued to inch forward, knives pointed forward, until I reached the walkway in the apartment that led to two doors. The door on the left led to the bathroom, and the other door led to his bedroom.

I was angry with myself for being in this situation and even angrier that Rumdog had brought me here, probably thinking that I would go without a fight. Then I reminded myself again that this whole thing had been my idea. I had insisted on intruding in his life. It was I that had come to him and asked to hear his story. Or did I? I had been thinking it, hadn't I? He had seemingly read my mind and asked the actual question, hadn't he? He asked me "You want to write my story, don't you?" I had swallowed the bait like a fish. But how had he known that it was exactly what I wanted to hear? Is my desperation and need for a story written all over my face?

Somehow, he had known. Now I was here, appropriately fearing for my life. Yet, the first time, I felt somewhat tough. I was ready to take on this psychopath and I had no idea where this sudden burst of courage was coming from. Then it dawned on me. I had consumed maybe half of a bottle of whisky during our long day together. I was drunk. I had always been someone that could hold my booze quite well, and even if I wasn't slurring and stumbling all over the place, it didn't mean that I wasn't drunk. Now that I had been walking about the apartment a bit, I had broken into a cold sweat and I could actually smell the alcohol seeping out of my pores.

From where I was standing in the middle of the apartment, I could see back into the living room by leaning back, and at the same time, I could still keep my eye on both doors that Rumdog was possibly behind. When we had started, the room was brightly lit with the light of day coming in through the windows. Now the apartment had an eerie light, not dark, yet not light anymore as I deduced that it was getting very close to night time as the sun set to the West. I could still see but my eyes were still trying to adjust and when I did peek into the living room, I saw that I had indeed drank quite a bit of the whisky. I was closer to three quarters of a bottle in, however, not the half bottle I had guessed earlier.

Ok, so I was drunker than I thought, but I was still very much in charge of my facilities. It did explain my beer muscles, the sudden uncharacteristic bravery I was displaying, but it did concern me that maybe I shouldn't be inebriated when my life might very well be on the line. I had often been accused of having a hollow leg, and that was where all the booze went, my friends would say, but I still knew that right now I was not in any position to take anyone on. I glanced towards the chair that Rumdog had sat in, trying to make out the rest of the landscape in the quickly darkening room. It was only then that I noticed that the bottle of Rum he had been drinking was still almost completely full. The cap was off, and there was a small glass sitting on the table, filled to the top with the clear liquid. He hadn't consumed

191

a single drop the entire time.

That was just great. Not only was I feeling increasingly shit-faced, but now I had the knowledge that my possible adversary was completely sober, as well as an experienced stone cold killer. The thought of suddenly referring to Rumdog as an adversary was completely mind numbing as I tried to get a grasp on my own panic. This was also his home turf, as if he needed any more advantages. I stood in the hallway, still waiting to hear some sort of furtive moment, but there was nothing at all. Was he lying in wait? Was he waiting patiently for me to stick my inquisitive head into a doorway, making a prime target of myself? I thought about turning the light on, but quickly though better of it. Why not just paint a bulls-eye on myself? I had to do something quickly, before the apartment was completely engulfed by darkness. I decided to try the bathroom first. I walked a little faster now, needing to beat the fast approaching darkness and got to the bathroom rather quickly. The bathroom door was slightly open and I could see no light or activity in the room, but I still had to make sure that it was empty. I reached for the door slowly and carefully, trying not to make any noise. I placed my hand against the cool painted wood and I was instantly enthralled by how good the coolness felt against my hand. I was sweating profusely and my ears felt like there were burning against the sides of my head. I thought of placing the side of my face against the cold plane, but then the image of a knife or a bullet going right through my ear quickly dissuaded me of that notion. I took a deep breath, and I pushed the bathroom door open. The door swung ajar without a sound or complaint from its hinges. In the movies, even the doors wish to be noticed as more than an extra, and always announces its opening with a slow scary squeak. Thankfully, the only sound it made was when it bumped softly against the tile wall behind it.

The sound, in the quiet soundless apartment, sounded to me like a stack of plates crashing to the ground. I winced and silently cursed myself for pushing the door just a bit too hard and waited for the repercussions. Nothing, still. I crept into the bathroom and towards the shower curtain, fully expecting the surprise of my life to be lying in wait behind it, so I moved forward without a sound and with both knives pointed forward. I was taking no chances. I held my breath as I finally reached the shower curtain and with one knife remaining menacingly pointed forward, I used the other knife to slowly slide the curtain over till I was sure that no one was standing behind it. I was still alone and that meant the bedroom was the only room left unchecked.

By the process of elimination, it was the only room that Rumdog could possibly be in. I spun slowly in order to walk out of the bathroom, as I was much too terrified to back myself out of there. Oddly enough from my right, I suddenly felt Rumdog's obtrusive and oppressive stare baring down on me and it made me freeze in my tracks. I didn't spin around this time, but slowly rolled my eyes to the right just in case he had magically appeared in the room. If I moved too quickly, he might know that I saw him, thus eliminating the element of surprise. There was nothing to my right except the bathroom mirror that I had just passed upon my exit. I took another deep breath of relief and continued to creep out of the bathroom.

I was losing the light of day much too fast for my liking and to my dismay, I knew that I would have to turn on a light at some point. I felt somewhat cloaked in the darkness, my eyes having already adjusted to the lack of light, and being spotted easily and in my drunken state was certainly not to my advantage. I was now standing right in front of his bedroom door and always having a wild imagination, I suddenly envisioned a hail of bullets blasting through the door and hitting me in several different parts of my body. I crouched down and bladed my body sideways as to make myself a smaller target. The sound of my heartbeat was completely deafening again. The option of hyperventilating and passing out was also a possibility, but I hoped that wouldn't come into play. That would be the very definition of laying down and dying, but I had already made up my mind that I wasn't going to go quietly. I reached for the doorknob and again was startled to alertness by just how cool it felt in my hands. My body felt as if it were ablaze with fever, but I didn't feel the ache in my joints that usually accompanies sickness.

I was simply burning with anticipation. Let's not forget that I was also drenched as my body attempted to cool itself with alcohol tainted sweat. My arms felt heavy, my legs felt shaky, and I was quickly spiraling towards an anxiety attack, something that hadn't happened to me in a very long time. It also dawned on me that despite my newfound liquid courage, my current physical state was as good as it was going to get. That very thought is what finally propelled me into Rumdog's bedroom. It was now or never.

I burst into the room, knives forward, fully expecting darkness and death to envelop me. I ground my teeth so tightly that I actually heard some of the top layers of my teeth chip off slightly under the immense pressure. The one thing that was unexpectedly to my favor was that the back of the bedroom faced the direction of the sunset, so there was still some natural light filtering through the windows and into the room. It was barely enough to see, but enough that I wouldn't have to give up my position being fully illuminated. I wasn't sure of what to think, even after I had scanned the room from left to right and back again, stopping suddenly as my eyes gazed upon the nightstand next to the bed.

I've never been a man of war, but I knew a gun when I saw one. It was black. It looked like a sizable weapon, much better than the two kitchen knives I had in my hands. The weapon, laying conspicuously on the nightstand, still kept its deserved command for respect and reverence. Interestingly enough it had its own presence in the room, ominous and deadly, yet quiet and unassuming, just like Rumdog himself. Other than that, I was alone. And confused.

I was never comfortable around guns, maybe because it was a reminder of just how fragile and vulnerable a human life was. One little squeeze of that tiny trigger and a life was erased with relative ease. And along with the spirit, it also took a lifelong of dreams, plans, hopes and memories with it. An unaccomplished To-do list is all that's left behind. Death is usually accompanied by an obscene amount of wilting flowers. I never understood the correlation between death and flowers, but maybe it was suggested as a symbol of us returning to the ground as to fertilize the earth, hence the term "Pushing up Daisies." Or maybe, the natural perfume that flowers exude were meant to disguise the smell of death in the room. Either way, it made no sense to me.

Who knows why I was thinking about these things at that very moment, considering I had bigger fish to fry. Maybe I was moments away from a hysterical panic attack, but for now, I had to keep moving and ensure my survival. I moved quickly and quietly towards the nightstand and looked around and behind myself one more time.

I put the knife on the table and picked up the firearm. The weight of it in my hands made me feel menacing and powerful. I put the second knife down and decided to inspect the gun. I had to make sure it was loaded, as it definitely felt heavy enough, but how the hell would I know what a loaded gun felt like. I hit a little button on the side and the magazine slid out partially from the bottom. I pulled out the magazine from the well and it was indeed loaded. I slid it back in and decided that maybe I should make sure that there was a bullet in the chamber, had I the need to use this firearm tonight. I pulled back on the top of the weapon, something that I must have seen on television, to see if there was anything in there and a single bullet was ejected from the side of the weapon, landing noisily on the ground. I grimaced slightly having made that much noise, but at this point I was almost certain that I was inexplicably alone in the apartment. I repeated the action on the gun and another round came flying out. I was also aware that I was inexplicably comfortable handling it.

I turned the bedside lamp on and decided that I would go with the gun in one hand and the smaller, easier to handle kitchen knife in the other. I took a step toward the bedroom to door and thought better upon my exit. I put the smaller knife in my back pocket and handled the larger knife. No need to leave any possible weapon behind. Then I noticed a picture frame lying on the bed. The pounding in my ears came to a soundless halt. My body, heart, and brain completely froze. Laying on the bed was a picture frame. My picture frame, that I kept on my own nightstand. In it was a collage of photographs of my children.

Therein, Lies the Rub

It was as if someone had used a device to remove all of the air from inside the bedroom. How could this be? How did he get his hands on that picture frame? What was he trying to tell me? Was it a warning? Did he intend to do to me what he had done to his friend Peter? I had known Peter in high school. I had seen him from time to time while I was bar hopping in my twenties, but he had never been my cup of tea. There were rumors in school that Rumdog had rigged the high school election in favor of Peter and even though it sounded like something Rumdog was entirely capable of doing, I would think that he would have done it for monetary reasons and not out of friendship. I would never put those two together as cronies, much less paired in some sort of kinship.

Then again, I don't think anyone would ever put Rumdog and me together as well. He was, as I have mentioned before, everything that I was not. I had heard of Pete's death somewhere along the grapevine some years after high school. How many years had it been? By then, everyone was pretty much out of touch with each other anyway. It had been an ugly scene. A gory triple homicide, involving a hooker. Just minutes ago, I had become very much informed about just what had gone down that faithful morning. God knows what had happened among them in between those years but whatever it was that Rumdog had harbored, the man certainly held a grudge. Now, here I was trapped in his apartment, unable to get out. I was just like the young woman he had snatched the life out of, after she almost cut his ear off.

Yet, it didn't explain why he had left all these weapons laying around for me to use to protect myself. Was he a homicidal maniac, or was he of the suicidal variety? Did he want to die? Was it his intention to hurt my children, then return to tell me the details of his atrocities, knowing full well that I would be armed upon his return? Was he not crazy enough to take his own life? I have heard of suicide by cop, which is what happens when someone doesn't have the moxie to pull the trigger themselves, so they call the cops and make a complaint of someone with a gun. When the police arrive, they turn the gun on the cops with no intention of pulling the trigger of course, but with all the hope that the police will shoot them down and end their misery. Is that what he wanted?

I have never been fortunate enough to have any part of luck. Again, I thought to myself that this thing, this entire dilemma, was something that I had brought upon myself and my loved ones. I had sought him out and he had decided to finally introduce himself to me without a doubt. My mind was racing, my heart was about to explode and I felt like I was going to pass out with fear at any given moment. My bravado was gone. The mere thought of my children being hurt was enough to defeat any fight I had left.

He was a man of atrocities. That was the word that kept popping into my head over and over. He was capable of emotionless atrocities. I slowly began to cry, as I involuntarily leaned my backside against the wall. I slowly slid down the wall as the strength to stand left my body and I accepted what was to come. I heard the sounds of what sounded like a sobbing teenage boy, before realizing that it was me that was making that foreign sound, as I was bellowing with pained regret and mournfulness of the horrors I had unwittingly unleashed on my loved ones. Afterward, I did the one thing that we all do once all hope has been abandoned. Believer or not, it is almost always that sheer desperation that finally pushes us to reach out for the miracle that is God, once you have arrived at that point of no possible human circumvention. I slowly sank to my knees, praying for the mercy of God, and I wept.

I wept for my children. I cried out loud for the fate that was to befall them and I wept for their futures that may never be. I also felt as powerless as any man could ever feel. Even if I could break a window and start screaming for help, there was no way the police would ever get to them in time to stop Rumdog from doing exactly what it was that he did. He had never even been a suspect in those killings he had committed and try as I might, I could not think of one time that I had ever talked to Rumdog on the phone. Did he even have a phone that I could use to summon help? He was a ghost. I knew that I was helpless to stop any harm that was heading in their direction and as soon as I could muster the courage, I knew I had to prepare myself for the fight of my life. As angry as I was, all I could do was cry, because I knew that regardless of the outcome, I was nearing some degree of an end. I sank. Slowly but steadily, I descended into the sadness of realization one might have on his death-bed. I didn't have the strength and pride that some people do as they look forward to the end of the suffering, but I knew that the end was near. I had begun, as Rumdog had suggested once, to accept the inevitable.

"What the hell are you doing on the floor?"

Rumdog's voice exploded into my ears. I know that he spoke to me in a fairly monotone manner, but it had been so quiet and still in the apartment that any sort of sound seemed to echo in my ears. It also scared me to my feet, as I jumped up with both the nine millimeter in one hand and the knife in the other. It was no wonder that Rumdog had never been caught in anything that he did. He had an uncanny ability to move with silence and stealth through any room. He wasn't exactly thin, yet he had the footsteps of an experienced and honed burglar. God knows how long ago he had exited the living room and left me there to write, but I had never heard so much as a creak of the floor nor his weight shifting off the chair he had been seated in. I tried to sound as menacing as possible.

I said, "Stay right there! If you come any closer to me, I will blow your fucking head off."

My voice was shaky at best. I had never been so scared in all of my life, but I felt somewhat empowered by the two deadly weapons in my hands. Until he smiled, that is.

He looked at the weapons in my hands and seemed genuinely amused by the sight of me quivering like a frightened rabbit. It occurred to me that Rumdog had been threatened and beaten many times in his life. He had also informed me that he had taken a machete to the side of his face without much of a fuss. I had a gun pointed straight at his face but that didn't seem to matter much to him. On the contrary, he looked rather comfortable and unfazed by the barrel of the gun pointed directly at his head. I'm sure he was one hundred percent confident that I didn't have what it takes to kill another human being. He thought that there was no way I was ever going to pull that trigger. He was wrong. If push came to shove, I was completely ready to do whatever it was I had to do to walk out of here alive. First, I had some questions.

We stared at each other for a few moments as he did his usual appraisal with his eyes. I took advantage of those precious seconds as I tried to steady my own voice, and not sound like a fledgling teenager. If only I could stop shaking. I was in charge here, wasn't I? I had the gun. I had the knife. All the while Rumdog remained right in front of me completely empty handed. So why was I the one trembling uncontrollably, while his demeanor hadn't changed one bit? I did a few mental checks in my own head and decided that I was sure that the gun was indeed loaded. I saw no safety of any kind along both sides of the gun so by all intents and purposes, I was ready to rock and roll. Also, if there was some sort of misfire or jamming of the weapon, I was still very much in range to plunge the knife into whatever body part Rumdog left unprotected. Still, his utter neutrality was making me increasingly uncomfortable. I was certainly out of my element and despite being armed to the teeth, I was feeling more and more like prey.

I finally worked up enough nerve. I asked him, "How did you get that picture of my kids?"

He looked at me with a newfound wonder and while I could still tell that he was entertained, his tight smile and expression had changed to something that resembled pity. He let out a single breath and shook his head. It was enraging. A guttural sound escaped my throat as my anger erupted from me as I had never felt before. I took a few steps forward and pointed the gun right between his eyes.

I growled, "Don't you shake your head at me like you have no clue what the fuck I'm talking about. Don't you dare lie to me, where did you get it?"

Rumdog answered, "Why don't you calm down?"

I thought I had been angry before but apparently, I had just scratched the surface as the rage in me exploded outward like the summit of a volcano.

I screamed at the top of my lungs, "I will kill you, I swear it, if you don't answer me right now. How did you get that picture of my children?"

That coy, condescending smile escaped his face immediately as he seemed to realize that I meant business. His eyes never left mine, however, and I knew that while he was still unafraid, he certainly felt that I was much more formidable than he originally believed. He was suddenly solemn, and addressed me like he actually cared for my well-being.

He said, "Jerry, I will tell you everything that you want to know and maybe even everything that you need to know. You need to calm down, hold on to the gun and the knife if you'd like, but you should really calm down. You might even want to sit down pal."

I wasn't about to do any such thing. I could tell that he was doing his best to look as harmless as possible and even though I wasn't buying it outright, I couldn't say that his face didn't seem honest and as genuine as I'd ever seen it. He was telling the truth. That was about the only thing I was sure of for some reason. However, the one thing I wasn't sure of was what he planned to do with me afterward.

I lowered the gun slightly, and made eye contact with him again over the front sights of the weapon. I asked him, "Did you hurt my kids? I need to know, right now before you say another word. Are my kids ok?"

He smiled at me reassuringly and nodded.

Then he replied "Your uh, the kids are fine Jerry. I would never hurt them. I'm capable of a lot of things. Things I'm not proud of and things that I can live with just fine. But I have never hurt an innocent person, especially not a child. So please, believe me when I say that the kids are fine. Ok?"

I believed him. Of course I wanted to believe him, but there was one thing that I had known about him for the countless years that we had been friends. He had always been an honest man. He was unpredictable, volatile and probably one of the strangest human beings I had ever come across, but he had always been brutally candid. My kids were ok. He hadn't hurt them. I was still confused and hopelessly lost in the point of all this, but the one thing I could take solace in was that regardless of what was to happen here, my babies were fine. I breathed a visible sigh of relief and the next thought in my head was "Now what?"

Rumdog had always been able to read me quite easily and I never even had to say the words, because just when I allowed myself a second to slow my heart rate he said, "You're probably asking yourself, now what? Aren't you?"

What could I say? He knew me very well. I nodded, and that was as much as I could rally in a response.

Again, his eyes portrayed something that if I didn't know any better, resembled compassion. Now it was my turn to appraise Rumdog, as I tried to decipher what was going on in his head, and if I was going to have to pump him full of lead in the very near future. He smiled warmly, which I thought was very strange considering I was standing in his bedroom, gun and knife in hand, and in a rigid stance waiting to pounce on him.

He nodded his heads towards the living room and said, "Come here, I want to show you something."

I didn't move an inch. After a moment he saw that I was not in motion, and realized that maybe, he should give me a little bit of space.

He repeated, "Come here" and moved out of sight and towards the dining room. I remained frozen for a few seconds as I tried to decide whether this was a trap or not. I don't think it mattered much anyway, because one way or another, I was going to have to get out of this room. He had also given me the room I needed to do so when he backed away from the door. I decided to move. As they say, "Now or never".

Those ten feet I walked from where I was standing seemed like miles. My legs were heavy and I felt as if I was walking through wet cement. I counted my footfalls and subconsciously made note that I too, was now moving as quietly as a thief in the night When I reached the doorway to the bedroom, I found myself frozen again. I couldn't coax myself to walk through the threshold. I imagined a few scenarios, as to what awaited me when I crossed out of the safety of the room. I would have my back to the wall and could not be surprised, but none of them were good. I imagined an ax to my chest, or perhaps a sword chopping off my arm that held the nine millimeter, right at the wrist. What if he had another gun and he was trying to lull me into a security that did not exist. There was no other way out of this room, so it's not like I had many choices. I made a decision. I was going to count to three, then burst out of the room and run. That was it, no looking back. I started to count, and rock back and forth to get some momentum, when I stopped counting in my head.

He had a double lock on his front door. My plan was no good. I had to get my hands on that key to get out. I would have to kill him for it, or he would just have to walk over and let me out voluntarily, perhaps wishing me well and giving me a hug as we shared a warm farewell. I didn't believe the latter was an option based on reality.

I would have to take it, literally, one step at a time. Get out of the room Jerry, that's your first move. You're going to survive this, one way or another and maybe even one day tell this story as an old and reminiscent fellow. "Did I ever tell you about the time…" Yes, that's how it would start. I can see it, but for the time being, I needed to move.

I heard his voice, "Are you coming out or what?" and that gave me a small amount of hope for my survival.

He was not in the dining room or waiting to dismember me on the other side of the door. From the sound of his voice, I guessed that he was about fifteen feet away at least. Sounds in a quiet place tend to echo and his voice carried throughout the apartment, bouncing off all the walls and ceilings and into my throbbing eardrums. There was definitely a bit of distance. So that ruled out any hand to hand combat. If he had a weapon, it certainly wasn't an ax or another sharp instrument that would be useless from that distance.

In my head, I decided, if he had anything, it would have to be another gun. Oddly enough, that little deduction brought me yet another glimmer of hope. Of all the possibilities, it was down to one weapon. A gun, and since I had a gun and a knife, I was on top right? It wasn't exactly "Rock, Paper, Scissors" but it was all I had to go with. Again, I had to prepare myself to exit the room. I counted silently again in my head and completely committed to barging out of the room on three. This was it. It was a very long and deliberate countdown. The kind you see at fixed wrestling matches every weekend on television. Nonetheless, at three, I burst through the door and tried to spin towards the living room so that I could have my weapon pointed at Rumdog right away. And I tripped.

There was a two inch risen lip between the doorway and the hallway that I simply had not accounted for. A huge tile mantel separated both rooms and after catching it with my front foot, it was more like I fell through the doorway then actually walked out. I bounced off a linen closet door and tried to right myself too fast. I jumped to my feet and backed up instinctively, slamming my back against the bathroom door. There was no place else to go. I was dead. I was sure of it. I expected to hear something, gunshots, screaming, my own at least as I was hit with slug after slug, but instead there was nothing but silence. What I heard was equally terrifying. Rumdog was laughing. Not a chuckle neither, he was actually laughing so hard that it was coming out high pitched.

He stopped briefly and took another look at me, and spit out "What the fuck are you doing?" before he started to laugh again.

He wasn't quite the fifteen feet away as I had surmised, it was a little closer to ten to twelve feet, as he was standing by the living room entrance with one arm leaning against the doorway. More importantly, he was completely empty handed. He was having himself a good old laugh and that really made me shift from fear to anger. He was actually enjoying this. I heard the screaming before I realized that it was my voice making all the racket.

I yelled, "You think this if funny? You think this is funny somehow, you mother-fucker!"

He put one finger up in the air, apparently needing a moment to compose himself. He glanced at me again and started to laugh again but without so much gusto. His finger remained in the air for a few moments, before he steadied himself and spoke again.

"Just calm down brother and please come here, I need to show you something." He still had a shit eating grin on his face and it was making my blood boil, but whatever the case, killing me didn't appear to be on his agenda just yet.

I started to inch toward him but when I covered about the half of the distance between us I said, "I just want the key. Give me the key, so I can grab my stuff and get out of here. You know what? Keep my shit. I don't care, I just want the key. Let me out. That's all I want."

He broke eye contact and stared at the floor as he seemed to be pondering my request. I knew that he was speaking to himself, in his head and trying to decide if he should let me go.

I said, "That's all I want man. I want to get the fuck out of here. I won't say anything. I won't repeat a word you said to me. Fuck the book, forget about it. I will never repeat another word. I just need to go. Now, please!"

He took a deep breath, and looked at me. He said, "Ok, you can go whenever you want. I'm not going to stop you. You were always free to go. I can't stop you Jerry. You're the one with all the weapons right now, aren't you? You're the big bad killer right? The only one acting like a maniac is you. I'm just standing here, talking to you and you're cursing and screaming at me."

I yelled, "You locked me in here. Don't act like I don't have a good reason to be scared. After what you just told me, you're just going to lock me in here and let me see a picture of my kids that you stole from my house? What does that mean? What are you trying to do to me?"

Rumdog had the bewildered look again, as he cocked his head to the side one more time.

Then he said, "Did I really lock you in here, all alone? I didn't go anywhere. I was here the entire time, from the time you started writing till right now."

I started to yell again but then steadily I lowered my voice so I could be steadier in my demands. "Bullshit! I searched the entire place and you were nowhere to be found. You fucking locked me in here. If that door wasn't locked from the inside, I would be long gone by now. Don't tell me you were here the whole time, because you weren't. Now, are you going to let me out, or do I have to shoot you? I don't want to, but I promise you, I will shoot you dead. What's it going to be?"

Rumdog looked at me and said, "Why don't you just let yourself out?"

I was utterly confused at this point. He showed no aggression. He showed no more amusement. He showed me no more than an honest question and suddenly I felt like the one who was losing my mind. What was I missing? The door had been locked shut, of that I was sure. Was there another door that I had somehow missed in my hysteria ridden search? I tried to speak again, but all of a sudden, my throat was completely dry. I didn't want to speak. My voice would surely crack and the tough guy persona I was displaying would crack along with it. I knew it. He knew it, and again that damn face of compassion was back on his face.

Rumdog said, "Would you like something to drink?"

It pissed me off to no end that he was so calm. Yet, it seemed so genuine. He was honestly worried about me and my frame of mind. Why? What did he know that I didn't? Wait. It was the whisky. Had he put something in the whisky? Was I tripping on some sort of hallucinogenic, which had made me wonder all over his apartment looking for a way out when the front door was open the whole time? Again, I took a gander at the door and it certainly seemed shut to me.

My head was spinning as my heart palpated out of control. I don't know what I was so anxious about. The fight for my life was certainly real in my head, yet

Rumdog seemed completely serene and non-apprehensive. Was this whole thing going on solely in my head? It had to be the whiskey. That was the only explanation. I had brought the whisky to his apartment? Hadn't I? For some reason that seemed to be unclear to me as well. It was only a few hours ago, wasn't it? Why couldn't I remember buying the whisky and bringing it over? And how did he manage to put something in it without me noticing? Whatever he had hit me with, it must have been in the glass before I began to drink out of it. That was the only plausible explanation. I suddenly remembered his friend constantly complaining about someone putting some kind of drug in his drink.

Involuntarily, I uttered the words "The fucking whisky."

He shook his head like he didn't understand what I meant. He asked me "What about it Jerry?"

I asked, "Did you put something in the whisky?"

He seemed annoyed by my question. His expression displayed dismay that I had even dared to ask him such a thing, as if he were incapable. He gave me a very stern look and inexplicably, I actually felt ashamed that I had hurt his feelings somehow.

He nodded his head in the direction of the living room and said, "Look" as he again asked me to set my eyes on something that he had been trying to show me for the last few minutes.

I had closed the distance between us slightly, hoping to make a bolt for the door, and so that I could see into the living room right from where I was standing. On the table, just like before was a full bottle of rum and a little less than half of a bottle of whisky. My laptop was on the table. My bag was on the floor. My pocket recorder was on the table as well, along with several of my composition books that I constantly use to jot things down in fear of forgetting them later. Everything was as I had left it. I could swear I had packed everything earlier.

Nothing was out of the ordinary so I couldn't quite comprehend what it was that he was trying to make me see. I shook my head, and glanced at the door again, still locked, then back at Rumdog.

I asked him, "What? Do you want me to grab my bag and my computer? Fine. I'll take it and go. Would that make you back off and let me leave?"

He shook his head again in frustration. He then asked me "What do you see, on the table, besides your belongings? Tell me what you see!"

I was honestly completely lost. I had no clue what he was getting at but maybe the answer he was looking for was the obvious. I looked at the table again, and took inventory of everything that was on it. All my stuff, and the two bottles of liquor. Was that the answer he wanted? Was that the answer that was going to end this nightmare once and for all? I gave it a shot.

I replied "Aside from my things, there's a bottle of rum, and a bottle of whisky. Is that what you are asking me here? What the fuck is your point?"

That answer seemed to buoy his spirit. He said, "That's right, good."

Then his stern look was upon his face again and his next sentence truly shocked me as it seemed to be the most random question anyone has ever asked me, especially in the situation that we were in.

He asked me, "Do you remember the day your kids were born?"

I was at a loss. What the hell did that have to do with anything? What kind of game was he playing? I didn't understand the question or why it was asked?

He seemed to notice my confusion and asked me in a different tone, as if he were a disappointed parent dealing with a stubborn child. "Do you remember the day that Jenny and Jonathan were born?"

He had never referred to my children by their names before and just hearing him say it sent chills down my spine, further hindering my fragile emotional state. I didn't know what he was getting at, and my level of anxiety managed to skyrocket past the previous levels I had achieved before. For good reasons, I might add. It is never comforting when a confessed killer starts to quiz you about your children. I don't even know why but for some reason I felt compelled to answer him.

I said, "My daughter was born in April, and my son in March. What the fuck is your point man?"

The look he gave me could have killed me a thousand times. I had never been looked at like that in my life. I could see that he wanted to rip my head off and I backed away involuntarily, I retreated more out of my own instinct for survival. I backed up towards the bathroom door when I really should have been making a run for the front door.

Weapons or not, it didn't really seem to matter to Rumdog. He wasn't afraid of me, not one bit. The disdain he expressed for me snuffed out my fire, as well as all the piss and vinegar I had been exuding earlier. He ripped it right out of me. Out of my chest, through my shirt and stepped on it with one single look.

He said, "I think you should stop cursing at me now. You understand me? I won't tolerate that for much longer. You've been yelling at me, threatening my life and accusing me of ugly things. I've taken that, but don't think that you can talk to me like I'm some lowlife piece of shit. Do you understand me?"

That look again. His eyes were spewing fire and venom at me, which instantly made me feel like prey. I might as well have handed Rumdog the knife and gun because I was certainly the meek and he had suddenly felt the need to flex his superior stature. I had recently found out just how easily he could dispose of someone, without much thought or angst, so I could only imagine what he could do to me when he was truly angry.

He paused for a moment, perhaps to give it a minute to sink into my head, or to give himself a minute to cool off. Slowly, but noticeably, his face softened, as he decided, internally but with no oral declaration, that he would forgive my manner of addressing him.

Then he said softly, "No Jerry, I didn't mean your kids respective birthdays. Perhaps, I should clarify. What I mean to ask you is, do you remember anything about it, the circumstances? The ride to the hospital, or anything else that happened that day? Do you remember the actual day?"

What kind question is that? My children being born are for certain the two biggest days of my life. It was my validation as a human being. Regardless of my failed marriage, my kids continued to be the one thing in this world that I considered "meant to be" and I'm not at all a believer in fate. My children represented the ensured future of my name and my teachings. Everything that I believed in and cherished, lay right there among them. They are great kids. Of course, I remembered the days my kids were born. Didn't I? Jenny was born in …. A hospital? Which hospital? The hospital in downtown Brooklyn! It's changed names once or twice, of that I'm sure, but when Jenny was born, it was definitely downtown. Wasn't it? Wait, perhaps that was Johnathan and I was just getting the days confused.

Damn it, why did I drink so much? I usually liked to drink myself into a hazy, but not quite useless inebriated state of mind when I did my writing. At times, I would go countless consecutive days without calling anyone or leaving the house. I saw these binges coming and I would stock up on all the booze and food I would need for the upcoming days ahead. I would vanish into my laptop and write whatever I needed to pry out of my subconscious until I had lost track of the time and days that I had been at it. The amount of booze I had consumed today was not even scratching the surface of what I was usually able to drink on any given day. Yet, I was dizzy, disoriented and losing my grip on my shit so to speak.

While I suspected that the whisky had been spiked somehow, I should still be able to remember the day my kids were born. I just needed to concentrate. Concentrate on my two favorite little humans on this entire planet, and focus on the task at hand to make sure I walk out of here to give them the biggest hug and kiss they have ever received. Daddy loves you both, very much. And I'll be home soon, I promise.

I must have lost track of time. How long had I been beating my brain against the wall trying to remember things that I should know off the top of my head? Before I actually realized it, Rumdog was saying something to me which I could not make out for some reason or another. I could see his lips moving, but I was losing it. I no longer felt armed and dangerous, and I no longer felt like I was in charge. What I did feel was dangerously close to passing out. God knows what would happen to me if I were to succumb to my own anxiety and lose consciousness. His lips were moving, but I could not focus on whatever it was he was saying. He snapped his fingers directly in front of my face and it quickly brought me back to the living. It also made me acutely aware of just how close to me Rumdog was standing. He had quickly and as always silently closed the distance between us without me even noticing his movement. I was also aware that had he wanted, he could have disarmed me quite easily without me putting up much of a fight. Yet, he had allowed me to keep the weapons I still had in my hand.

I wondered if he had done it because he knew I was not built like him and would probably never harm anyone if my life depended on it, or if he had just wanted to let me feel the least bit of security by letting me pretend that I could actually defend myself if the occasion were to arise. I was alert, at least for the most part and I again attempted to back away ever so slightly. It was only about an inch before I felt my back against the door, but it made me feel better. He was literally right in front of me. His words slowly filtered into my jumbled brain and he was saying that he always liked me. Could that be right? I shook the cobwebs out of my head and tried to focus on the ever dizzying room.

He asked me "Hey, you with me? You ok brother?"

I nodded out of necessity to respond at all. Something was definitely wrong with me, but I could not figure it out. This was worse than anxiety. Then the strangest thing happened. I didn't see Rumdog anymore. My vision was picture perfect, but it felt like the lights in room burned much too brightly, giving it and everything in it a hazy contrast. Out of my eyes, I was looking at directly at myself.

I saw myself from Rumdog's point of view and I was a complete wreck. I was shaking and scanning my orbs all over the room like someone who had recently lost his vision. It was no wonder that Rumdog had taken pity on me. I was a frightened harmless rabbit. I looked skinny, and weak. I took a step towards …myself?

I asked, "Hey, you with me? You ok brother?" but it wasn't my voice that I heard.

It was Rumdog's. The panic I saw in my own eyes from this vantage point was truly disheartening. I reached towards myself, to perhaps put a reassuring hand upon my shoulder, when the other me I was looking at repelled from the touch and backed away until there was no place else to go.

The other me seemed to be on the verge of a nervous breakdown, and scurried into the bathroom. I saw the bathroom door open and slam shut right in front of me, my arm still outstretched in mid reach, as I pulled my hand back as to not get my fingers broken.

Suddenly I was in the bathroom. What the hell was going on? I caught a glimpse of my haggard, worried face in the bathroom mirror and admittedly, I looked like total shit. What kind of trip was I on? I had just had a genuine out of body experience. I put the knife and gun down on the sink and turned the water on. I needed ice cold water to snap me out of this. I needed to be awoken from this nightmare. Yes, that was it. I was dreaming. I've heard that you can wake yourself up from a terrible nightmare by just convincing yourself that the dream wasn't real. By snapping yourself out of it and into the conscious world. The cold water would do just that.

I bent over and started to practically drown myself in the basin as I poured cold water all over my face, on my head, and down the back of my neck. It gave me chills when some of the water trickled down the back of my shirt and down my backside. I realized that I was making small involuntary moans as I continued to pour copious amounts of ice cold water onto myself, hoping to wake up at any moment in my own bed in a cool pool of sweat. This wasn't going to work. I needed to try something else, perhaps a jolt of pain. I pulled my head out of the water, and reached up to shut the valve, when I heard his voice in the room.

"You know that's not gonna help any brother."

I jumped back and tumbled backwards against the wall as I slammed my back against the towel rack, snapping it into two pieces. I clumsily reached for the gun again and dropped it into the pool of cool water I had created in the basin. Undeterred, I reached into the water and pulled out the dripping wet nine Millimeter and pointed it straight at Rumdog again, who had not made a move at all. He was sitting calmly on the toilet, smoking a cigarette, as if we were having an everyday conversation. He had an unperturbed demeanor about him again, not one bit worried. He even seemed to be smiling again, but not quite.

He said, "Careful with that, it will still fire even if it's wet. As a matter of fact, I've heard it will fire even if it's underwater. I don't know if that's true, but I wouldn't want to find out in a pinch, you dig?"

My hands were shaking uncontrollably as I was wiping the water that kept trickling out of my hair and down my face, and into my eyes. As I shifted the gun from my right hand to my left, I again noticed how incredibly comfortable this weapon felt in my hands. My left hand was usually useless, and the few times that I had tried to playfully write my name, it resembled the writing of a two-year-old who had just learned to write his name in a made at home birthday card. It was a scribble at best. Yet, I could manipulate this weapon as if I had been practicing with it for years.

Would it fire? Soaking wet after being submerged in the sink? I hoped to god that he was right, and I sure hoped that if I did have to pull the trigger, there would be more than just a click. He would surely kill me then, wouldn't he?

I asked him "How do you do that? How do you go in and out of rooms without making a sound? I know I closed that door behind me. I saw…. I saw myself slam the damn door shut. Yet, here you are."

His trademark half of a smile, began to slowly branch out to the rest of his face. It was creepy. He was nodding his head and smiling like he was very happy with what I had said. I didn't get it.

He seemed to reflect for a moment, took a long drag of his cigarette and then looked back at me and said, "As I was saying earlier, I always liked you. At first, I was very confused and maybe even a little resentful of you, but I always knew that you were good, you know? You were something good and pure, you would never do me or anyone any harm. The one thing I didn't like about you and I guess I really can't blame you, is how selfish you can be. But aren't we all selfish in one way or another? Who would I be to judge, right?"

I had no clue what Rumdog was talking about or what he was getting at. I really had no response to anything he was saying or to him accusing me of being selfish. I wasn't in the mood to debate him about it so I said the only thing that came to mind.

"Ok?" was all I could respond with.

He nodded and said, "Sure, you're definitely a good egg Jerry. At first, I didn't know who you were, or where the hell you came from, but as the years passed, I started to realize that you were probably the only steady and positive thing in my life. Now that you've heard all about my childhood, you know that it was certainly not the best of times. Especially for a poor kid like me. You were always there, for as long as I could remember. But when the shit was bad Jerry, when my life would take one fucked up turn after another, you were nowhere to be found. I was on my own."

I immediately felt a pang of guilt over what he had just said. I always wondered about him, even as kids and was just always too afraid to reach out to him. He was always so volatile and though he had never been so towards me, I always felt it best to befriend him, from a distance. That's the way the relationship had remained throughout all the years I knew him. He seemed to be a magnet for random violence and I had done my best to avoid all of those situations when we were growing up. Fighting had never been my cup of tea and for people like Rumdog, it seemed to be

211

all that they knew. All that they liked. I admittedly had never thanked him or shown him any appreciation when he would stick his neck out for me and my friends and I guessed that I probably owed him an apology for never doing that.

I said, "I'm sorry, I didn't know. I didn't know your life was so bad, I was just a kid. How could I have known?"

Whatever I had just said didn't seem to register with him at all. He didn't acknowledge my apology at all. I didn't regret saying it, but I did feel like perhaps I was talking to a wall. A wall built of years of resentment and guilt. Perhaps not directed at me, but certainly the clueless, happy go lucky world that I reside in.

Suddenly he said, "Then I figured out where you came into play. I figured out where you had come from and things started to make sense."

I shook my head and said, "I still don't know what you mean brother, I'm sorry, but you have me very confused. I don't know what's going on here, but I don't want to hurt you at all and I hope that you don't want to hurt me. I just want to go home. Can you please, just give me the key, or let me out. What happened here tonight stays here. That's it!"

He looked at me, slightly disappointed again and said, "Why don't you look in your pocket?"

I gave Rumdog a long stare and shook my head. I stared at him and said, "Why would I look into my pocket? What am I going to find?"

He shrugged his shoulders. This was a ploy. It had to be. Maybe he wanted to distract me, or wanted me to put the gun down and take it while I fished into my own pockets looking for God knows what. He obviously wasn't talking so I had a choice to make yet again. He had had many chances to take the gun from me but never made any effort whatsoever to disarm me. He definitely could have taken it from me when I was in my out of body stupor outside of the bathroom and didn't try then neither. I had to accept that he didn't mind me having the weapon, but what was so important that he needed me to check into my own pockets? I had the gun in my right hand, so I used my left hand to pat my left pocket down and felt nothing.

Rumdog remained still as if he sensed my apprehension. I then switched the gun to my left hand, and used my right hand to search. Still nothing. Wait, at the very bottom of my pocket, there was something? I established eye contact with Rumdog again and he slowly raised his arms over his head in mock surrender. I slowly reached deep into my pocket and closed my hand around something small and metal. I didn't want to believe it, but I already knew what it was before I pulled it out. I didn't have to see it, but my eyes pretended to need convincing as well. There was a small key in my hand, but not the normal long ended key. It was small and silver, and had a rounded circular edge to it which you inserted into a special lock. Yes, a double sided lock. How in the world had he managed to sneak that key into my pocket? And just how long had I been in possession of it? It had to be in the hallway, when he was close to me. I had nearly fainted. He could have easily slipped it into my pocket then, without me noticing. He had touched my shoulder. Yes, he had certainly done it then, when I had been distracted and disoriented. He was no magician.

I asked, "You still think this is a game? You're having a good old time with me aren't you?"

He smiled and said, "I've always been quite amused by you, Jerry. You are really entertaining. Please don't take that in a bad way. That's what I always liked about you. You were good and funny, and happy. Everything that I could never be. But that's the circle isn't it. You're everything I'm not. I'm everything you're not. See? It is perfect and symbiotic. You know I owe a lot to you. I could never have the things I had or the people in my life, not without you. I mean, once they get a wind of the real me, nobody sticks around, but hey at least we have good times for a little while. Why do you think the Hoff and Cee don't come around anymore? Someone like me, I can only keep it going for so long, before the real me rears his ugly head."

I could not help myself but to ask Rumdog, "So this isn't the real you? You're different, somehow?"

He started to laugh again, and this time he didn't give a shit that he was going to make me mad.

He was almost mocking me as he did it. When he was done laughing heartily he suddenly asked "You loved Henry, didn't you?"

I was totally blindsided by that question. Henry? From Rumdog's childhood? Had I met him at some point and forgotten? I shook my head and started to speak when a flash of memory came across my mind. Henry was driving a van, and I was in the

213

passenger seat. He was telling me how sorry he was, but the matter simply wasn't up to him. He was explaining to me that if he had his choice, he would raise me as his own child. He would let me live with him for as long as I needed. He would cloth me, feed me and send me to school along with his own children. All I had to do was pull my own weight, but I did have a mother and she wanted me home in New York City. I was barely a teenager, but for the first time in my life, I had experienced happiness. I had spent the entire summer in Upstate New York and I had the time of my life. There was no hunger, no beatings, nothing but a kid finally being allowed to act like a kid. It was the happiest two months of my young life and now it was all coming to an end. I was looking out the window and listening to Henry's soothing voice as he tried to make me feel better about going back home. I was entirely heartbroken and imagining going back home to everything that I hated. A single tear ran down my face as I sat in the van staring out of the window at the rolling mountains that I was sure I was seeing for the last time.

The memory was gone. I was in the bathroom again and there were tears streaming down my face. I uttered "Henry" in a strained whisper. I had loved Henry. How could I have forgotten the man he was to a fatherless boy? Rumdog was no longer smiling. He stood up slowly and came face to face with me.

He said, "Yeah, you loved him quite a bit. He was great to me, great to us. But I couldn't love him. I was unable to love. But you, you knew how to love somehow. That's where you came from. You came from the very little bit of good in life. You came from the love for Gilbert, who protected us no matter how many times I got us into trouble. You came from the only sister I have left, who still tries to see me and spend time with me no matter how hard I try to push people away. You come from love, but not me. I…I come from sorrow and sadness, and pain. When Indio was beating Gilbert senseless and I stepped in, that's where I come from. You could never do that. That is the difference between us. You were made from Henry's unconditional love and I come from kneeling on raw rice every single day for an entire fucking summer. Do you even remember the things that were done to me when we were all homeless and bouncing from place to place? Do you know how much that hurts, still? Can you imagine the holes in my knees and how much it hurt to straighten out my legs to go to sleep? No! You don't know what that's like because you were nowhere to be found. Those memories are mine."

I could now remember the pain. I remembered Gilbert slowly using a toothpick to pick the hard strands of rice out of his knees first, then mine. We didn't even know what we had done wrong. Sometimes we got smart and wore jeans, no matter how hot it was, just to have cloth in between the hard floor and our skin. Sometimes she made us take them off, as she inflicted the same corporal punishment she instilled on her own son. I remembered thinking to myself that given the choice between sleeping in a bed and suffering this torture or being homeless, the thought of living in a filthy subway tunnel didn't seem too bad of an option.

Rumdog was now in directly in front of me but the vivid memories were flooding my mind and preventing me from seeing anything going on directly in front of me. I was tuned in to whatever channel was showing "memory lane" and I was having a hard time keeping my emotional core intact. I suddenly felt Rumdog's hand grab a hold of my face and he was talking to me.

He said, "You never lived in reality, you were always a dreamer. I lived in the real world where life, our life, was hard. Try being me, for one God-damned day. Try going to sleep every single night not just knowing that you're going to lose the moment you wake up, but knowing full well that you have already lost. That's my life, Jerry. Things like love, hope, and fairness stopped pertaining to me a long time ago. God stopped giving a shit about me the day I was born, no matter how much I have needed him. Not for you though, you had a whole other version of what real life was like. You took other people's stories and made them your good memories. You borrowed other families and made them your own. Just like Henry. He was a great man, but he wasn't ours."

He had a tight grip on me as we stood face to face, close enough to smell each other's breath. I smelled something very familiar. He continued as I struggled to escape his grasp on me "He wasn't ours, you loved him, but he wasn't ours. He wasn't ours."

As he said that, my out of body vision had returned. I had a grasp on my own face, and I was talking to myself. I was standing directly in front of myself, with my hand gripping the other me by the face. I kept repeating, "He wasn't ours" in another voice. Then, in another vision, I had switched places and it was me that had a grip of Rumdog's face. Both of us repeating the same mantra, reaffirming that Henry had never been our father. Then there was two of him, two Rumdog's face to face, each with a vice like grip on each other's face, repeating "He wasn't ours." Finally, as if that wasn't enough, there was now two of me standing face to face. Both repeating the same phrase as the prior set of twins had been chanting earlier.

The room began to spin and before I even realized I was doing it, I pushed the other me away as hard as I could. I didn't know which one was me or which was the carbon copy, so I simply pushed. The broken contact seemed to work as I was suddenly very aware of my individual self and I could see that Rumdog was thrown against the toilet tank almost knocking the top off of it. Again, out of reflex and certainly not passed practice, I raised the gun and pointed it at Rumdog.

I said, "This can't be real. What the fuck did you put in my cup? This isn't real!"

Rumdog started laughing again and said, "After everything I just said, you still think you drank the whisky? You didn't drink anything my friend, I did."

I said, "No, that can't be true. I'm drunk. That is the only possible explanation."

I exploded and without warning, I found myself screaming at the top of my lungs. "No! No! No! This can't be true. It just can't! If what you're saying is true, then I'm a crazy person. Is that what you are saying? Is that what you want me to believe? You're saying I'm a crazy motherfucker and you're nothing but a figment of my imagination. Is that it?" Rumdog's rebuttal took all the wind out of my sails.

He looked at me, quite sadly again and said, "No, you silly fuck! I'm saying that I'm very much schizophrenic, and you are a figment of mine."

I'm sure we're all familiar with the term "The world crashing down upon you" and we never seem to fully comprehend what it must really feel like. The weight of his words coupled with his stoic demeanor almost deflated me to a point of non-cohesion. I hated him for saying it. I still didn't know if what he was saying was true but I certainly couldn't believe that my whole life had been a lie. Not even a lie actually, but an entire mythical creation of another person's sick, hopelessly damaged mind. He would have me believe that my entire existence had been a by-product of his own pain and suffering and an inability to cope with it on his own. No, this simply could not be possible. I could not accept this, no matter what he said, and if there was ever a time to pinch myself and wake up from this nightmare, there would be no better time than right now. Yet, I could not deny the sudden flood of memories coursing through my mind.

I was real. I had a family, of that I was sure of, for the love and care I felt for them was as real as the air that we breathe. As real as the hair on my head and as real as the tight embrace I gave each of them every night when I put them to bed. That seemed like so long ago all of a sudden, but I was sure that I had tucked them in, safe and snug in their own beds, just last night. Hadn't I?

I looked back at Rumdog and asked in an unassured manner, "My kids! Are they even…."

I could not bring myself to say it. The mere thought of losing that pure love that we shared was enough to tear my heart in two.

Rumdog looked at me and replied, "I really hate to kick you when you're down buddy, but you are a dense prick. You don't have any kids. I mean, the kids are certainly real, but they are my kids, not yours. I brought them into this world, not you. Like I told you earlier, you have a habit of taking people's beautiful little stories and making them your own. Somehow, you seem to thrive off of it. Truth is, neither one of us has seen Jenny and Johnathan in a few years. You see, I could only hide this little condition of mine from the wife for so long. When she got wind of who I really was, she packed the kids for Florida and got a court order to keep me from them. I write them a letter every once in a while and send them a few bucks on their birthdays, but everything always comes back, undelivered. I went there once to surprise them, but I lost my nerve when I got there. I just watched them play from a few houses away. I watched as another man came home and played with them, pretending to be their dad. I wanted to hurt him, but then they too would meet the real me. I couldn't let them see that part of me. I miss them Jerry. I miss them so much."

I could tell that this was something he could never make up. The sudden flood in his eyes were all I need to see to know how much pain Rumdog was in. He didn't cry however, and seconds later I was looking at his cold emotionless eyes again. I should not have felt so angry with him but instead of sympathy, all I felt was rage.

Then RumDog said, "He took my place, Jerry. But you don't remember that, do you? No, that one's all mine and you're welcome."

"I hate you." The words came out of my mouth before I realized I was speaking. "I should kill you. I should point this gun right at your fucking head and end your miserable existence right now."

Rumdog could never be frightened easily could he? He looked at me and said, "Well why don't you?"

He said it in the same manner that he had told me to look in my pocket for the key to the front door. I had forgotten about that. All I had wanted was to high-tail out of here as quickly as possible, and when I had finally gotten the key, I had not moved a muscle to escape this hell hole I was in.

That, in itself was interesting, but what I found more intriguing was Rumdog's complete confidence that I wasn't going to shoot him. Was this another ploy? Did he really want to die and was he trying to entice me to end his life for him? I must say, after the things he had said and done to me tonight, I would fully oblige him at this point. He was daring me to shoot him.

I had tolerated enough of this torture. "You don't think I'll do it, do you?"

His response, again, was a simple shrug of his shoulders. Ok, I was finally keen to this little game of chicken. My hand was shaking but not quite as badly as before. I pointed the muzzle of the gun inches away from his face, not expecting him to cower in any way but his reaction still caught me by surprise. He tilted his head, thrusting his jaw forward and opened his mouth. I slowly inserted the barrel of the gun into his mouth and he offered no resistance. Instead, he bit down on the end of the weapon, to ensure that I could not pull it out of his mouth if I tried. Then he said something that I could not make out because his mouth was full of metal. I wanted to hear him beg for his life.

This part of me I had never seen before, but I was suddenly angry enough to shut his lying mouth for good.

I asked, "You got something to say?"

He still managed a smile although he had his mouth wrapped around the gun. Then he repeated "Nice tattoos asshole."

It was then that I noticed that my entire right arm was covered in tattoos. I had never once in my life got so much as a needle at a doctor's office, but I was suddenly covered in tattoos. The same tattoos that encompassed the right arm of

Rumdog. I tried to recoil from my own arm as the sight of seeing myself covered in ink shocked me. And when the gun went off, I imagine that it shocked us both.

The explosion of sound almost made me deaf, as the gunshot echoed loudly in the naturally acoustic bathroom. My eardrums pulsed in my ears but all I could hear was that distinctive ringing that follows and accompanies an unusually loud occurrence. When I was younger, I remember having small bouts of tinnitus, but this was much worse. The pain coursed and pulsed throughout my ears and head so strongly that I could not open my eyes, as I stood there with both hands covering my ears. It was the equivalent of shutting the barn doors after the horses got out, but it was all I could do prevent my brains from tumbling out of my head. My right ear was leaking fluid, which I suspected to be blood, but since I couldn't open my eyes just yet, I'd have to live with that assumption. Slowly the pain began to subside, but jolts of pain still pulsed throughout my head as I tried to open my eyes. I had temporarily forgotten about Rumdog and because of the sudden mind-bending pain, I had absentmindedly put the gun down on the sink to cover my ears. It probably didn't matter, for I imagined he was sitting on the toilet still, lifeless, with the top half of his head sprayed all over the bathroom wall. He wasn't going to be any more trouble.

I opened my eyes slightly and the vertigo kicked right in. For those of you who don't know this, you may learn very quickly just how important two functioning eardrums are to maintaining your balance and equilibrium. I had just received a crash course as the room began to spin and I fell through the shower doors, not shattering them but certainly knocking them off the rails. Perhaps my luck was about to change, since the glass shower doors didn't shatter, thus creating shards that would have cut me to pieces.

I lay there for a moment, trying to establish my balance and sure enough the room stopped spinning. I would have to remain motionless, but it was better than creating any more of dizzying nausea that accompanies vertigo. I steadied my eyes and focused on the toilet where Rumdog had been sitting with his teeth clenched tightly around the gun. There was no blood. There was no gore dripping down the walls or any sign that anyone had been shot. There was nothing.

Well, that wasn't exactly true now, was it? There was a hole in the tile wall. And in the adjoining wall, there was another hole and crack where the bullet must have ricocheted. I couldn't see where the bullet had finally finished its course, but I suppose I was lucky that it wasn't embedded in me somewhere. As a matter of fact, I really wasn't sure that this wasn't the case so I began a visual and physical inspection of my body to make sure that my ear wasn't the only thing bleeding. I was halfway through my check up when I was suddenly pulled to my feet, making the room spin even harder this time. The abrupt movement created an explosion of pain and vertigo through my entire brain. Standing right in front of me, with an incensed and crazed look in his eyes, was Rumdog. No bullet holes in him at all. Looking none the worse wear, with a huge maniacal smile spread across his face. He was yelling, but he wasn't angry. He was screaming at me, of this I was sure, but if I were a betting man, I would put it all on the fact that he was spewing words of … praise?

He was yelling, "Look at you finally showing some fucking balls. I can't believe it. Holy shit, look at the huge fucking balls on you Jerry!"

He had me by the collar, both hands holding me them tightly and keeping me upright. If he had not had such a tight grip on me, I would be laying on the floor, or still in the shower. He was elated. He was shaking me and jumping up in a strange celebration. Suddenly he kissed me right on the mouth, and I tasted and smelled Whisky.

Suddenly, he purposely changed his voice to that of a woman and mockingly said, "My Hero!" And then he was back to his normal speaking voice, "Where have you been all my fucking life?"

I had tried to shoot him and he was proud of me. The look in his eyes conveyed complete adoration, but I was in no mood for celebrations. I grabbed his hands and tried to steady my eyes to look into his but he kept shaking me. I uttered the words "Please stop shaking me," and he stopped suddenly.

He stood me upright in front of the mirror to let me get a good look at myself. In the reflection I could see that he was still standing right next to me and he was whispering loudly into my left ear, the one that wasn't bleeding.

He was saying, "You're starting to see now, aren't you? You see who we are, finally!"

I couldn't help but notice the heat emitting from Rumdog's mouth. It felt like the hot whispers of a lover directly into your ear, which sent shivers down your spine. He was there, in the room and yet he wasn't. He couldn't be, because if he was actually there, he'd be dead. The bullet would have hit flesh and skull, not just the cold dead tile. I also noticed another little detail in the mirror that send the final pulse of ice down my back and it spread throughout my skin, giving me goose bumps from head to toe. My left ear looked to be much tighter against my head than the right ear. I couldn't see a scar, but there was certainly a difference from the ear that was bleeding. I raised my left land and slowly, as my hands shook, used my fingertips to trace along the ridge where my ear met my head. Along the crease, it felt jagged and coarse. It felt like scarring from stitches being clumsily and hurriedly applied to what was once a gaping wound.

My stomach did somersaults, but I was determined to see the truth. I leaned into the mirror and pulled my left ear down a bit. I saw the jagged scar above my ear, along the cartilage that attached it to the side of my head. The scar was long, from the top of my ear to the back of it. There was no denying that it had been once reattached, leaving it slightly disfigured but functional. And then I saw her face. The girl with the machete, her beautiful face, her perfect body and her one discolored eye. I saw her, in perfect detail and I could no longer deny that I had been in the room. My mind jumped to Peter and his brother, and I began to cry because I knew if I tried at all, I would recall the memory of taking their lives. I wanted nothing to do with this, but I knew that it wouldn't be too hard to pull it out of the archives and I just didn't want to see. I, despite my good will and best intentions, was a cold blooded murderer. I was a killer, I realized, as another flash of the girl entered my head. I pulled the trigger and the spray of blood drenched me, flying straight into my mouth. I remembered. I tasted it. I suddenly felt the urge to vomit and I did, into the sink. I vomited nothing but Whisky. After a moment, the stomach convulsions subsided and I turned the water on to wash the remnants of stomach bile out of my mouth.

When I stood upright, I was staring at the mirror and Rumdog was looking right back at me. He wasn't laughing or smiling anymore. He was all partied out, it seemed. I raised my hand to wipe my face, and Rumdog mimicked me. I wiped the trickle of blood that oozed from my right ear and his little game of pantomime continued.

I stared at him intently and said, "You don't have to play this game anymore. You've made your point. I know exactly who I am."

I could hear my own voice doing the talking, but in the mirror Rumdog was doing a perfect lip synch to my every word. I knew who I was. I knew that I had been the one who had coldly taken three lives that Father's day without so much as an ounce of guilt. Well, it had really been the consciousness of Rumdog, but that didn't really matter anymore. We were one and the same, were we not? He was me, and I was him. Both of us would rot in prison, then in hell for our sins regardless of who exactly was pulling the strings that day. While that was something very hard to live with, what felt worse to me was the fact that I was never a parent. I didn't have my own children. Maybe he did and by default that sort of made me a parent as well, but the realization that I was never going to be allowed to see my own children again, if I could still call them that, was my very own proverbial nail in the coffin. I began to mourn immediately and as the tears streamed down my face, I saw that Rumdog was crying in the mirror as well. I felt sorry for him. I had just arrived at this realization, but he had dwelled here and lived with this for the past forty years. He had been here for all of his life.

That's where we differed. He was always so strong and willful. And I was just not that resilient. Knowing all that I knew now, was enough to trigger my emotional and psychological surrender. I looked at Rumdog in the mirror and I pitied him. I thought of my own despair as well. My own self-pity being too much of a burden to withstand, so I thought that I would just do us both a favor. I picked up the nine millimeter and pointed it straight at the mirror, but Rumdog's expression did not change. It was one of sadness and grim determination, a face I had never seen him wear.

I looked up to my God, crossed myself and sealed it with a kiss and a touch to my heart and said, "Jenny and Jonathan, I love you so much, with all my heart. I'm so sorry."

I then turned the gun and pointed it straight at my own head. Suddenly Rumdog's face changed as he realized what my intentions were. Impossibly, he reached out

222

from the mirror and tried to move the weapon away from my head but he was too late. I heard him yell "NO" and that was the last thing I heard. For the second time that day, I pulled the trigger. It was just like Rumdog had said, nothing! Just a fade to black.

Missa Defunctorum

I am Rumdog, and I am almost done with my story.

An old Cherokee is telling his grandson about a battle that goes on inside of people. He tells his grandson that the battle is between two wolves inside us all. One is Evil. It is anger, envy, jealousy, sorrow, regret, greed, arrogance, self-pity, guilt, resentment, inferiority, lies, false pride, superiority, and ego. The other is good. It is joy, peace, love, hope, serenity, humility, kindness, benevolence, empathy, generosity, truth, compassion, and faith. The grandson thought about it for a moment and then asked his grandfather "Which wolf wins?"

The old Cherokee simply replied, "The one you feed."

There are two reasons why I am quite fond of this proverb. The first reason is that I have witnessed, as in seen with my own two eyes, the very face of evil, and somehow managed to survive the encounter. I know just how authentic it is and will never doubt its existence or power. The other reason is that I also had two wolves fighting for the fate of my soul. Gilbert was the good wolf, always protecting me and making sure that I ended up on a straight path. Even if I resisted, he would come down on me, whether I appreciated it or not and grabbed me by the nape into safety. My oldest brother Indio was the bad wolf. He taught me about stealing. He taught me about drug use. He gave me daily lessons in violence, anger, and contempt and indifference towards my own family. He tried his best to corrupt me, to break me, so that he could use me in whatever way he needed. Gilbert and Indio are both gone now, but each of them took with them a little more of me with them than I could afford. Nonetheless, the pieces of me are gone, but the battle of the two wolves still resides within me.

I also share this because the eternal battle that rages within is not without casualties. Regretful as they may be, I know that some losses are for the better of me. Some losses will remain a thorn forever lodged in every ventricle of my beating heart, for as long as it does so. I've lost my children. I've lost some very good friends and family, as well as some good women. However, with my condition being what it is, I never really know what is real and what is not. Sometimes it takes me months to figure out if someone is a real live human being, or if they are just another manifestation of my sick and polluted mind. I know that the Hoff and Cee were real. I've been to their respective homes and seen pictures, wedding albums and such that proved that I was actually there with them at some point or another. It was years, however, before I realized that Jerry was just another piece of me that I created to somehow cope with the ever-changing topography that was my emotional state. I don't know how. I don't know why, but at some point, a separation had occurred and Jerry managed to carve out a little existence of his own. I would go months without seeing his face and then he would be sitting on my couch, watching the game alongside me as if he had never left. On other occasions, I had no recollection that he had been around at all. I admit that I would awaken sometimes and realize that I hadn't been aware for days at a time. I would come to, needing a shave and not remembering what I had done for the past several days. I surmised that Jerry had been at play again and it was happening too frequent for my own liking. Apparently, he liked being the main attraction and the more he appeared, the more time he wanted. I would wake up other days surrounded by pages and pages of Jerry's writing. Countless volumes of the things Jerry was trying to express, things that were important to him but mindless drivel to me. Finally, I awoke one morning with a fresh tattoo of a bottle of ink and a quill on my chest. I had not sanctioned this at all. Jerry had always more than a bit squeamish whenever we had spoken about all of my body art so it could not have been his decision. Another consciousness, a meld of the both of us had to responsible for the new tattoo. Naturally, this posed a problem for me. I could live with Jerry operating right alongside me and helping me navigate through life with this debilitating condition. He had been with me for as long as I could remember. But I certainly took issue with someone else taking the reins and pushing both of us aside. While I never thought it would come to this, something was bound to happen. It happened in a big way that day.

I came to on the bathroom floor. My ears were ringing and I was in an incredible amount of pain. I could taste blood in my mouth and I could tell that were fragments of tooth sprayed all over my mouth. I wasn't dead, of this, I was sure. There was no way I could be in this much pain and be dead. I touched the right side of face and a new slew of fireworks and excruciating pain radiated throughout every nerve ending in my body. Ok, let's try not to touch that anymore. I slowly and carefully sat up, but was hit with a dose of vertigo, reminding me that my eardrum was most likely perforated by the loud explosions that had occurred in the closed and acoustic bathroom. I spun slowly and that's when I realized that the left side of my face was in extreme pain as well. The left side of my face was caked in blood, and I deduced that this was most likely an exit wound. I slowly took a peek to my left and saw a small bullet hold in the bathroom door, directly at head level. It came back to me, slowly. Jerry had tried to kill me. Kill us actually, as if he had any right to make any managerial decisions. I had not seen it coming. At the last possible moment, when I saw the reflection in the mirror of the gun pointed at my temple, I had tried to intervene, but I wasn't quite fast enough. At least I had managed to alter the direction the gun was pointed at and when he had fired, the bullet had ripped right through one cheek and out of the other. It had taken a few of my teeth with it. I saw my reflection in the mirror and I was a mess. I needed to get out of this bathroom. I glanced down. On the floor next to the gun was Jerry, laying in a pool of blood that was streaming from his face. He looked to be lifeless, but I was in no condition to check. I picked up the gun, slowly and carefully so that I wouldn't agitate the vertigo and stepped over his body as I opened the bathroom door. Yes, there had certainly been a separation between us. I took a few steps and used the wall to steady myself, leaving bloody handprints all along the hallway to the dining room. I would have to repaint that at some point, I thought to myself. I stopped in my tracks. I could be mistaken, but I could swear I heard the sound of a woman crying.

I looked back at Jerry's body, but it was still there. He wasn't making a sound nor would he ever make any sort of complaint. I took a few more steps forward and sitting on my bar stool, four seat dinner table was a crying and bleeding Nina. Oh no. My beloved Nina, not you too!

She was rocking back and forth on the chairs, her knees folded up to her chest, and blood was pouring profusely from her face. She had the identical entry and exit wounds that I had on my own face. She placed her shaking hands along each side of her face and then looked at her hands in disbelief. She then displayed both of her hands to me, covered in blood, just in case I didn't believe that she too had been severely injured. She tried to speak, but her mouth was not functioning the way it should. She sounded like she was speaking through clenched teeth.

She cried "Are you happy now? I always tell you to let things be, but look at this now. Look at what you've done."

She was crying, sobbing heavily as I turned away from her slowly, needing to sit down all of a sudden. It all made sense now. I could never meet her family because there was none to meet. She was not ashamed of me. The shame was my own. My poor darling, Nina. How could I not see?

I dragged my wounded self into the living room and fell into the recliner that I usually liked to relax in. It was more like I collapsed into it than actually sat down, but I was impressed that I accomplished that much after being shot in the face. I wiped my hands as best I could and did a remarkable job of getting a lot of the blood off my hands and onto my shirt. I didn't want to ruin my favorite chair.

My head was pounding, and I was hyper-aware. I could actually hear the filament in the bulbs burning. I sat there and thought that I should call a doctor pretty soon before I bled to death. It was a call that I hadn't had to make in many years, but I still remembered how it was done. I heard the tip tap of nails suddenly and though I didn't have any pets, I knew that by the frequency of the footsteps, that it was a four legged creature approaching me, not the two legged kind like myself. Out of the kitchen and across the tile floor of the dining room, the small and quick footsteps continued until the origin of the noise crept into my field of vision. It was my old friend, the same dog that had haunted and tormented me ever since I was a little boy. He was all teeth. He was still big and black, and as formidable as he had always been. He approached me slowly and growled as he got to the doorway that separated the dining room and the living room in which I sat. I stared at him and it at me. While he continued to growl, he dared not take one step closer to me. I imagined that maybe it was because I still had the nine millimeter in my lap, but that certainly didn't make any sense to me. This creature was from beyond and a man-made weapon like this would not ever strike any fear whatsoever into its cold black heart.

I was tired and I had no fight left in me whatsoever. I picked up the gun with my left hand and carelessly tossed it on the couch, far away from my reach. I was finally ready to go. The dog once again tilted his head to the side and looked at the weapon as it bounced off the cushions and then as it landed and remained motionless. Still the dog did not approach. I almost laughed as it became all too clear.

I patted my right leg, and coaxed the hound, "Come here boy" and immediately the dog sat up and came to sit at my side.

I ran my hand along his snout and I heard his whine as the hound winced from the pain. My hand was once again wet and sticky and when I brought it up to visually inspect what it was, I noticed that my hand was covered in blood.

Well, isn't that something? A quick inspection cemented what I already suspected. The dog was bleeding from both sides of his snout. Immediately, I though of an old Spanish proverb, "More grows in the garden, than the gardener knows he has planted." This was true indeed.

I needed to make a phone call. I needed to call a doctor and it had to be someone skilled and discreet. I also needed to call my sister. I would have to disappear for a while and if she couldn't get in touch with me, she would come check on me. If she ever saw me in this condition, she would most certainly have me committed, again. It had been a long time since I had been handcuffed to a hospital bed, but I remembered that I didn't like it at all. I knew I had to act soon, but not just yet. Instead, I was content to sit there, still alive and somewhat intact. Truthfully, I just needed a little more time to process the slew of new information. I have been unimaginably bent by circumstances in my life, but I had not broken. I have survived. Therefore, I have won. No?

Yes, I win simply because I still am. I am battered, but I am still alive. I'll make all the calls I need to make very soon, but not just yet. For now, I shall sit here with my new found friend at my feet, listening to every single light bulb burn much too brightly, and to the haunting sound of Nina crying.

Special Thanks

A very special "Thank You" to the lovely and professional Rana Davis of Global Reign Productions for helping me weave through this story and lending me the patience to properly present my word to the world. Your input and guidance have truly been invaluable. May this work be the first of our many.

Big Thanks as well to my dedicated and passionate book reading team. I am eternally grateful to Rachel Ruda, Tiffani Stevens, Robert "Chi-Chi" Gonzalez, Tanya Spaulding, James Bell Jr., Peter Sciortino, Jason Tibbets, Toni Stallings and Jonisha Rios.

My utmost appreciation to my I.T. and Web design team that consisted of Brenda Perez and Joshua Colon, & Julia Ford. Your work on this project was undeniably priceless and made me realize just how little I know about computers and technology.

I would also like to thank all the people that came together to help me create the infinitely scary but still somewhat lovable Rumdog. My Director of Photography, Robert Rodriguez of PartyRecap.com. The incredibly talented photographer, Thomas Mester. Last, but certainly not least, the incredible multi-faceted Film & Make-up extraordinaire Adinda Dharma and Elizabeth Andrea Rivera.

Made in the USA
Middletown, DE
21 May 2017